1

Dortmunder sat in his living room to watch the local evening news, and had just about come to the conclusion that every multiple-dwelling residence in the state of New Jersey would eventually burn to the ground, three per news cycle, when the doorbell rang. He looked up, surprised, not expecting anybody, and then became doubly surprised when he realized it had not been the familiar *blatt* of the hall doorbell right upstairs here, but the never-heard *ing* of the street-level bell, sounding in the kitchen.

Rising, he left the living room and stepped out to the hall, to see May looking down at him from the kitchen, her hands full of today's gleanings from her job at Safeway as she said, 'Who is it?'

'Not this bell,' he told her, jabbing a thumb over his shoulder at the hall door. 'The street bell.'

'The *street* bell?'

Dortmunder clomped on back to the kitchen, to the intercom on the wall there that had *never* worked, that the landlord had just repaired in a blatant ploy to raise the rent. Not sure of the etiquette or operation of this piece of machinery, for so long on the inactive list, he leaned his lips close to the mouthpiece and said, 'Yar?'

'It's Andy,' said a voice that sounded like Andy being imitated by a talking car.

'Andy?'

May said, 'Let him in, John.'

'Oh, yeah.' Dortmunder pressed the white bone button, and yet another unpleasant sound bounced around the kitchen.

'Will wonders never cease,' May said, because Andy Kelp, who was occasionally Dortmunder's associate in certain enterprises, usually just walked on into their place, having enjoyed the opportunity to hone his lockpicking skills.

Dortmunder said, 'What if he rings this one up here, too?'

'He might,' May said. 'You never know.'

'It's an awful sound,' Dortmunder said, and went down the hall to

5

prevent this by opening the door, where he could listen to the echoes as Andy Kelp thudded up the stairs. When the thuds stopped, he leaned out to see Kelp himself, a sharp-nosed cheerful guy dressed casually in blacks and dark grays, come down the worn carpet in the hall.

'You rang the bell,' Dortmunder reminded him – not quite an accusation.

Kelp grinned and shrugged. 'Respect your privacy.'

What an idea. 'Sure,' Dortmunder said. 'Comonin.'

They started down the hall and May, in the kitchen doorway, said, 'That was very nice, Andy. Thoughtful.'

'Harya, May.'

'You want a beer?'

'Couldn't hurt.'

'I'll bring them.'

Dortmunder and Kelp went into the living room, found seats, and Dortmunder said, 'What's up?'

'Oh, not much.' Kelp looked around the living room. 'We haven't talked for a while, is all. No new acquisitions, I see.'

'No, we still like the old acquisitions.'

'So,' Kelp said, crossing his legs, getting comfortable, 'how you been keeping yourself?'

'May's been keeping me,' Dortmunder told him. 'She's still got the job at the Safeway, so we eat.'

'I figured,' Kelp said, 'you didn't call for a while, probly you didn't have any little scores in mind.'

'Probly.'

'I mean,' Kelp said, 'if you *did* have a little score in mind, you'd call me.'

'Unless it was a single-o.'

Kelp looked interested. 'You had any single-os?'

'As a matter of fact,' Dortmunder said, as May came in with three cans of beer, 'no.'

May distributed the beer, settled into her own chair, and said, 'So, Andy, what brings you here?'

'He wants to know,' Dortmunder said, 'have I been working without him, maybe with some other guys.'

'Aw, naw,' Kelp said, casually waving the beer can. 'You wouldn't do that, John.'

Dortmunder drank some beer, in lieu of having something to say.

May said, 'What about *you*, Andy? Anything on the horizon?'

'Well, there is one little remote possibility,' Kelp said, which of course would be the other reason he'd happened to drop by. 'I don't know if John'd be interested.'

Dortmunder kept the beer can up to his face, as though drinking, while May said, 'What wouldn't he like about it?'

'Well, it's in New Jersey.'

Dortmunder put the beer can down. 'They got a lotta domestic fires in New Jersey,' he said. 'I was just noticing on the news.'

'Family feared lost?' Kelp nodded. 'I seen that sometimes. No, this is one of those big box superstores, Speedshop.'

'Oh, that,' Dortmunder said.

Kelp said, 'I know you had your troubles with that store in the past, but the thing is, they're having this giant television sale.'

'Got one,' Dortmunder said, pointing at it. (He'd turned it off when all the bell-ringing started.)

'Well, here's my thinking,' Kelp said. 'If they're gonna have a giant sale on these things, it stands to reason they're gonna have a bunch of them on hand.'

'That's right,' May said. 'To fill the demand.'

'Exactly,' Kelp said to May, and to Dortmunder he said, 'I happen to know where there's an empty semi we could borrow.'

'You're talking,' Dortmunder said, 'about lifting and carrying a whole lot of television sets. Heavy television sets.'

'Not that heavy,' Kelp said. 'And it'll be worth it. You see, I also happen to know a guy out on the Island, recently opened up a great big discount appliance store out there, Honest Irving, not one item in the store is from the usual channels, he'll take everything off our hands but the semi, and I might have a guy for that, too.'

'Honest Irving,' Dortmunder said.

'His stuff is just as good as everybody else's,' Kelp assured him, 'same quality, great prices, only maybe you shouldn't try to take the manufacturer up on the warranty.'

'Speedshop,' Dortmunder said, remembering his own after-hours visit to that place. 'They got a lotta security there.'

'For a couple guys like us?' Kelp spread his hands to show how easy it would be, and the phone rang.

'I'll get it,' May said. She stood, left her beer behind, and headed for the kitchen, as the phone rang again.

'I know I'm wasting my breath,' Kelp said, 'but what a help for May it could be, I give you a nice little extension phone in here.'

'No, thank you.'

'One phone in an entire apartment,' Kelp said, and shook his head. 'And not even cordless. You take back-to-basics a little too far back, John.'

'I also don't think,' Dortmunder said, 'I wanna buck Speedshop, not again. I mean, even before the question of Honest Irving.'

Kelp said, 'Where's a question about Honest Irving?'

'The day will come, an operation like that,' Dortmunder said, 'all of a sudden you've got this massive police presence in the store, cops looking at serial numbers, wanting bills of sale, all this paperwork, and whadaya think the odds are, we're there unloading television sets when it happens?'

'A thousand to one,' Kelp said.

'Yeah? I make it even money,' Dortmunder said, and May came in, looking worried. He looked at her. 'What's up?'

'That was Anne Marie,' she said, referring to Kelp's live-in friend. 'She says there's a guy in the apartment, says he wants to see Andy, just waltzed in, won't give a name, just sits there. Anne Marie doesn't like it.'

'Neither do I,' Kelp said, getting to his feet. 'I better go.'

'John will go with you,' May said.

There was a little silence as Dortmunder reached for his beer can. He lifted his eyes, and they were both looking at him. 'Uh,' he said, and put the beer can down again. 'Well, naturally,' he said, and got to his feet.

The Road to Ruin

The Road
to Ruin

Donald E. Westlake

ROBERT HALE · LONDON

© Donald E. Westlake 2004
First published in Great Britain 2005

ISBN 0 7090 7748 3

Robert Hale Limited
Clerkenwell House
Clerkenwell Green
London EC1R 0HT

The right of Donald E. Westlake to be identified as
author of this work has been asserted by him
in accordance with the Copyright, Designs and
Patents Act 1988.

2 4 6 8 10 9 7 5 3 1

Typeset in 10/12½pt Plantin by
Derek Doyle & Associates, Shaw Heath.
Printed in Great Britain by
St Edmundsbury Press, Bury St Edmunds, Suffolk.
Bound by Woolnough Bookbinding Ltd.

2

Since the time, a couple years ago, when Anne Marie Carpinaw's husband, Howard, decided to walk out on her in the middle of a vacation trip to New York City from their home in Lancaster, Kansas, and while drowning not her sorrows but her befuddlement in the hotel bar she had met and taken up with Andrew Octavian Kelp, life had become odder and more interesting than it had ever been with Howard or in Lancaster (or in D.C., for that matter, where she'd also partly grown up while her daddy the congressman was still alive), which meant things were usually pleasant and went a long way toward making life worthwhile. But now and again, in the orbit of Andy Kelp, life became a little *too* interesting, and this was one of those moments right now.

The guy in the living room wasn't menacing, exactly, but he wasn't explainable either, and that's what had Anne Marie upset. The doorbell had rung, and when she'd opened the apartment door there he was, short, aged maybe fifty, bandy-legged and skinny-armed but with a big barrelly torso, like a cartoon spider. He was balding, with very pale skin that had maybe never seen the sun, plus watery blue sunny-side-up eyes and a kind of blunt fatalistic manner, as though he would be hard either to surprise or please. There was something in his manner that reminded her of John Dortmunder, except that John almost never got mad, but you could imagine with no trouble at all this guy getting mad.

At the moment, he was cheerful, brisk, and indifferent to her. 'Hi,' he said, with a smile, when she opened the door to him. 'Andy in?'

'Not at the moment. I'm—'

'I'll wait,' the guy said, and slithered in past her.

'But—'

It was too late; he was across the threshold. With an empty smile over his shoulder at Anne Marie he said, 'I'll just sit in the living room here, wait'll he comes back.'

'But—' Helplessly, she watched the guy look at the available furniture and go directly to the chair she thought of as hers. 'I don't know you,' she said.

Settling into Anne Marie's chair, the guy said, 'I'm a friend of Andy's.'
He smiled at the living room: 'Very nice. The woman's touch, huh?'

'Is he expecting you?'

'Not for maybe twenty years,' he said, and laughed. 'Don't mind me,'
he advised her. 'You go on what you're doing.'

'I'm not sure when Andy's coming back.'

'I got nothing but time,' he said, and suddenly looked bitter, as though
he'd reminded himself of something unpleasant. Something that might
make him mad.

'Well . . .' She thought, maybe she should placate him somehow. Even
though he wasn't at all threatening, he did look as though he might get
mad, even if not at her. The truth was, he barely seemed to notice she was
there. She was, she knew, an attractive person, but he gave no indication
at all that he'd remarked it. Which was also unsettling.

So, not wanting to, but feeling she should, she said, 'Do you want a cup
of coffee? Glass of water?'

'No, I'm fine,' he said, and pulled a *Daily News* out of his jacket pocket,
all folded in on itself like origami. Unfolding it, he said, 'I'll just sit here,
read my paper, wait for Andy.'

So that's when she left him there, went to the kitchen, and called John
and May's place, because Andy had told her he wanted to see John today,
so maybe he was still there. She got May, and Andy was still there, 'but I
don't need to talk to him,' Anne Marie said. 'Just tell him what the situation is here.'

May said, 'What *is* the situation there?'

So Anne Marie told her, and May said, 'Ooh. *I* wouldn't like that.'

'Neither do I.'

'I'll send Andy home right now.'

Which meant Anne Marie spent the next fifteen minutes in the
kitchen, a place where she normally didn't spend a whole lot of her time.
It was very small, to begin with, and what could you do in there except
cook and eat?

What she did do, for the next quarter hour, was fret. *Was* this man a
friend of Andy's? Was it Andy he was potentially mad at? Had she inadvertently permitted all kinds of trouble into the house? It was so hard,
sometimes, to know what to do in Andy's world.

Finally, she heard the apartment door open, so she hurried out to the
living room to be present for whatever happened next, because, of course,
she was partly responsible for whatever happened next. As she entered the
living room, suddenly breathless though it was a mere half-dozen steps
from one room to the other, she saw that Andy was here, that John had
come along with him and was closing the apartment door, and that the

stranger was getting to his feet, doing origami again with his newspaper. And he was smiling.

And so was Andy! It was with great relief that Anne Marie saw that smile, and heard Andy say, 'Chester! Whadda *you* doing out?'

'Believe it or not,' Chester said, 'I been out almost four years.'

'Well, I'll be.' Andy seemed genuinely happy to see this strange man, which Anne Marie knew shouldn't surprise her, though it still did. Shaking hands with Chester, he said, 'You met Anne Marie?'

'I didn't wanna push myself forward,' Chester said, and turned to offer a smile and a nod and a 'How are ya?'

'Anne Marie Carpinaw,' Andy introduced, 'Chester Fallon.'

'Hello,' she said, thinking, You didn't want to push yourself forward? You walked right into the house!

On the other hand, it was now clear Chester Fallon was not a threat or a problem, but a friend of some sort. And once he was Chester, somehow, he became much less threatening.

Meantime, Andy was saying, 'I don't think you know John,' and made the introductions, and Anne Marie noticed that John was very neutral toward Chester, like herself, shaking Chester's hand, looking him straight in the eye, and contenting himself with a 'Harya.'

'Not so good,' Chester told him, and said to Andy, 'I take it Anne Marie's with you, and John's one of us guys.'

'You wanna tell a story?' Andy asked him. 'In confidence? Be confident. Siddown. Everybody wanna beer? I'll get them.'

So Andy left, and the other three sat, and Anne Marie said to Chester, 'I wish you'd told me.'

Chester looked surprised. 'Told you what? I'm a friend of Andy's, I said that.'

'But there was no . . . conversation.'

'Well, Anne Marie, if I can call you Anne Marie—'

'Of course.'

'I didn't know you, did I? It could be you're the lady of the house, it could be you're a bill collector, process server. No offense, I seen cops look like you.'

'Not enough of them,' John said.

'Very true,' Chester told him. 'John, is it? You're right when you're right. Most cops, what they look like, they look like what *you* would look like if, your whole life, you never ate anything but Big Macs.'

Andy came back then to distribute beer, take his own seat, and say, 'Chester, I haven't seen you in years. More.'

'You know I went up,' Chester said.

'It wasn't your fault,' Andy assured him.

'Of course it wasn't my fault,' Chester said, 'but I was still doing large time.' Including John and Anne Marie in his explanation, he said, 'I'm the driver, it can't be my fault, unless I turn around and drive back to the bank. The thing is, I started in life as a stunt driver.'

Anne Marie, surprised, said, 'Really?'

'You may have seen the one,' Chester said, 'where the guy's escaping in the car, they're after him, the street becomes an alleyway, too narrow for the car, he angles sharp right, bumps the right wheels up on the curb, spins sharp left, the car's up on two left wheels, he goes down the alley at a diagonal, drops onto four wheels where it widens out again, taran-to-rah.'

'Wow,' Anne Marie said.

'That was me,' Chester told her. 'We gotta do it in one take or otherwise I'm gonna cream the car against some very stone buildings. I liked that life.'

John said, 'Was it you in the rest of the picture?'

'Nah,' Chester said, 'that was some movie star. They even had to bring in somebody else to do his swimming. Anyway, the problem was, that career dried up. They don't need the guys like me now, they got computers to do the stunts.' He shrugged, but looked disgusted. 'People wanna look at a *cartoon*, a car on a diagonal down the alley, nobody at the wheel, nobody's life at stake, what I say, it isn't the pictures got worse, it's the audience. But don't let me get off on that, that's a pet grievance, or it would be, except now I got a new pet grievance.' Turning to Andy, he said, 'And frankly, that's why I'm here.'

'I was wondering,' Andy admitted. 'You say you've been out four years, but I haven't heard anything about you, so I don't think you're driving any more.'

'Not away from banks,' Chester said. 'See, it isn't that I reformed, it's that driving in heists wasn't my first career choice to begin with. Movies, and some television, your circus in the slow periods, industrial films, I was making out OK. But then, when the computer muscles me outa there, how else am I gonna maintain my standard of living?'

'So,' Andy said, 'you didn't go back to it when you got out, because you got something else?'

'I did minimum time,' Chester told him. 'Kept my nose clean, all positive reports, got parole in one, with a placement bureau that actually did some placing for once. There was this rich guy, Monroe Hall—'

'I've heard that name,' Andy said, and Anne Marie felt that she too had heard it, but couldn't think where.

'It's been in the news of late,' Chester said, and sounded disgusted again. 'Let me get there.'

'Take your time,' Andy agreed.

'Monroe Hall,' Chester said, 'owns one of the major antique car collections in the world, out in his estate in Pennsylvania. Probably two million dollars on wheels, he keeps them in climate-controlled barns, he does exhibits sometimes, these are his babies. But himself he's not a great driver, so he hires a guy, like a chauffeur, to drive the cars, make sure they stay in condition. You just let a car sit around, the gasoline gums up, everything goes to hell. So around the time I'm getting out, Hall's previous chauffeur, that he's had almost as long as the cars, dies of natural causes and he needs a new guy. I've got one fall, I've paid my debt to society, I've got this movie background, it's exciting to Hall in every possible way. Movies, jail, bank robbery, you name it. So the placement bureau puts me together with Hall, I'm hired, I relocate the family out to Pennsylvania.'

Andy said, 'Family?'

Surprised, Chester said, 'You didn't know that? Well, I guess I kept that part away from the part you knew. Yeah, I got a wife and three kids, grown now, well, in their twenties, but outa the house. So the wife and me, we relocate, and I've got all these cars to play with, and I'm an employee of SomniTech.'

'Wait a minute,' Andy said. 'I've heard of that.'

'Sure you have,' Chester agreed. 'It's one of your huge corporations, they're in oil, they're in manufacturing, they're in communications, they're all over the place. It's what they call horizontal diversification, which to me sounds like a whorehouse that caters to all tastes, but if that's how they want to call it, fine. Anyway, Monroe Hall is one of the major executives there. And everything in his life is paid for by SomniTech. My paychecks are SomniTech. I get health insurance and a retirement plan, it's all SomniTech. The upkeep on the cars, paid for by SomniTech. His *pool* maintenance is a business expense, goes through SomniTech, his kids' dentist bills.'

'Something went wrong,' Andy said. 'I've read about this thing.'

'What he was doing,' Chester said, 'charging everything off to the company, turns out he wasn't supposed to do that.'

'Cheating the IRS,' Andy suggested.

'Well, that, too,' Chester said. 'But the main thing was, he was stealing from the company. That's shareholders' money, that's supposed to be profit, dividends, they just sucked it all out, him and like four other executives at the top of the heap.'

Anne Marie said, '*I* remember that! Wasn't he the white-haired man, testified in front of Congress?'

'Anne Marie,' Andy said, 'every white-haired man in America that owns a suit has testified in front of Congress.'

'But you're right,' Chester assured her. 'Monroe Hall was one of the people testified in those business ethics hearings.'

Andy said, 'So what happens? This Hall guy gets your old cell?'

'Not a chance,' Chester told him. 'You can't touch these guys, every one of them is surrounded by a moat filled with man-eating lawyers. He's still fat and happy there in Pennsylvania. But here's the *thing* of it,' he said, and Anne Marie saw that now he *was* getting angry. 'The deal he cuts,' Chester explained, 'he has to make *restitution*, partial *restitution*, and the reason it's partial, he's gotta plead poverty now, so he can't be a guy now that his hobby is million-dollar antique cars, so he gives it – here comes a charitable tax deduction, by the way – he gives it to a foundation. And guess who the foundation is. I mean, if you lift up the rock.'

Andy said, 'How does this affect you?'

'The foundation takes over maintenance on the collection,' Chester said, 'with some federal education money, and the foundation can't hire an ex-con.'

Andy said, 'You're out of a job.'

'I'm out of everything. My job is gone, my medical insurance through SomniTech is gone, my retirement is gone, everything's gone. I asked him, on account of my faithful service, find a spot for me somewhere, all of sudden I'm not allowed on the property, nobody wants to talk to me on the phone.'

'Jeez,' Andy said.

Chester shook his head. 'My first career is still dead, my second career still contains certain risks, and I don't feel like getting a job at a car service in Manhattan, to be the guy out at the airport holding up the sign: *Pembroke*.'

Andy said, 'You have a different idea.'

'I do.'

'And you think it includes me,' Andy said.

'I hope it includes you.'

John said, 'What is it you want to steal?'

'His fucking cars,' Chester said, and nodded at Anne Marie. 'Excuse the French.'

3

'I tell you what,' Monroe Hall said. 'Let's throw a party.'

'They won't come,' Alicia said, and walked on past him toward the stairs.

Monroe had been standing about in the upstairs west wing hall, not thinking of much of anything, when his wife emerged from the music room with a triangle in her hand. Seeing her, the party thought had just popped into his head, fully formed, and now it was as though a big happy party was what he'd been wanting forever. Forever. 'Why not?' he called after her. 'What do you mean, they won't come?'

She turned back to give him one of the patient looks he detested so. 'You know why not,' she said.

'*Who* won't come?' he demanded. 'What about our friends?'

'We don't have any friends, darling,' she said. 'Not any more.'

'*Somebody* has to stand by me!'

'I'm standing by you, dearest,' she said, this time with the sad smile that was only marginally less detestable than the patient look. 'I'm afraid that will have to do.'

'We *used* to throw parties,' he said, feeling very forlorn and put-upon. Nearby, the clock room erupted into a hundred cuckoos proclaiming the hour – ten (a.m., though the cuckoos didn't know quite that much) – and Monroe and his wife automatically moved on down the hall.

'Of course we used to throw parties,' she agreed, raising her voice a bit above the cuckoos. 'You were an important and successful and rich man,' she explained, as the cuckoo chorus raggedly wound itself down. 'People wanted to be seen with you, to have the world think of them as your friend.'

'That's who I'm talking about,' Monroe said. 'Those people. We'll invite them. You'll do clever wording on the note, something about how the little unpleasantness is over and we can all get back to our lives again, and— *Why* are you shaking your head?'

'They won't come,' she said, 'and you know it.'

'But I'm still important and successful,' he insisted. 'And I'm still rich, come to that, though I admit I can't quite flaunt it the way I used to. But I'm still who I was.'

'Oh, darling, no, you're not,' she said, with the little sympathetic head-shake and cluck that was *also* on the detestable list. 'What you are now, Monroe,' she told him, 'is notorious. What you are now is a pariah.'

'Oh!' he cried, terribly hurt. 'That you'd say *that*!'

'No party, dear,' she said. 'We can watch movies on the television.'

'What about the lawyers?' he demanded. 'They made enough off me, God knows. What if I invited *them*?'

'They'd be happy to come,' she said.

He smiled. 'See?'

'For three hundred and fifty dollars an hour.'

'Oh, damn!' he cried, and actually stamped his foot. A soft man of middle height, middle age, and middling condition, his jowls rippled when he stamped his foot, which he didn't realize and which his wife was too kindhearted to tell him, unfortunately, because it made him look like a turkey, and if he'd known that, he might have stopped doing it. But he didn't know about his comical jowls, so he did stamp his foot, and cried out, 'I can't do *anything*! I can't leave the country, I can't even leave the *state*. I can't go into the office—'

'You don't have an office any more, dear,' she said.

'That's why I can't go into it.'

'If you did go to the headquarters of SomniTech, Monroe,' she told him, 'the remaining employees there, the ones who lost their retirement benefits, might very well string you up.'

'For God's sake!' he cried. 'Why can't they all just get *over* it? What did I *do*? The same thing everybody else did!'

'Well, a little more so,' she suggested.

'A matter of degree.' Monroe shrugged it all away. 'Listen, what about the fellas? You know, the old bunch from the shop? *They* can't high-hat me, they were indicted, too.'

'If you will recall, Monroe,' she said, with the detestable patient look, 'the judge was very forceful on that topic. You and the boys are not to asso-ciate with one another any more.'

'Associate!' he cried, as though he'd never had any such idea in his mind. 'I don't want to associate. How can a fellow play golf? I want to play *golf*? You can't play golf by yourself, then what is it? Just you and these sticks and the ball, and you hit and walk and hit and walk and it's *boring*, Alicia, it's the most boring thing on earth, golf, if you're just doing it by *yourself*. The whole point of golf is hearty laughter with your chums. And where *are* my chums?'

'Not in jail,' she pointed out, 'and neither are you, and you can all consider yourselves extremely lucky.'

'Bosh,' he said. 'That wasn't luck, that was money. Give a whole lot of money to the lawyers, stand back, let them work out the deal. So they worked out the deal. But how long do I have to – *Pariah!* How long does *that* go on? It is like being in jail, Alicia!'

'Not quite,' she said, with the detestable sad smile. 'Not quite, Monroe, though I do understand. I too would like a little fun in my life. Would you like to go for a drive?'

'Where?' he demanded. 'If I leave the compound, you never know when some reporter's going to pop out from behind a tree with those smart-alecky questions. Or even a disgruntled stockholder, some of *them* are still out there, too, with their horsewhips.'

'Around the compound, then,' she said. 'We could take that Healey Silverstone, that's such a fun car to drive.'

'I don't feel like it,' he said, and stuck out his lower lip. What he was feeling, in fact, was sulky. Since he'd been born rich into a family that had been a long time rich, he'd never known the need to suppress his feelings, so he pouted completely and might even have stamped his foot again, except he sensed that a kind of lumpish stillness might better illustrate the sulk he'd fallen into.

'Well, *I* think it's a good idea,' she said. 'Zip around in the Healey. Wind in our hair.'

'I don't like the cars as much any more,' he said.

'Because you had to let Chester go,' she suggested.

'We all *knew* he was an ex-convict,' Monroe reminded her. 'He was one of my good deeds, one of my many good deeds that no longer *counts* any more. But, no. I have to pretend I've given the cars away and do all that foundation rigmarole so they won't be lost in the settlement, and fire the only person who ever really understood the cars and could make them just tick right along. I loved it when *he* drove me. *I* don't want to drive me. I'm afraid of banging them into things.'

'*I'll* drive you,' she offered.

'I'm afraid of *you* banging them into things.'

'Nonsense,' she said. 'I've never banged a car into anything in my life.'

'Famous last words.'

'I'm going for a drive,' she decided, 'with you or without you. In the Healey. I love that car.'

'Associate,' Monroe said, pursuing his own thoughts. 'There's that "associate" word again. I can't associate with Chester because he's an ex-convict, surprise, surprise, so now I don't even get to enjoy the cars any more.'

'Coming, Monroe?'

'No,' he said, remembering he was sulking, and again stuck out his lower lip.

'Well, in that case,' she said, with a smile, 'I might even drive off the compound. Nobody bothers *me*. Here, put this away, would you?' she said, and handed him the triangle. 'I won't practice with it, after all. That's how bored I was, Monroe. But a quick spin in the Healey is a *much* better idea than ting-ting-ting, sing Johnny One-Note. I'll be back for lunch.' And off she went, down the hall toward the stairs and the great world outside.

Because Monroe was rich, Alicia, who was his first wife, looked like a second wife, so, even when sulking, he watched her walk with a great deal of pleasure. One of the few pleasures left to him, Alicia. He knew he was lucky she'd stuck by him, when all the other rats deserted like . . . well, the ship thing.

She was gone. He was alone in the hallway, with nowhere to go and nothing to do. Can't even have a party.

God, he told himself, I wish something would happen.

4

When Dortmunder walked into the O.J. Bar & Grill on Amsterdam Avenue at eleven that night, Rollo the bartender was nowhere to be seen. The regulars, clustered as usual at the left end of the bar, were continuing without him, like a conductorless orchestra.

At the moment, the discussion concerned global warming. 'The *reason* for global warming,' one of them said as Dortmunder leaned his front against the bar somewhere down to the right of them, 'is air conditioners.'

Two or three of the regulars wished to object to this idea, but he with the most powerful voice won out, speaking, perhaps, for the group as a whole: 'Whadaya mean, air conditioners? Air conditioners make things *cold*.'

'*In*doors,' the first regular said. 'What happens to all the heat used to be indoors? It's outdoors. It's what they call vent. All the cold air's inside, all the hot air's outside, there you go, global warming.'

A third regular, who'd been outshouted the last time around, now said, 'What about in the winter? Nobody's got their air conditioner on then, they got furnaces, they're keeping the heat inside.'

'So?' the first regular demanded. 'Is there a point in this?'

'A point?' The third regular was astounded. 'The point is, no air conditioners in the winter, so how does that make for global warming?'

'Come on, dummy,' the first regular said. 'There isn't any global warming in the winter, everybody knows that. It's *cold* in the winter.'

'Not in South America,' said a fourth regular.

'Dummy?' said the third regular. 'Did I hear "dummy"?'

'Not you,' the first regular assured him, 'just in general.' And to the fourth regular he said, 'OK. So maybe in South America they got global warming in the winter. In *our* winter. It's their summer. It's the same thing.'

The third regular, trying to fix his stance in all this, muttered, mostly to himself, 'Dummy in general?'

Meanwhile, a fifth regular had chimed in. 'It isn't air conditioners, anyway,' he informed the group. 'It's coal mine fires.'

Nobody liked that one. The third regular even forgot his 'general dummy' dilemma to say, '*Coal* mine fires? A couple little underground fires in Pennsylvania, you think that makes global warming?'

'Not just Pennsylvania,' the fifth regular told him. 'In Russia you got coal mine fires. All over the world.'

The second regular, whose loud voice had not been heard for some time, now said, 'What it mostly is, you know, is holidays. I mean, those other things may help, I wouldn't know about that, but your basic cause is holidays.'

The first regular, the air conditioner stalwart, turned on this new theorist, saying, 'What do *holidays* have to do with anything?'

'There's too many of them,' the second regular said. 'You got a holiday, everybody gets in their car and drives, or they take a plane. All that fossicle fuel everybody's burning, that gives off a lotta heat.'

Before anybody could comment on that, the third regular said, 'What I wanna know is, how come all the holidays are on Monday? I mean, does it just work out like that, or is this a conspiracy?'

Conspiracy; huh. They all thought about that. Then a woman from the regulars' auxiliary, a little farther down the bar, said, 'Thanksgiving isn't on Monday, it's on Thursday. I been known to cook it.'

'All the others,' the third regular told her. 'All the ones you can't remember their names.'

'Christmas,' the first regular suggested, 'isn't always on Monday, it's all over the hell. I remember there was a Christmas on a Sunday once, threw everything outa whack.'

Rollo the bartender came in then, from the street, wearing over his high-calorie apron an eleven-foot-long Bob Cratchit scarf, even though it was balmy late May outside, just past the Monday on which, or so the politicians thought, Memorial Day – remember that? – had been 'observed.' Seeing Dortmunder, he said, 'Be right with you.'

'Take your time.'

Rollo would anyway, but he said, 'Thanks.' Going around behind the bar to his usual location, unwinding and unwinding the scarf, he held up a little package and said, 'I ran outa D'Agostino bitters.'

'Right.'

Now that he was facing the bar, Dortmunder noticed, on the backbar, some kind of strange glittering machine that seemed to be half cash register and half television set, except the program showing was simply a set of squares and rectangles in different shiny colors. He pointed his forehead at this thing and said, 'What's that?'

'That?' Rollo turned to look at the machine, considering his answer. 'That,' he decided, putting the bitters bottle in pride of place next to the grenadine, 'is the new computerized cash register. The owner put it in, for the efficiency.'

'Computerized?'

'Yeah. Let's say, for instance,' Rollo said, 'you asked for a beer. I know you didn't, but let's just say.'

'Fine,' Dortmunder agreed.

'What it does,' Rollo said, turning to the machine and not quite touching its glittery screen, 'it reads your order, depending where I touch the screen.'

'You touch the screen?'

'Not unless you actually order the beer,' Rollo said. 'But say you did.'

'I got that part,' Dortmunder said.

'Right.' Rollo demonstrated, his meaty forefinger never quite making actual contact with the multicolored screen as he said, 'I press *beer*, I press *domestic*, I press *eight-ounce*, I press *sale*. Then the order shows up down here, in this rectangle, the yellow one.'

'I see it.'

'It says one domestic beer, eight ounces, and then it says, "Press *here* if correct, press *here* if incorrect," and I press *correct*, and then I press *cash*, and then I press *sale*, and then the cash register drawer opens.'

'The cash register drawer *is* open,' Dortmunder said.

'Yeah,' Rollo agreed. 'I keep it that way. It's simpler.'

At the other end of the bar, the regulars were trying to figure out what ever happened to Armistice Day. 'It used to be,' the third regular said. 'I remember it.'

The second regular, the one with the voice, intoned, 'The eleventh minute of the eleventh hour of the eleventh day of the eleventh month.'

The third regular said, 'Maybe if that ever shows up on a Monday, we'll get Armistice Day again.'

'So what happened,' the fifth regular inquired, 'when all those elevens came up?'

'Why, the war ended,' the second regular told him, with great solemnity.

'What war?'

'The war they were having at that time.'

The buttinsky from the regulars' auxiliary said, 'What if it's the *tenth* minute of the eleventh hour of the eleventh day of the eleventh month, and the lieutenant tells you to take a peek over the top of the trench, see if the Germans are still there?'

Darkly, the third regular said, 'I had a lieutenant like that.'

'Yeah?' The first regular was interested. 'What ever became of him?'

'Friendly fire.'

'I take it,' Rollo said, placing on the bar in front of Dortmunder a round enameled Rheingold Beer tray, 'you're meeting some of your associates in the room in the back.'

'Yeah,' Dortmunder said, as Rollo put two thick squat glasses and a shallow ironstone bowl with ice cubes in it and a bottle of murky brown liquid labeled *Amsterdam Liquor Store Bourbon – Our Own Brand* all in a row on the tray. 'We'll have the vodka and red wine and the beer with salt and the other bourbon,' he said, because Rollo knew his customers strictly by their liquid preferences. 'And a guy with like a barrel chest and skinny arms and legs, answers to Chester, I don't know what he drinks.'

'*I'll* know,' Rollo said. 'The minute I look at him.' Pushing the tray closer to Dortmunder, he said, 'You're the first.'

Good; that meant he'd get to sit facing the door. 'Thanks, Rollo,' he said, and carried the tray past the holiday debate team, who were trying to decide if Arbor Day was an actual holiday or a typo for Labor Day. Leaving the front part of the bar, Dortmunder went down the hall with doors decorated with black metal dog silhouettes labeled POINTERS and SETTERS and past the phone booth surrounded by graffiti of hacker's code and on into a small square room with a concrete floor. The walls were hidden, floor to ceiling, by beer and liquor cases, leaving just enough space for a battered old round table with a stained felt top that had once been pool-table green but now looked mostly like Amsterdam Liquor Store Bourbon. The table was surrounded by half a dozen armless wooden chairs.

This room had been dark, but when Dortmunder hit the switch beside the door, one bare bulb under a round tin reflector hanging low over the table on a long black wire let you see all you wanted to see of the place.

Dortmunder walked all around the room to sit in the chair that most directly faced the door – the prize for being first. Then he added an ice cube to one of the glasses, poured in a little murk, and sat back to await his crew.

As far as Dortmunder was concerned, holidays were mostly an opportunity to improve your luggage.

5

Dortmunder had left the door open, which turned out to be a good thing. It wasn't a good thing for the view it offered, which was of the opposite wall of the corridor, constructed many ages ago, apparently out of cooling lava, possibly with small life forms ambered within, but because the door being open made it possible for the next arrival to arrive.

He couldn't have done it otherwise. With both of his hands encumbered as they were, a glass of beer (domestic, eight-ounce) in the right, a half-full glass saltshaker with metal top in the left, he might have found it a little tricky to deal with that round smooth doorknob requiring a half turn to the left. It's bad luck to spill salt, as everybody knows, and even worse luck to spill beer.

The bearer of these objects, a blocky ginger-haired man with freckles on the backs of his hands, gave Dortmunder a sour look and said, 'You got here first.'

'Hi, Stan,' Dortmunder said. 'You're right on time.'

Stan came around the table to sit at Dortmunder's right hand, which meant he would have anyway a three-quarter view of the door. Putting down his beer and his salt, he said, 'I woulda been OK, I mean, I plotted it out ahead, I know the BQE's no good, they're putting in a bicycle lane—'

Dortmunder said, 'On the BQE? Impossible. The slowest car on the BQE is doing Mach two. You're gonna put bicycles up there?'

'A bicycle *lane*,' Stan corrected. 'It keeps the greens happy, now they got a bicycle lane, it keeps the construction industry happy, now they got useless work at union wages, and if a green ever tries to *use* it, there's another cause for happiness. Anyway, the Van Wyck's no good because they're putting in the monorail—'

'I don't know,' Dortmunder said, 'what's happening to New York.'

Stan nodded. 'You wanna know what's happening to New York?' he asked. 'I tell you what you do. You go to a used-magazine store, you look at the covers of science fiction magazines from the thirties. *That's* what's happening to New York. Anyway, I figured, the old streets are still OK, I'll take a straight run up Flatbush Avenue, come to Manhattan that way. I've got ten-ten-wins on, to tell me anything I ought to know, this is the radio station they say, "Give us twenty-two minutes, we'll give you the world." What about the demonstration at Flatbush and Atlantic? Isn't *that* part of the world?'

Dortmunder said, 'Demonstration?'

'The people that want Long Island to secede from New York State,' Stan said, shrugging as though naturally everybody knew about *that*, but before Dortmunder could ask the first of several questions that came to mind, Andy Kelp entered, empty-handed, followed by Chester Fallon, carrying a glass of beer much like Stan's, but without the side order of salt.

They both scoped out the seating situation pretty fast, but Kelp was quicker, and slid in to Dortmunder's left, leaving a less-than-half view of the doorway for Chester at *his* left as he reached for the 'bourbon' bottle and the other glass and said, 'Tiny'll be along in a minute.'

Dortmunder said, 'Where is he?'

'Out in the bar,' Kelp said, 'arguing with some people, is Decoration Day a national holiday.'

Surprised, Chester said, 'That guy? He's with *us*? I wouldn't argue with him.'

Dortmunder said, 'The arguments don't run long.'

Kelp said, 'Some of the people out there think it's Decora*tor* Day, which is kinda muddying the issue.'

At this point a man-monster entered the room. Shaped mostly like an armored car, but harder, he held in his left hand a tall glass of red liquid while his right hand was to his mouth as he licked his knuckles. He left off the licking to glare around the room and say, 'I was *born* in this country.'

'Of course you were, Tiny,' Dortmunder said. 'Come on in. This is Chester Fallon. Chester, Tiny Bulcher.'

'Harya,' Tiny said, and stuck out a hand like a Christmas ham, with wet knuckles.

Chester studied this offering. 'Did you hurt yourself?'

'I don't hurt my*self*,' Tiny told him.

So they shook hands, Chester winced, and Tiny shut the door, then sat with his back to it, not giving a damn.

Stan said to Chester, 'We weren't introduced. I'm the driver, Stan Murch.'

Chester looked at him in surprise. '*You're* the driver? *I'm* the driver.'

Stan gave him the critical double-o. 'Then where's your salt?'

Chester said, 'Salt? You expect icy roads? In May?'

'The driver drinks beer,' Stan told him. 'Like you, like me. But the driver doesn't want to drink *too* much beer, because he's gotta know what he's doing when he's at the wheel.'

'Sure,' Chester said, and shrugged.

'But the thing with beer,' Stan said, 'it won't last. You just sip it, sip it, one time you look, it's flat, head's gone, tastes like shit.'

'That's true,' Chester said.

Stan picked up the saltshaker. 'Every once in a while,' he said, 'you tap in a little salt, gives it back its head, gives it back its zest, you can pace yourself.' He demonstrated, tapping a little salt into his glass, and they all watched the head improve.

Chester nodded. 'Pretty good,' he said. 'Not exactly driving expertise, but useful. Thank you.'

'Any time,' Stan told him, and sipped beer.

'Anyway,' Dortmunder said, 'this time around, we need more than one driver.'

Stan said, 'Why? What are we taking?'

'Cars,' Dortmunder said.

Stan looked interested. 'Yeah?'

Dortmunder turned to Chester. 'Tell Stan and Tiny the story.'

So Chester told them the story, and at the end of it Tiny said, 'Would you like it if this guy Monroe Hall got chastised a little along the way, as long as we're there?'

'I wouldn't mind that a bit,' Chester said.

'It sounds,' Tiny said, 'like he's overdue.'

'What we're here for now,' Dortmunder said, 'is, Chester tells us the layout, we see how we can do it. Or, you know, *if* we can do it.'

'For now,' Stan said, 'let's stick with *how*. I wanna see Tiny chastise that guy.'

'OK,' Dortmunder said. 'Chester, what's the layout?'

'Well, that's the thing,' Chester said. 'It isn't easy. I wish it was, but it isn't.'

Tiny said, 'Just tell us.'

'Sure,' Chester said. 'It's a big place, don't know how many thousands acres, rolling land, some woods, different buildings, roads. It's like its own little country. In fact, it's almost the entire county.'

'Everything,' Kelp suggested, 'except the "R".'

'Uh, yeah,' Chester said, and told the rest: 'Part of it used to be a dairy farm, there's still a part with horses, there's these special buildings for the cars, other buildings for the other collections—'

Kelp said, 'Collections?'

'This guy's a collector,' Chester explained. 'Not just cars. Some of the collections he keeps in the main house, like the music boxes and the cuckoo clocks, but some have their own buildings, like the model trains and the nineteenth-century farm equipment.'

Dortmunder said, 'Wait a second, Chester. While we're there taking these cars, is there stuff we should be putting *in* the cars?'

Kelp said, 'I was just thinking the same thing. Small, valuable, fit right in the car, backseat and trunk. Chester? They got stuff like that?'

Chester said, 'I'm not a collector, I don't know what all that stuff is worth.'

'We know people that do know,' Dortmunder told him. 'Give us a list of the collections. Not now, later.'

'OK.'

Tiny said, 'OK, never mind what we put in the cars, we know we can deal with that. But let's say we got the *cars*, these six cars you think are the best, worth a lot of cash. Who do we sell them to?'

'Insurance company,' Chester said, so promptly it was obvious he'd been thinking about it.

Dortmunder said, 'That's what I figured, too. That's the natural customer.'

Kelp said, 'And they don't argue, insurance companies, all they want is to minimize the expense.'

Stan said, 'They do cooperate with the authorities, though.'

Kelp shrugged. 'We expect that, we account for that. But all along they know, they give us ten percent of the value, it's better than giving Monroe Hall a hundred percent.'

'Twenty percent,' Dortmunder said.

'No, John,' Kelp said, 'they gotta reimburse the owner the full value.'

'Twenty percent to *us*,' Dortmunder said.

Kelp perked up. 'You think so? We could hit 'em for that much?'

Chester said, 'All they have to do is say no once, we pick the least valuable of the six, put it in a field, burn it up, call the insurance company, say you can go pick up that one right now, and by the way, the rest'll cost you twenty-five percent.'

Admiring, Dortmunder said, 'Chester, that's pretty tough. Somewhere you learned to be a hell of a negotiator.'

'From watching Monroe Hall,' Chester said. 'He'd coin-toss his mother for a returnable soda bottle, and knife her if he lost.'

Stan said, 'So we just need a place to stash these cars while everybody talks it over.'

Tiny looked doubtful. 'Then it's like a kidnapping,' he said. 'It's step after step, the phone calls, the ransom, the pickup, the return.'

'That's OK,' Dortmunder said. 'We can handle that.'

'No problem,' Kelp said.

Tiny considered that. 'Maybe,' he decided. 'Maybe no problem. But before that there's a problem.' He turned to Chester. 'Tell us about the problem.'

'Well, the security,' Chester said.

Tiny nodded. 'There's always gonna be security' he said, 'where you got valuable stuff.'

'But they beefed it up,' Chester said, 'since the scandal broke. You got a lotta people out there, not just us, wouldn't mind chastising Monroe Hall. He's what they call a pariah. So now they got electric fence around the whole compound, miles of it, motion sensors, big lights that light up, private guards.'

'So the first question is,' Stan said, 'how do we drive a bunch of cars off the property without anybody seeing us or hearing us.'

'Well, no,' Chester said. 'The first question is, how do you get *on* the property.'

'I give up,' Stan said. 'How do we?'

'I never planned any stuff,' Chester told him, 'back in my life of crime. I was just the driver.'

'So what you're saying,' Stan suggested, 'is, you don't know how we get in.'

'Come on, Stan,' Chester said. 'You said you're the driver. Do *you* ever know stuff like that?'

'I leave that to John here,' Stan said.

Chester nodded. 'Good. Then so do I.'

Everybody looked at Dortmunder. He nodded, accepting the weight. 'So we gotta see the place,' he said.

They looked alert, watching him, waiting.

'OK,' Dortmunder said. 'So the first thing we do, we steal a car.'

6

They whiled away the empty hours in the little brown Taurus singing the union anthem:

'Who will always guide the way?
Give us comfort in the fray?
Gain us benefits and pay?
The A C W F F A!'

At which point Mac interrupted, saying, 'Here comes the Healey.' He was in the backseat, looking toward the guard-shacked entrance to the Monroe Hall compound that stretched away behind them.

'And here we go again,' Buddy said, pessimistic as hell, but he did switch on the Taurus engine.

'You know it's just the wife,' Ace said, up front in the passenger seat.

'It is,' Mac said, seeing her blond hair fly as the Healey picked up speed once it reached the county road, coming this way as the compound's gate closed behind her.

'Follow her,' Ace said.

Buddy said, 'Again? Why? What's the point?'

'Maybe he's hiding in there,' Ace suggested.

Buddy snorted. 'In a two-seater? Where? Besides, he never did before.'

The Healey zipped past then, still accelerating, and Buddy's point was made. The Healey was so small and so open you could see the wife's brown suede purse on the passenger seat to her left, the Healey being a British car, with right-hand steering. It was a beautiful car, in truth, small and neat, over fifty years old and still looking like a spring chicken. It was topless, with a wide rectangular windshield – windscreen, its makers would say – edged in chrome and tilted back. The slightly raised air scoop on the hood, like a retroussé nose, had twin low flaring nostrils over a gleaming grill shaped like an Irish harp. The body was a creamy white, like very good porcelain, and the fenders, standing out to the side of the body, were arched like white leaping dolphins. With the beautiful long-

28

haired blonde at the wheel, flashing through the lush green Pennsylvania countryside on the first day of June, it was a sight to make you glad there's evolution.

Mac and Buddy and Ace had seen that sight enough – in fact, too much. What they wanted to see, and so far had not seen, was the man himself at the wheel, Monroe Hall, come out to meet his judgment.

Once or twice a week the wife emerged, usually in the Healey though sometimes in one of the other cars, the 1967 Lamborghini Miura or the 1955 Morgan Plus 4, for example, and in her automobile of choice she would drive apparently aimlessly around the rural back roads surrounding the compound.

Mac and Buddy and Ace had discussed among themselves whether or not these trips actually were aimless, merely the random actions of a bored woman stuck in a gilded cage the size of Catalina Island, or if there were some purpose to them after all. So far as they knew, she'd never stopped anywhere on any of these jaunts, never met anybody, never did anything but drive around for an hour or so, and then back to the Monroe Hall compound.

That was as far as they knew. Unfortunately, they didn't know everything. From time to time, on these trips, on some particularly empty back road, the wife would floor it, apparently just for fun, and all at once the Taurus would be alone on the road, poking along, following nothing. That's when Ace started calling the Taurus the tortoise, which Buddy, who owned the car, took offense at, not even cooling off after Mac pointed out that the tortoise had won that particular race.

Something had to be done. They'd been staking out the Hall compound for weeks now, months, and except for the occasional gallop with the Mrs they had nothing to show for it. They could only keep this stakeout going until their unemployment insurance ran out, which would be in just a very few weeks. Something had to be done.

As they drove along the country road, well back from the gleaming white Healey, the wife taking her time today, so far not zipping off unexpectedly over some hillock and out of sight, Mac said, 'Listen, something has to be done.'

'We know,' Ace said.

Mac said, 'OK. What if we kidnap *her*?'

Ace shook his head. 'He'll never pay.'

'She's his *wife*.'

'He won't pay,' Ace said. 'You know the guy as well as we do, and he won't pay. We could send him her fingers, one at a time, and he wouldn't pay.'

Mac scrinched up his face. '*I* couldn't send him her fingers.'

'Neither could I,' Ace said. 'Even if it would do any good. I'm just saying.'

'Besides,' Buddy said, steering around curves, keeping the Healey just barely in sight, looking from time to time in the rearview mirror, '*he's* what it's all about. That was the agreement at the beginning.'

'None of us,' Mac said, 'thought it would take this long.'

Ace said, 'Sure. We thought he'd go out sometimes.'

'There used to be all these pictures of him in the magazines,' Mac said, 'at the opera, at charities—'

'Hah,' Buddy said.

'Who knew,' Mac said, 'he'd suddenly turn into a hermit?'

'It's the publicity,' Ace said. 'These days, he isn't famous, he's infamous, and he's afraid to go out.'

'I don't know,' Mac said. 'I don't wanna give up, but what are we *doing* here?'

'And it isn't just for us,' Ace pointed out. 'It's for the whole local.'

'Hold on,' Buddy said. 'Come on, lady, stop, then go.'

Up ahead, the Healey had reached an empty intersection, two minor roads crossing among evergreens, no houses or businesses around. The road they were on had the stop sign, and the Healey had stopped, but now it wasn't moving on.

Buddy had slowed, not wanting to get too close, not wanting her to make a note of the Taurus and maybe remember it some other time, but he was also looking in the mirror again. 'I got a guy behind me,' he said, 'so I can't slow down too much.'

Up ahead, a gasoline truck went slowly by, from left to right, explaining the wife's delay, and once it cleared the road the Healey shot across the intersection and headed off around the next curve. Buddy accelerated to the stop sign, hit the brakes hard, the Taurus jolted to a stop that made Ace reach out to brace himself against the passenger air-bag compartment, and a black stretch limo crossed the intersection, also from left to right, very slowly.

Well, no. It didn't *cross* the intersection; it entered the intersection, filled the intersection, and stopped.

'Now what?' Buddy said, and honked his horn. 'Come on, Jack!'

Twisting around, Ace looked past Mac out the rear window. 'What's going on?'

Mac twisted around as well. Behind them was a big black Lincoln Navigator SUV, the most carnivorous vehicle on the road, the Minotaur of motoring. Both of its rear doors were open, and a man in a business suit and tie was getting out on each side. Both men wore sunglasses and were tall and thin and maybe forty.

'Holy Christ!' Mac said.

'God damn it!' Buddy cried. 'They tipped to us!'

'Following the wife too much,' Mac decided, watching the men walk forward, taking their time, in no hurry.

'Lock the doors,' Ace said.

'Oh, come on,' Buddy said. 'We're past *that*.' And he rolled his window down.

The two men had reached their car now. The one on Buddy's side bent down, hand on the Taurus roof as he smiled at Buddy and said, 'Good afternoon.'

'Afternoon,' Buddy agreed.

'We thought maybe you'd like to join forces,' the man said. Across the way, the other man smiled at Ace through the window of his locked door.

So, Mac thought, these guys aren't goons from the compound after all. This was something else.

Buddy said, 'Join forces? Whadaya mean, join forces?'

'Well,' the man said, 'we've got a stratagem aimed at Monroe Hall that doesn't appear to be working out, and I'd say you gents also have some sort of plan in mind involving Monroe Hall that *also* isn't working out.'

Buddy said, 'Monroe who?'

The man's smile was kindly, you had to say that for it. 'You three have been staking out Hall's place for weeks,' he said. 'We've got enough Polaroids of you to fill a bulletin board. We've traced the registration of this car, so we know who *you* are, Alfred "Buddy" Meadle, and we can pretty well guess who your friends are. Former coworkers. Mrs Hall isn't going to do anything interesting, she never does. We've got a nice stretch here, why not come on over, get comfortable, we can discuss the situation.'

'What situation?' Buddy asked him.

'I think we should do it,' Mac said. He didn't know who these people were, but they looked to him as though they just might be the something that had to be done.

'The situation where we pool our resources,' the man said. His smile as he looked the Taurus up and down was pitying. 'I believe we have more resources than you do. Your friend is right, you should do it. Why not leave your car on the side of the road here, and we'll go for a spin in the stretch?'

7

It was a while before Alicia realized she'd lost the Taurus. She was just so used to it being there, in her rearview mirror, keeping its humble distance like a footman in a palace, that she hardly actually saw it any more, so it took a little while to realize she *wasn't* seeing it. Her mirror was empty, like a vampire's.

Had they given up, after all this time? She couldn't believe it. They were so faithful in their fashion, following her everywhere, except for those moments when, just for the fun of it, she took them out to some extremely remote part of the countryside, suddenly accelerated, and zip, left them there. Other than that, they were always with her, like old dog Tray.

In fact, she mostly thought of them as the Three Stooges, bulky men hunched in their little tan Taurus. When the siege started – she supposed it had to be called a siege, however ineffective – they'd all worn plaid shirts, like lumberjacks on holiday, but as the weather had warmed they'd switched to T-shirts with words on them. She'd never been able to study those shirts, but she supposed most of the words were about beer.

The stop sign, that must be it, where she'd lost them. She'd had to wait for that gasoline truck to go by, but then she'd managed to dash across the intersection before that tasteless stretch limousine had arrived, and what was *that* thing doing in this neck of the woods?

It must have been the limousine that had made them lose her. Lord knows how long a thing like that would take to cross an intersection, so by the time the Three Stooges could once again take up the chase, their quarry was gone. What a shame.

Well, she'd been out and about long enough for today, anyway, so why not go back along the same route, have another look at the intersection? Wouldn't it be funny if the Stooges were still there, stuck, lost, unable to decide which way to turn? She could sail on by, pretend not to notice them, but give them plenty of time to get back into position in her train. Of course they *wouldn't* be there, but it was fun to think of them that way, and why not drive back past there in any case?

She knew all these roads around here by now, knew them as well as she'd once known Madison Avenue, so she didn't have to U-turn. A left here, and another left farther on, and so forth. The next thing you knew, she'd be at the intersection, and the *next* thing you knew, she'd be home again, home again, jiggety jig.

Home. Not such fun, these days. If only Monroe didn't have those travel restrictions on him, there were so many lively places they could go. Nowhere among old friends, of course, but still. Monroe could grow a beard, call himself something else. Almost anything else. Monroe Hall was a stupid name, anyway; Alicia had always thought it made him sound like a private school dormitory.

Of course, *she* could go if she wanted, and anywhere she wanted. She could even go among their friends, who would sympathize with her, and press her for gossip, and offer their tin sympathy, and praise her for having left the monster, but she didn't *want* to go by herself. She didn't want to leave Monroe, unfortunately.

Yes, that was it. She loved Monroe, unfortunately. Also, he'd covered for her, which had been very good of him. Back in the heady days of their massive rip-off of SomniTech she had been a willing, even eager, coconspirator, using her remembered expertise from the world of advertising to help them gloss, shift attention, misdirect. Company reports, or at least the most fictitious ones, had been mostly written by her.

And yet, through all his subsequent travail, Monroe had never once pointed a finger in her direction. Yes, it was true that bringing *her* down wouldn't have been of any help to *him*, but apparently this was one instance where misery did not love company, and Monroe had faced the music all alone.

For that, by itself, he deserved to have her stand by him. But even without that, the fact was, she loved him. She knew everything that was wrong with him, she knew he was a selfish, infantile, coldhearted monster, because, with absolute openness, he had let her see to the depths of his black heart. But she also knew that *she* was the one spot of color he was able to see in the world outside himself.

What love he contained, Monroe had given to Alicia. He had made her rich and happy. They were still rich, and she could hope that some day they would once again be happy. And out of the compound, Lord, please.

The intersection. Coming to it from the other direction, slowing for the stop sign, she was startled to see that the Taurus *was* parked just off the road over there. Good heavens, were they *that* lost?

Behind the Taurus was another vehicle, a black Lincoln Navigator, like the bigger fish behind the smaller fish, mouth open to eat it. *That* car she'd never seen before.

There was no other traffic. Slowly she drove across the intersection, frankly staring at the Taurus, and was further surprised to see it was empty. Its driver's window was open.

The Navigator was occupied, by a uniformed chauffeur at the wheel, reading a copy of *Harper's*. He didn't look up when Alicia drove by.

There was something odd about all that. Driving on, frowning at her mirror, Alicia watched the empty Taurus and the chauffeured Navigator recede, then disappear around a bend in the road.

What was *that* all about?

8

Seated behind his partner Os in the forward seat of the stretch, just behind the driver beyond his soundproof partition, Mark Sterling surveyed the trio from the Taurus, now arrayed across the forward-facing rear seat as though they really should be doing see-no-evil-hear-no-evil-speak-no-evil. They were not an inspiring lot. Years of factory jobs interspersed with bowling had left them soft and paunchy, with blurred round faces. Their T-shirts were walking billboards for Miller Lite, Bud, and the Philadelphia Eagles football team. They did not, at first blush, look like anything a truly serious conspirator would want in his cabal.

Well, this had been Mark's idea to begin with, Os being on the fence vis-à-vis the proposal, leaning toward the negative. So now was the moment of truth, the plunge, the spin of the wheel.

'I should begin,' Mark said, smiling in his clubby fashion at the trio, hoping to put them a bit more at their ease, since at the moment they couldn't have looked less at their ease had they been seated in a tumbrel surrounded by people speaking French. 'We should introduce ourselves,' he said, then gestured gracefully at Meadle, saying, 'Well, Buddy, we've already introduced you. It is Buddy, isn't it? You don't use Alfred much?'

'Not much,' Meadle admitted. Seated in the middle – hear-no-evil – he was blinking a lot.

Time to move the process along. 'Well, I'm Mark Sterling, Mark to my friends, of whom I hope to soon count yourselves, and this is Osbourne Faulk, known as Os to friend and foe alike.'

'Mr Os to foe,' Os said.

'Yes, of course,' Mark agreed, bouncing his negotiator's smile off Os's prominent cheekbone. 'If you'd like to introduce your friends, Buddy,' he went on, and spread his hands in a welcoming way, 'even if only by nickname at this moment, it would certainly help us to move forward.'

'I'm Mac,' said the fellow on the left: see-no-evil, of course.

Buddy turned to look at the profile of his other friend, who now looked like a man in a swarm of gnats, intolerably pestered yet unwilling to open his mouth to complain. Buddy said, 'You want *me* to innerduce you?'

35

'I don't know what this is all about,' cried speak-no-evil. 'What are we *doing* here?'

'Introducing ourselves, at the moment,' Mark told him, pleasantly enough. 'What we are doing here in a larger sense, however, if I take that to be your question, I believe we have all been brought to this corner of the world by a desire for revenge against one Monroe Hall.'

Mac gave him a skeptical look. '*You* didn't work for Hall.'

Oh, so that was it. Buddy was the driver, but Mac the natural leader. Mark remembered it had been Mac, from the rear seat of the Taurus, who'd said, 'I think we should do it.' Therefore, addressing Mac more directly now, Mark said, 'No, indeed, we didn't work for Monroe Hall, at least we were spared *that*. However, we did invest with SomniTech.'

To Mark's left, Os made that little *grr* sound he'd often make when about to lose control at tennis. Patting that knee – it quivered a little – Mark went on, 'It has been our hope, since pitching our tent outside the Hall compound, to, one way or another, recoup our losses.'

'Us, too,' Buddy said.

Surprised, Mark said, '*You* invested?'

'Everything,' Buddy told him. 'Life insurance. Health insurance. Pension plan.'

Oh, those things. They hardly mattered in the grand scheme of existence, after all, but Mark could just see that Buddy and his friends might treasure them more than they were really worth. Symbolic value, and so on. Sympathy at full bore, he said, 'So you see, we are in a similar situation.'

'I'm Ace,' abruptly said speak-no-evil, sitting up straight like a drum major, frowning massively at Mark.

Mark smiled upon him. 'Welcome to the group, Ace. Have you something to add?'

'How do we know,' Ace demanded, 'you aren't a cop?'

The limo, rented, like the Navigator, for its flash effect, traversed a climbing curve. The view outside, lovely enough, was sufficiently unchanging so as not to distract from the conversation within. His most open and boyish smile on his face, Mark said, 'Ace, all I can tell you is, no one in my entire life has ever mistaken me for a policeman.'

Mac said, 'Ace, these aren't cops. These are – whatchucallit – venture capitalists.' Raising a thick eyebrow at Mark, he said, 'That right?'

'Very good, Mac,' Mark said. 'Yes, we are investors by trade, though at rather a low level, in comparison with some of the names you'll read in the newspapers. We've had our wins and our losses, a nice win in a particular kind of rear window SUV windshield wiper, an unfortunate loss on a kind of nonflammable Christmas wreath available in every color except green—'

Os *grr*ed again, and Mark moved smoothly on: 'But rarely have we trusted any company as much as we trusted SomniTech, nor any smooth-talking son of a bitch as we trusted Monroe Hall – yes, Os, we know – and I'm afraid we severely overextended ourselves there, so that our little company at this moment is in ruins at our feet.'

'Too bad,' Buddy said, though without what sounded like much real sympathy.

'Yes, it is bad,' Mark agreed. 'Os and I are living on relatives, an unpleasant alternative in any circumstance. To make capital, as everyone knows, you must start with capital, and capital is just what we don't have at this moment. All sources, familial and institutional, had already been exhausted before the final blow fell. Long after Monroe Hall was taking money *out* of SomniTech, he was still urging us to put money *in*. Yes, Os.' Mark patted that quivering knee once more, then told the trio, 'It is only here, with our hands on Monroe Hall – yes, Os, on Monroe Hall's throat – that we can hope to recoup, to raise the capital that will finance a few extremely promising opportunities about which we have been made aware, but I'm sure you'll understand if I refrain from discussing in this venue.'

Os spoke for the first time, his throat partly closed by the intensity of his feelings, so that his voice had a rather clogged aspect: 'It might be enough for you three to just beat the bastard up, but we need him to put the blood back in our veins.'

Mac said, 'Beat him up?'

Oh. Had they been wrong about these three? Mark said, 'Os and I, having been aware of you three for some time, had assumed simple physical revenge was your plan. Were we wrong?'

'That depends,' Mac said, belatedly being cagy.

'I know there are others in the neighborhood with that sort of idea,' Mark told them. 'There's a fellow sits in the lobby of the Liberty Bell Hotel down in Dongenaide with a horsewhip, tells anybody who'll listen he's a former stockholder, wiped out, intends to horsewhip Monroe Hall within an inch of his life. How he expects to horsewhip Hall in the lobby of the Liberty Bell Hotel in Dongenaide I have no idea, but there he is.'

Os said, 'Not to kill him, though. I mean you three. I don't want you killing him. Not before he lays the golden egg.'

Mac said to Mark, 'You told Ace nobody ever mistook you for a cop. How many people you think mistake us for killers?'

'Point taken,' Mark said. 'But you haven't been hanging around here for your health. You have *some* scheme in mind. I tell you what. I'll tell you ours, and then you tell us yours. Deal?'

The three looked at one another, then Buddy and Ace looked at Mac, and then Mac looked at Mark and said, 'You go first?'

'That's the proposal,' Mark agreed. 'Right now, if you'd like.'

'Sure.'

As the Taurus three adjusted themselves, getting more comfortable because they were about to be told a story, Mark said, 'Monroe Hall did not drain the life out of a large and viable corporation out of personal need. He did it out of an excess of personal greed. In truth, Monroe Hall was born rich, as his father had been before him, and his father before him. In truth, despite the devastation he has caused to all around him, Monroe Hall is still rich. Some of his relatives who trusted him have a bit less than the cushion they'd always assumed would be there, but Hall himself is sitting on a pile.'

Buddy said, 'That's what we want some of.'

'Good,' Mark said. 'It is always a good thing when partners share a goal. Now, *our* scheme is dependent upon Monroe Hall's offshore holdings, untouched by the federal prosecutors, untouchable by American courts.'

Mac said, 'Offshore holdings? What's that?'

'Bank accounts, real estate, government paper, all in places closed off to American law.' Gesturing at the tinted windows, Mark said, 'You've heard of them as tax havens.'

Mac said, 'And where those dictators stash their loot, before they get thrown out. Numbered accounts.'

'Numbered accounts, exactly. Untraceable, untappable, even unprovable.'

'Not,' the constricted Os said, 'with our hands on his throat.'

'This is the idea, yes,' Mark said. 'We know how these money instruments work. Once we get our hands on Monroe, we can force him to make irrevocable transfers from *his* accounts to *our* accounts.'

Shaking his head, Mac said, 'The minute he walks into a bank—'

'No bank,' Mark told him. 'In fact, no travel. Really, all the best banking these days is done on the Internet.'

'You mean,' Buddy said, eyes clouded with confusion, 'hack into his bank accounts?'

'Certainly not,' Mark said. 'That's why we need the physical presence of Monroe Hall. Given Os's volatile personality, as you have no doubt remarked it, Monroe himself can be persuaded to make the transfers. After all, he knows his passwords, his identification numbers, just where to access which holdings.'

Mac said, 'You're gonna put his feet to the fire, you mean.'

'We considered that as a method,' Mark said, 'but it's too hard to explain a fire in June. There are other ways. And Monroe knows Os, he can guess what he's capable of.' As the trio soberly assessed Os, considering what he might be capable of, Mark said, 'But now it's your turn.'

Again they all exchanged looks. Ace asked his friends, 'Do we tell them? There's two of them, so they can be each other's witness, if they wanna turn us in.'

'There's three of *us*,' Mac pointed out, 'if *we* wanna turn *them* in. Why would we?'

Ace frowned, searching for an answer, while Buddy shook his head and said, 'Oh, go ahead, Mac, tell them.'

'Sure.' Facing Mark and Os, Mac said, 'Hold him for ransom.'

'Ransom?' Mark considered that. 'You mean a straight kidnapping?'

'Almost.' Mac nodded at his friends. 'We're all members of ACWFFA, and—'

'I'm sorry, the what?'

'Our union,' Mac explained. 'There's over twenty-seven hundred union members just from ACWFFA lost everything with SomniTech. So the idea is, we grab him, we hold him for ransom, but we don't want the ransom for us. The ransom goes to the union.'

'Ten mil,' Buddy said.

'What that is,' Mac said, 'it's a little over three grand for each and every union member.'

'Outa his pocket,' Ace said, 'and into ours.'

'I know three grand doesn't seem like a lot to you guys,' Mac said, 'but our union members could use it, and it would be like a symbol. Justice got done.'

'Admirable,' Mark said, and meant it. 'I admit you surprise me, Mac, I hadn't expected selflessness. I admit I'm feeling abashed. But I'm afraid there are problems with your idea.'

'Yeah,' Ace said. 'We can't get our hands on him.'

'In addition to that,' Mark said.

Os made one of his rare appearances, saying, 'Who'd pay for the son of a bitch? Not ten mil, ten bucks. Who'd pay for him?'

'His wife,' Mac said.

Mark said, 'It's possible you're right about that, Mac, but if her, surely she's the only one.'

'One will do,' Mac said.

'Except not,' Mark told him. 'If she tried to raise the ransom, what assets would she use? Her husband's.'

'That's the idea,' Ace said.

'But,' Mark said, 'if Alicia Hall – that's her name – if she reached out to her husband's unseized holdings, if she withdrew ten million dollars from anything at all belonging to him, and brought it into the country, the courts would take it away from her long before she could get it to you and the . . . your union.

'ACWFFA,' Mac said, helpfully.

'Yes, them,' Mark said. 'The money might get to Alicia Hall, if she asked for it, but it would never get *through* her. Our idea has a much better likelihood of success.'

Mac said, 'Then why'd you want to talk to us? If you've already got your success.'

'Because,' Mark said, 'while we have the *likelihood* of success, which you do not, so far we do not have the actuality of success. But with three strong, gifted, imaginative, and, if I may say so, noble fellows like yourselves joined to us, success might still be in the offing.'

'An extra ten mil to you,' Os threw in.

'Exactly,' Mark said. 'So long as we're having our way with Monroe's offshore accounts, there's no reason we can't drop an additional bundle into the coffers of, uh, the, your union.'

'ACWFFA,' Mac said.

'Exactly.'

'What we've been thinking recently,' Mac said, 'is, it might be what we got to do now is go in there into that compound and just bring him out.'

Mark turned a hugely beaming countenance upon Os, who himself was very nearly smiling. 'There, you see?' Mark said. 'Great minds *do* think alike.'

9

Andy Kelp trusted doctors. Not so much on the medical side, though some of them were pretty good at that, too, but on the question of automobiles. As far as he was concerned, if you trusted a doctor's judgment when it came to his personal wheels, you were not likely to go far wrong.

Doctors have a deep understanding, for instance, of the difference between comfort and pain, so they're unlikely to choose a car with a badly designed driver's seat or misplaced steering wheel or one of those accelerators where your knee begins to hurt after a hundred miles. Also, doctors have a perhaps too-vivid picture in their minds of the aftereffects of high-speed physical impacts, so they're mostly going to wrap themselves in products that will (a) avoid accidents where possible, or (b) survive them when necessary. Thus, when Andy Kelp went shopping in the streets and parking lots of greater New York for transportation, he always went for the sign of the MD plate.

Today, however, Kelp had a second criterion to include in his search, which was that he needed not just a car and not just a doctor's car, but a *large* car currently owned by a doctor. This wasn't because the car would be carrying five travelers, but because one of the travelers would be Tiny.

It was, therefore, a distinct pleasure to him when, the morning after the meeting at the O. J., while roving the outer reaches of long-term parking out at Kennedy International Airport, a place where you're pretty much guaranteed to have a few days' head start if you choose a vehicle with no dust on it, he saw ahead of him a Buick Roadmaster Estate, seven or eight years old, an antique the day it was built, a nine-passenger station wagon with not only room enough inside for a bowling team but room enough for that team to bowl. And proudly below that broad rear window and door, a . . . yes! MD plate.

This grand vehicle was a color not seen in nature, nor much of anywhere else except certain products of Detroit. It was a metallic shimmering kind of not-chartreuse, not-gold, not-silver, not-mauve, with just a hint of not-maroon. It was in effect a rendering in enamel of a restaurant's wine list descriptions. But even better, from Kelp's point of view,

41

the Roadmaster was dust-free.

It's amazing how many people don't want to carry their parking lot ticket with them when they travel, preferring to 'hide' it behind the sun visor instead. Even some doctors. Kelp was happy to pay the two-day parking fee, explaining to the ticket-taker's surprised look, 'Emergency at the hospital.'

'Oh, too bad.'

Kelp took his change, took the Van Wyck Expressway toward the city, and while stopped by the monorail construction phoned the troops. 'I'm on my way,' he told them, not completely accurately.

Still, they didn't have that long to wait, at Ninth Avenue and Thirty-ninth Street, before Kelp slid the Roadmaster in at the curb next to them. Once he got there, it didn't take them long to sort themselves out. Chester and Stan, of course, had to ride up front with Kelp, because they'd be the drivers on the day and Chester knew how to find Hall's place. Tiny, of course, had to sit on the back seat; *all* of the back seat. And Dortmunder, of course, had to open the rear door and climb over the tailgate and sit on the backward-facing final seat, as though he'd been bad in class.

'Been waiting long?' Kelp asked, after everyone was in and the door closed.

'A while,' rumbled Tiny from behind him.

'They waved down a couple real doctors,' Chester said, between Kelp and Stan. 'I think one of them's gonna send a bill.'

'We'll fight him to the Supreme Court,' Kelp said, and accelerated to and through the Lincoln Tunnel and across New Jersey without looking at it, and halfway across Pennsylvania.

'There it is,' Chester said.

'There what is?' Kelp asked.

'The compound. Hall's land, it started just back there.'

Tiny said, 'Pull off, let's look at this.'

'Right,' Dortmunder said, from way in the back.

This was a fairly straight county road, rolling along with the low hills to either side, some of it farmed and some of it forested. This stretch was forested on both sides. The right shoulder was wide enough for a car to pull off, but just beyond the shoulder was an old low stone wall that suggested this land too had at one time been farmed, or at least settled. Beyond the wall was second-growth forest, tall but skinny-trunked trees with a lot of bramble and shrubbery underneath.

'This is it here,' Chester said. 'The main entrance – well, the only entrance now – is a couple miles farther on.'

Kelp peered past Chester and Stan at the empty forest. 'Where's the security start? Down by the entrance?'

'No, it's here,' Chester said. 'Not right out by the road, in behind the wall about ten feet. Stan, open the window, would you?'

So Stan, next to the door, rolled the window down and said, 'I don't see anything.'

'You can't see the wires,' Chester told him, 'but you can see the uprights.' He pointed past Stan's nose at the trees. 'See them?'

Stan sighted along Chester's forearm, closing one eye. 'Oh, yeah,' he said.

Kelp squinted, looking past Chester and Stan, glance roaming among the trees; then all at once he realized he was looking at a slender black metal pole, about six feet tall. Off to the left, a little farther, a little farther, there was another one. 'I see them,' he said. 'Very discreet.'

'They didn't want it to look like a penitentiary or something,' Chester explained.

Dortmunder, from way back there, said, 'I don't see them.'

Tiny said, 'What kinda wire?'

'Electric,' Chester said. 'Not enough to kill you, but enough to make you go away. Like a deer fence. But if a wire gets broken, there's a signal in the guardhouse, tells them exactly where, between which two posts. And there's lights in the trees, you can't see them from here, but if the wire gets broken at night, they can switch the lights on, it's like high noon in there.'

'I don't see them,' Dortmunder said.

Stan said, 'Just one wire?'

'No, three,' Chester said. 'At two feet, four feet, and six feet.'

'Hey,' Dortmunder called. 'I'm back here, remember me?'

Kelp looked in the mirror and saw him way back there, waving for attention. 'Oh, hi, John,' he said. 'Almost forgot about you.'

'I noticed that,' Dortmunder said. 'What I don't notice is these posts you're all talking about.'

'They're right there,' Tiny said, and waved a paw at the woods.

'I don't see them,' Dortmunder insisted.

Chester said, 'OK, John, you and I can get out, I'll show it to you.'

So that's what they did. Stan had to get out first, to let Chester out; then he leaned against the side of the car, leaving the door open, while the other two stepped over the stone wall and walked in among the trees. The occasional vehicle went by, mostly pickup trucks, but nobody paid any attention to the parked car or the strolling men.

With the door open, Kelp could hear Chester as he said, 'Closer in, they've got motion sensors, but not way over here. So we can walk right up to it. See it, John? See it there? *Stop*, you're gonna walk into it!'

'What? There's— I can't— Oh, *this*! It's metal!'

'Sure,' Chester said, and pointed away to the right. 'Metal poles. See them? Every so often, all the way to the cornfield back there, that's where Hall's property stops.'

'I thought it was gonna be wood,' Dortmunder said. 'I was looking for wood.'

'They did it in metal.'

'Yeah, sure, I get it.'

Dortmunder now squinted off to the right, holding a hand up to his brow to shade his eyes even though he stood under a whole lot of trees in full leaf. He said, 'So then it makes the turn and goes along next to the cornfield, is that it?'

'All around the property,' Chester said. 'Miles of it.'

'What happens if I touch the wire?' Dortmunder asked, and he could be seen to lean toward where the fence must be, as though touching it might be a good idea. 'Does it tell the guards?'

'Not unless you break it. But it'll give you a hell of a wallop, John, knock you back a few feet, probably give you a sore arm for a few days.'

Kelp called, 'Don't do it, John.'

'I wasn't going to,' Dortmunder said, and the two of them came back to the car, where he said, 'Now that we're here, maybe Chester or Stan would like to switch with me, I can ride up—'

'No, John,' Kelp said. 'We need Chester to describe it to us. '

Stan said, 'And I gotta keep my eye on the routes.'

Dortmunder sighed. 'Fine,' he said, and stumped away to get into the third tier again.

When they were all aboard and Kelp had them rolling once more, slowly, beside the forest and the stone wall, Dortmunder called to them, 'It's amazing to me how many grown men and women, if you're sitting back here, make faces at you. Stick their tongue out. Grown-up men and women, driving, think they're funny.'

'Pretend you don't see them,' Kelp advised.

'I do,' Dortmunder said. 'But I do see them. Waving their hands, thumbing their nose, yukking it up. It wears you down after a while.'

'If we find a store,' Tiny suggested, 'we can buy some carpet tacks, you can toss them out your window back there.'

'That's a very good idea, Tiny,' Dortmunder said. 'Thank you.'

Looking ahead, Kelp said, 'What's happening, now?'

The forest was coming to a ragged end, followed by a very large expanse of weedy barren land, with a few farm buildings very far back. The low stone wall continued, and so did the black metal poles bearing the electric wires, the poles more visible now that they weren't in among trees.

Chester said, 'They used to lease this part to commercial tomato grow-ers every year. These people would come in, a little earlier in the spring than this, plant a million plants, put chemical shit everywhere, go away, come back at the end of August for one harvest, middle of September for another, leave the rest of the tomatoes right where they are, you had this whole carpet of red here until frost. Very pretty.'

Kelp said, 'But they don't do that any more.'

'Well, they can't, with the security,' Chester said. 'Also, I understand it, the company didn't want to do business with Hall any more.'

Kelp said, 'People that fill up the food and the ground with chemicals, even *those* people won't deal with Monroe Hall?'

'He's not well liked,' Chester said.

'If they left the rest of the crop like that,' Stan said, 'there's probably volunteers growing in there now.'

'Never volunteer,' Tiny commented.

Soon the weedy field came to an end, with more farm buildings, some of them looking abandoned, and then a blacktop road that ran through a greater variety of landscape – parts with trees, cleared parts, buildings of different kinds, some looking like small residences, some like storage.

Kelp said, 'What've we got here now?'

'Some of the cars are in those buildings there,' Chester said, pointing. 'The ones without windows.'

'What about the ones that look like houses?'

'They're houses,' Chester said. 'Where the staff lives. See that nice green one? That's where *I* lived, me and my family.'

'It's like a little village in there,' Kelp said.

'Not as much occupied as it used to be,' Chester said. 'He lost a lotta staff.'

'Running out of money?'

'No, he'll never run out of money. It's just more people he screwed, like me. And other people left 'cause they just didn't like him any more. It's tough for him to hire people now. I hear he's trying to recruit in South Africa.'

Kelp said, 'South Africa?'

'Because they speak English,' Chester said, 'but they never heard of Monroe Hall. He needs people that never heard of him. Here comes the entrance.'

First there was a long one-story office building of gray stucco, with venetian blinds in all the windows, some up, some down, some crooked. Then there was a six-foot-high wall of gray weathered barn siding, and then a blacktop road, one lane on either side of a rustic guardshack that looked like a tugboat coming at you. Serious-looking metal rods were down across both lanes, and three people in rent-a-cop uniforms could be seen inside the big-windowed guardshack. The blacktop road wandered in among more village-type buildings and some not-well-cared-for lawns and plantings. And way in back just a glimpse could be seen of Tara, the house from *Gone With the Wind*.

Kelp drove on, past another barn-siding wall, as Dortmunder called, 'Was that it? The big white house back in there?'

Chester said, 'It goes for about another mile along this road, and then there's a shopping mall, by the intersection with the state highway.'

Stan said, 'Was that big white house back there where Hall lives?'

'Yeah, that's his place.'

'Andy! Andy! Hey, dammit, Andy!'

Kelp looked in the mirror, and there was Dortmunder again, waving like before, or maybe a little more desperately. 'Hi, John,' he said. 'You wanted something?'

'Find a place and *park*. Stop. I gotta talk to you people and I can't do anything back here.'

'Sure, John,' Kelp said. 'But maybe we oughta look at this mall first, see if there's a way in from there.'

'Forget the mall,' Dortmunder said.

Chester said, 'It isn't easier at the mall, Andy, it's worse. There's an eight-foot-high chain-link fence all along the property line there.'

'Forget the mall,' Dortmunder said. 'The mall doesn't matter.'

Tiny said, 'If we brought a truck in, we could go over the top of the fence.'

'Forget the mall, will you?'

Chester said, 'But you've still got the electric fence. That goes all the way around the property.'

'Forget the mall!'

'Well, we'll go on to the mall, anyway,' Kelp decided. 'See what things look like along the way. I think John wants to stop for something anyway, when we get there.'

'Yes, stop! That's right! Stop!'

Kelp said, 'Chester, is there anything interesting along this part, before the mall?'

'No, it's all pretty much the same.'

'I give up.'

So they drove on to the mall, and when they turned in at the entrance Kelp said, 'Any kind of store in particular you want, John?'

'A parking space,' Dortmunder said. 'Stop the car. Stop it. Make it stop.'

Stan said, 'That's a pretty big fence they got up there. Maybe we should get over closer to it.'

'Stop! Stop! Stop *now!*'

'That's what I'm doing,' Kelp said, and drove around a little, and then found a parking space not too far from the home appliance store, in case it turned out anybody needed anything. He switched off the engine, looked in the mirror, and said, 'John? Here OK?'

Twisting around, Stan said, 'John, it took forever to get out here. We don't want to waste too much time sitting around some mall. We gotta figure out a way to deal with that electric fence. We gotta figure out how to get in there and get back out again, with a whole lotta cars.'

'Forget that,' Dortmunder said. 'Forget the fence.'

Finally he had everybody's attention. They all twisted around to look at him, the ones in front banging each other up pretty well along the way, and then Tiny said, 'Dortmunder, we're outside. The fence is there, all around. We gotta get inside. We gotta get past the fence. We can't forget it.'

'This is what I've been trying to tell you,' Dortmunder said. 'There's no way to defeat the fence. We gotta do it another way.'

Chester said, 'John, there is no other way.'

'Well,' Kelp said, 'if John says there is, maybe there is. John?'

'Monroe Hall needs staff,' Dortmunder said. 'We hire on.'

10

Of all his clients, Flip Morriscone thought Monroe Hall was by far the one he hated the most. Oh, he hated them all, of course, flabby flatulent creatures, no self-discipline at all, expecting *him* to sweat for them, expecting his magic hour once a day or even once a week would make up for all the rest of their self-indulgent lives.

But of them all, Monroe Hall was the worst. Big self-involved baby, just too precious for words. And look at the *security* around La Manse Monroe – as though a movie star lived there, at the very least. But who would *want* to get close to Monroe Hall? As far as Flip was concerned, people would pay good money to stay away from the man. But no. So here we go again.

Flip drove his forest green Subaru Forester along the county road in the afternoon spring sunshine, perfectly on time for his three o'clock with Horrible Hall, turned in at the entrance and stopped before the iron bar, as he did three times a week, next to the guardshack.

And as also happened three times a week, every week, thirty-some weeks and counting, the sullen-faced guard came out, pretended he'd never seen Flip before in his life, checked his name off on the clipboard he carried like a tiny shield, and demanded identification. At one point, seven or eight weeks into the relationship, Flip had tried jollity, saying, 'Surely you remember me? From two days ago?' But the expressionless guard had merely said, 'Gotta see ID before you come in.' So since then Flip had merely flipped the Neanderthal a quick close-up of his driver's license, and thus gained entry.

Well, it wasn't quite that easy. First the clipboard, then the identification, then the call to the Master to confirm that yes, Flip Morriscone did have his usual appointment with the Big Cheese, all done with great solemnity, the required ritual, like a religious event or something.

But then at last, also as usual, the guard raised the metal boom and Flip could zip on in and up the long two-lane blacktop to the Big House, which is the way he thought of the sprawling white mansion that dominated the view within the compound. Drive up, follow the right fork of the blacktop to the parking area beside the house, then grab his long canvas bag from the back and carry it around to the front door. Heavy bag it was, flipped onto Flip's shoulder, the knuckles of his right hand as he gripped the two cloth handles resting on his trapezius, flexing both the pecs and the 'ceps.

The first two weeks he'd had this client, there'd been an angry man waiting for him at the front of the house, dressed in a uniform something like a United Parcel deliveryperson, to take the Forester from Flip and park it, but the third week United Parcel was gone and instead the butler called to him from the open front door, 'Park it around the side there, that's a good fellow.'

Good fellow. He'd lasted only a couple more months himself, the butler, and now it was Monroe Hall who opened the front door of the Big House to Flip three times a week. Staff seemed to be thinning out around the Big House.

Could Hall be getting a bit light in the coffers? It seemed unlikely, with evidence of the man's wealth everywhere you looked (though in Flip's experience that could be misleading, too), but in any case Flip was always paid promptly. And in cash, as well; no point getting the IRS mixed up in the transaction.

Once again, Hall himself stood in the open doorway, beaming out at him. How ridiculously happy the clients were to see him, as though he could possibly effect any real change at all in their lap-of-luxury lives. They all wanted to look like *him*, is what it was, so when they smiled him a greeting they were actually saying hello to the fantasy selves in their own minds.

The reality was considerably worse. Hall, for instance, was a moderately large man, probably a welterweight in his youth, now covered with flab like a duck waiting to be roasted. To make matters worse, every time he had a session with Flip, Hall wore yet another of his matching sets of sweats; today's were electric blue, with gold stripes up the arms and legs. Why he so wanted to look like a New Jersey mobster Flip would never understand.

'Good afternoon, Mr Hall,' he called breezily, as he came up the walk.

'A beautiful afternoon, Flip,' Hall told him, beaming all over his fat face. 'A pity to be indoors.'

'Oh, but it's time to work.'

'I know, I know.'

Hall closed the door, his smile turning sad, then immediately happy again. 'One of these days, Flip,' he said, 'you and I must go riding. Great exercise. In the great outdoors.'

They were walking toward, then up, the broad central staircase. Flip said, 'Riding? Riding what, Mr Hall?'

'Horses, of course!' Hall beamed like a man who'd just ridden a horse all the way from Monument Valley.

'Really?' Surprised (he didn't like the clients to surprise him), Flip said, 'I didn't know you rode horses, Mr Hall.'

'I'm learning,' Hall said. As they reached the second floor and moved down the wide corridor, he gestured vaguely off to the right. 'Got a couple sweet-dispositioned mares in a stable over there,' he said. 'Fixed up one of the barns for them.'

Flip stood aside to let Hall precede him into the gym, as somewhere a cuckoo said, '*Cuckoo*,' thrice. 'That one's late,' Flip said, and followed Hall through the doorway.

The petulance that was never gone from Hall's face for long came storming back. 'Something else I can't get fixed,' he said, as Flip put on the table his bag, filled with towels, liniments, small weights. 'You'd think people would *want* to fix things. Even sent it over with one of the guards, in mufti, claim it was his clock, but they knew. Recognized it, knew it was mine.' He made a disgusted sweeping gesture. 'So it runs slow, that's all. Runs slow.'

'But we don't, Mr Hall,' Flip reminded him, and waved at the side-by-side treadmills. 'Shall we start with a little jog?'

'I suppose we must,' Hall said, with the self-pitying sigh Flip knew all too well.

'Be right with you,' Flip said, and stripped down to his running shorts and tee.

'I've been meaning to ask you about that, Flip,' Hall said, hanging back as Flip moved toward the treadmill.

'Ask me about what? No stalling now, Mr Hall.'

'Oh, no, certainly not.' Hall approached, but did not get on, the machine. 'I *was* taking riding lessons,' he said. 'But that fellow isn't— He won't do it any more. I wondered, by any chance, do you know anybody who teaches riding?'

'Gee, I don't, Mr Hall,' Flip said. 'Most of my friends are human.'

Hall made a little laugh, more a whinny, as though he were becoming a horse himself. 'Just a thought,' he said.

'Come on, Mr Hall, step up here. Let's go for our jog.'

So they did, bouncing along side by side among all the equipment. Hall's gym was as complete as most professional spas, with the treadmill and Nautilus machines and barbells and anything your little jock's heart could desire. The machines were all several years old, though, and when Flip had first seen them they hadn't shown the slightest indication of any actual use. They were simply another of Hall's endless collections, and why all of a sudden he'd decided to *use* the health equipment, Flip neither knew nor cared. It was a job, that's all. The equipment was good, and he doubted it was ever used except when he was on the premises.

Hall could never do more than ten minutes on the treadmill, even with the dial set at barely more than a brisk walking pace. During that time, Flip observed himself in the mirror and, to a lesser extent, observed the client.

None of the clients wanted a mirror, but Flip insisted on it. 'You have to watch yourself,' he'd tell them. 'You have to see the progress you're making. You have to figure out where you need more work.'

All of which was true, but Flip had other reasons as well, which he saw no reason to mention. For one thing, it was punishment to make the slobs view their own hopeless efforts, punishment they richly deserved. And for another, it gave Flip the opportunity to watch *himself*.

Flip Morriscone would rather watch himself than anyone else on the planet, man or woman, and that was because he was in the absolute peak of physical condition; rockhard abs, rockhard butt, legs like a centaur's, neck like a plinth. On the treadmill, on the machines, anywhere, what he was really doing was not training the slobs. What he was really doing was watching himself, and getting paid for it. (In his dreams, he often walked beside himself, holding hands.)

After the jog, with Hall gasping and weaving, Flip gave a period on the leglift machine, so Hall would have a little opportunity to sit. While he groaned over the strain of lifting those weights, just from the knees down, his face streaming, sweats already living up to their name, Hall said, 'Flip, this is horribly hard work, but do you know, I look forward to it?'

'Well, sure you do, Mr Hall. It makes you feel better.'

'It makes me feel much worse, Flip.' Hall emitted another groan, then managed a ghastly smile as he said, 'Do you know what *does* make me feel better, Flip?'

'What's that, Mr Hall?'

'You being here.'

'That's what I'm talking about, Mr Hall.'

'No, not this torture, Flip. You *being* here. *You*.'

Good God, Flip thought, is he throwing a pass at me? That did happen from time to time (why not, with such perfection as his?), and it was repulsive in the extreme, and usually ended with Flip saying farewell to that client, walking out on the 'you must have misunderstood' malarkey. Was another client about to self-destruct?

'I don't follow you, Mr Hall,' Flip said, watching Hall's eyes like a panther watching a deer.

'I've learned over the years, Flip,' Hall said, 'that friendship is a some-time thing. People I thought were— Well, doesn't matter. I know we've become good friends over the last few months, Flip, and I just want you to know I value that. I'm glad we're pals.'

'Pals,' pronounced as though just learned from a foreign language. Flip smiled large in relief, it wasn't a pass after all. 'Of course we're pals, Mr Hall,' he told the client.

11

Anne Marie didn't like it when Andy brooded, because it happened so seldom that it had to mean something serious had gone wrong. He'd been his usual cheery optimistic self when he'd left for Pennsylvania with John and the others, but in the three days since, his mood had considerably darkened. Not unhappy, exactly, or angry. Mostly he seemed to be stymied, to have walked into a wall somehow, unable to move, and therefore unable to catch up with his regular buoyant self.

Generally speaking, Anne Marie left Andy to be Andy, with no interference from her. He was like a smooth-running but intricate machine whose workings were completely unknowable, and therefore not to be messed with. For instance, she knew how to drive a car and considered herself a good driver, but there were some special high-performance vehicles she wouldn't dare try to take control of, and that's what Andy was to her: too complex and abrupt to steer.

But this funk had been going on for three days, which was an eternity in the weather of Andy Kelp, and it showed no signs of improving, so finally, in the midafternoon of the third day, a Saturday, when yet again she walked into the living room and Andy was slumped in his favorite chair, gazing glassy-eyed in the general direction of the television set, which didn't happen to be switched on, she had to try at least kicking the tires a little: 'Hi, Andy.'

'Hi.' His smile was as chipper as ever, but there didn't seem to be anything behind it.

Feeling suddenly like the wife in a soap opera, although she was neither, she sat on the sofa, where she could see him most directly, and said, 'Andy?'

His eyes rolled toward her; his brows lifted slightly. The smile on his lips was small and nostalgic, as though he were remembering happy times rather than being in them. 'Mm?'

'What's wrong, Andy?'

He sat up straighter. He looked surprised. 'Wrong? Nothing's wrong.'

'Ever since you came back from Penn—'

'Oh, that,' he said, and brushed it away, as though now he understood what she was talking about and it was nothing, nothing. 'That's not my problem,' he said. 'That's John's problem.'

'What problem?'

'His.'

'Andy,' Anne Marie said, 'what's John's problem that you keep thinking about?'

'Do I keep thinking about it?' He considered that. 'Huh. Maybe I do, from time to time. You see, Anne Marie, we wanna get into this place—'

'I know,' she said. 'That's what you do.'

'Right.' Andy nodded. 'That's what we do. Get into a place, get what we want, get out, game over. The thing is, *this* place, you can't get in. I mean, you really can't get in.'

'So no game,' Anne Marie suggested.

'Well, the thing is,' Andy said, 'John came up with a great way to get in, a really great way. But now we're stuck. We can't make that way work. I mean, John can't.'

Anne Marie said, 'Do you went to tell me about it?'

'It won't do any good, but sure, why not?' He adjusted himself more comfortably in his chair, and said, 'The guy has this huge compound surrounded by electric fence and guards, no way through it without being seen and heard. The guy is also a rat, so the ships are deserting him. Not the ships, his crew, his staff, the people that work for him. So he's got like a skeleton crew there, and John's brilliant idea is, we hire on. We're working for the guy, naturally we're on the property.'

'Well, that is a brilliant idea,' Anne Marie said, 'if he's hiring.'

'Oh, he's hiring,' Andy said. 'Or he would be, if anybody'd show up. *Our* trouble is, anybody he hires has to be checked by the law. Chester couldn't work for him any more because he was an ex-con. *All* of us are ex-cons, Anne Marie, all four of us, John and Tiny and Stan and me. What we need is new ID, and we don't know how to do that. I mean, we know how to go to Arnie Albright the fence and buy a driver's license, a credit card, it won't burn to the ground for another two, three days, but that stuff doesn't survive an *inspection*. Not by a bankruptcy court or a lot of feds. How do you get a different identity that stands up? That's where John is down in the dumps about right now.'

'And you, too,' she told him.

'Well, maybe a little.' He shrugged. 'Still, it's John's brilliant idea, so it's John that feels so bad.'

She shook her head, surveying him. 'You just wasted three days,' she said.

He gave her his alert look, almost like the old days. 'I did?'

'We're gonna have to remember this, Andy,' she said. 'Any time you've got a problem, you've got to talk it out with me. Mostly, all I'll be able to give you is sympathy, but that's not so bad.'

'Not bad at all,' he agreed.

'But *this* time,' she said, 'I'm almost positive I can solve your problem.'

'Come on, Anne Marie,' he said. 'You're gonna run some birth certificates off on your computer? This stuff has to stand up.'

'That's what I'm talking about. Andy, you *know*, when I was a kid, my father was a congressman, in Congress, from the great state of Kansas.'

'Yeah, I know.'

'Well, for a lot of that time,' she said, 'and when I was in college, and after, he was on the Select Intelligence Committee in the Congress, to liaise with the FBI and the CIA and all of those other people in the intelligence community. The spooks.'

'Spies.'

'They call themselves spooks,' she informed him.

'They do?' Andy scratched an ear. 'Have they thought that through?'

'It's what they call themselves.'

'OK.' Nodding, he said, 'Select Intelligence, you said. What's Select Intelligence?'

'You have all this news coming in,' she explained, 'from all over the world, all this intelligence, what they call the raw data. Select Intelligence is when you select the parts that agree with what you already wanted to do.'

'OK,' Andy said. 'That sounds about right.'

'And my father,' Anne Marie said, 'got to know this guy called Jim Green that was a substitute identity specialist.'

'Jim Green.'

'He said he called himself that because it was the easiest name in the world to forget.'

'That wasn't his real name? What was his real name?'

'No one will ever know. Andy, Jim Green's *job* was to put together new identifications for spooks, identification packages so real, so secure, they could travel in foreign countries, they could be arrested, they could testify in court, they could do *anything* and the identification would hold up.'

'That's pretty good,' Andy allowed.

Anne Marie said, 'It's better than the Witness Protection Program. There's retired spooks now with murder charges against them, fatwas out on them, death sentences passed on them, living under a new identification that Jim Green gave them, they're safe forever, die in their own beds at a hundred.'

'Of what?'

'Old age. The point is, he could give you and John exactly what you need.'

Andy, doubtful, said, 'Why would he?'

'I knew him for years,' she said. 'He and my parents were neighbors in D.C. He's retired now, but I'm sure I could find him.'

'And you think he'd do this for you.'

'Oh, sure.' Laughing lightly, she said, 'He always liked me. He used to dandle me on his knee.'

'When you were a little girl.'

'Oh, seventeen, eighteen,' she said. Getting to her feet, she said, 'Let me make some calls.'

12

'Benson,' Jim Green said. 'Barton. Bingam.'

'Bingham has seven letters,' Chiratchkovich objected.

'Not without the "H".'

Looking surprised, Chiratchkovich said, 'We can do that?'

'We can do whatever we want,' Jim Green told him, 'as long as it's six letters long and starts with "B". Burger. Bailey. Boland.'

The room Jim Green and Anton Chiratchkovich sat in, almost knee to knee, was small, square, windowless, illuminated almost completely by the dials and screens on just about every surface. Jim Green, a lanky soft-edged man of indeterminate age, with features that faded away as you looked at him – nose-shaped nose, boring eyes, just enough eyebrow, thin but not too thin mouth, completely unnoticeble jawline, a rug that so thoroughly imitated the onset of male-pattern baldness in shades of tan and gray that it was impossible to believe it really was a rug, because who would go out of their way to make their head look like that? – perched on a metal folding chair, feet up on tiptoes to raise his lap slightly so he could better peck away at the laptop he held, its dim light rising from the surface of the screen to fade into the folds of his face.

Opposite him, seated on a sagging old oft-recovered armchair, waited Anton Chiratchkovich, bulky, sixtyish, heavy-browed, fat rolls on neck, overdressed in a too-tight black suit and white shirt and dark thin strangling necktie, who looked exactly what he was: a longtime small-time bully and embezzler who'd swum for years in the stew of a corrupt government somewhere east of the Urals until his string had run out, and who at the moment was being hunted down like a dog.

Well, not at the moment. Not in this secure room here, so deep within Jim Green's bland suburban development house outside Danbury, Connecticut, that it wasn't even within the house any more, but burrowed into the hillside behind it, reachable only through a long passage lined with both copper and lead, to keep intrusions out and radio waves in.

Unlike Chiratchkovich, Jim Green had never attempted to turn his government service into cash. He was an artist, identification manipulation was his art, and the United States government his patron. It had been sufficient for him to do his job better than anyone else in the world, to recognize the awe in the eyes of the cognoscenti who knew of his works, and to move like the shadow of a shadow through the greater world of the unknowing.

Green's own distant past contained secrets so horrible, so chilling, from the years before he'd learned self-control, that he himself couldn't stand to look in that direction. Like the volunteer in the French Foreign Legion, he had slipped into the persona of 'Jim Green' to forget, and except for the rare nightmare, he had forgotten.

He had been happy in government service, but times change, and sometimes a valued skill becomes less valued. When the enemy was German or Russian, there was much for Jim Green to do, because basically everybody in the cast looked the same. But when the enemy became Pakistani, or Indonesian, or Korean, the skills of identity morphing gave way to the skills of bribery and subornation. His final years with the agency, Green had less and less to do.

And yet, he loved his work, and wanted to go on doing it. Outside the government, there were still, as it turned out, many who needed desperately to be able to say, 'Here!' to a new name, and who had the money, a whole lot of money, to make it happen. Thus Jim Green became a freelancer, his work now as secret as his history.

Chiratchkovich, for instance, had come to him, as most of them did, through the recommendation of a previous satisfied customer. After preliminary telephoning, and Green's own background check to be certain Anton Chiratchkovich was (so far) who he claimed to be, they had met today in a parking garage in Bridgeport, where Chiratchkovich had submitted to the blindfold and the handcuffs and the trip in the trunk of Green's no-color Honda Accord. In his own attached garage outside Danbury, he'd helped his guest out of the trunk, then led him, still blindfolded and cuffed, through the invisible door at the end of the garage, down the cement steps, along the metal corridor, and into this secure room, where he'd removed the cuffs and blindfold, both had sat down, and Green had gone to work.

Photos had been taken, eyes scanned, blood tested, voice recorded. Some of Chiratchkovich's more blameless history had been noted down, to adapt to the new persona.

Chiratchkovich had a slight but noticeable eastern European accent, which meant he couldn't present himself as native-born American, but that wouldn't be a problem. In some ways, it made the job easier.

Every day, the web of information grows thicker, more convoluted. When so much is known, what can still be secret? But the very complexity of the knowledge stream at times betrays it. Here and there, in the interstices of the vast web of details covering the globe, there are glitches, hiccups, anomalies, crossed wires. Jim Green could find those like a hunting dog after a downed quail. He could find them and store the knowledge of them for later use.

Now, for instance, he could use one of those lacunae in order to insert into the system, as though he'd always been there, a naturalized American citizen who had shortened and anglicized his name to something of six letters that started with 'B.' All Chiratchkovich had to do was choose the name he would answer to the rest of his life.

'Buford. Bligen. Beemis,'

'Beemis!' said the customer.

Green looked up at him. 'Beemis?'

'Beemis!'

'You're sure.'

'It feels like *me*,' Chiratchkovich said, and breathed it like a drawn-out prayer: 'Beeee-mis. Yes. I like.'

'Fine,' Green said. 'Beemis it is.'

'Ah, but the first name,' the new Beemis said. 'What do I do for a first name?'

'Keep your own,' Green advised. 'You're used to it. Americanize it. Anthony. You'll be Tony.'

'Tony. Tony Beemis.' The heavy jowls parted for a heavy smile. 'I know that is me.'

'Good.' Green made a note. 'In two weeks, I'll have your paperwork.'

'And I,' Tony Beemis assured him, 'shall have the gold.'

'I'll phone you,' Green said, 'at the same number.'

'Yes, of course.'

Green closed his laptop, rested it on the floor, and leaned it against the front of a cupboard. 'And now,' he said regretfully, getting to his feet, 'I'm sorry, but we'll have to button you down for the return trip.'

'Certainly,' Beemis said, rising, extending his hands for the cuffs. 'I understand.'

It was when he returned home after delivering Beemis to his car in the garage in Bridgeport that Green found the message on his answering machine from little Anne Marie Hurst: 'Hi, Jim, it's Anne Marie Carpinaw. Remember when I was Anne Marie Hurst, my father was your neighbor, the congressman from Kansas, John Hurst? I've got a question that, gee, you're the perfect guy to ask on this. I hope I'm not intruding, I got your number from Fran Dowdy, remember her? She's still a secretary there at the agency, isn't that something? Let me give you my cell phone number, and I hope you'll call. Be nice to talk to you again.'

Copying down the number as she reeled it off, Green couldn't help but grin. Oh, yeah, he remembered little Anne Marie Hurst, all right. Not even that little. Just right, in Jim Green's estimation.

It had been years, though. He wondered if she was at the peak of perfection these days, or maybe just a little over the hill. Oh, sure, he'd call her, all right. Nice to see little Anne Marie again.

It didn't even occur to him to wonder what she wanted.

13

'They aren't gonna do it,' Os said.

This troubling possibility troubled Mark as well, but he was hoping against hope. 'But it's the right thing to *do*,' he insisted.

'They aren't gonna do it,' Os said. He sounded pretty sure of himself.

The two were seated in the knotty pine rec room in the basement of Mark's mother and stepfather's home in Westport, the rec room being just next to the lumber room he was unfortunately bunking in these days. It was difficult enough to have to move back in with one's parents at the age of forty-two – and a bit irritating to the old folks as well, as they had subtly but relentlessly made clear – but it was even worse to have to live in the *basement*.

That huge house above him contained room after room, yet not one of them was considered appropriate housing for a prodigal son. True, this was not the house in nearby Norwalk where he'd grown up, nor the Daddy he'd grown up with, so he wasn't actually *returning*, but why couldn't there be a comfy bedroom upstairs somewhere, with a view?

But, no. Mum had made that perfectly clear. 'You're not to clutter up my sewing room with your tubular socks, and Roger needs the library for his research as you well know, and the keeping room is out of the question, being right in everybody's traffic pattern,' and on and on, till it began to seem, if they'd had a manger, there wouldn't have been room for him there, either.

What was he to say? That he hadn't worn tube socks in twenty years? What good would that do?

Besides, the unspoken recrimination in all this was that some of the money that bastard Hall had siphoned out of Mark had, in fact, come from Mum and Roger. So the basement lumber room, with its faint essence of heating oil, was not the extent of Mum's beneficence; there was her silence, as well.

Mark sighed. *When* would he get his own place back, his independence back, his life back? 'They ought to do it,' he insisted. 'They're a *union*. They're a *workforce*.'

'Mac and the others won't ask them,' Os insisted right back.

'But why not? Mac says they have over twenty-seven hundred members in their W-whatchacallit. How many would we need? Twenty? Less.'

'Fewer,' said Os, who was a stickler for the language. 'And they won't do it.'

'A tunnel,' Mark reiterated. 'Way in the back where nobody can see anything. Late at night, along that dirt road by the cornfield. How long a tunnel would we need, just to get under the electric fence? A bunch of men with shovels, a few pickup trucks to carry in the shoring and carry out the excess dirt, and we're *into* the compound.'

'They won't do it.'

'Lickety-split across the estate,' Mark went on, not even caring that he was repeating himself, just loving the concept from beginning to end. 'Into that white elephant of a house of his, *truss* him up like a Christmas tree, cart him back to the tunnel, pop him *out* of there like a champagne cork, and off to the hideout.'

'We don't have a hideout,' Os said.

'We'll *have* a hideout,' Mark said, brushing that off. 'By then, we'll have one. Os, twenty-seven hundred members! Working men, strong horny hands, powerful backs. I'll bet you, they all have their own shovels.'

'They won't do it.'

'It could be like one of those prisoner of war escape movies. Many hands make light work.'

'They won't do it.'

'Why do you keep *saying* that?'

'Because it's true. Because Mac is just a little too noble for our own good.'

'Oh, please.'

'He is, Mark,' Os said. 'And if you suggest this thing to him, we'll lose the three of them, never mind the twentyseven hundred. He'll decide we just want to use them.'

'We *do* just want to use them.'

'Collaboratively,' Os said. 'That was the agreement. Think about this, Mark. That fellow Mac and his friends are sacrificing themselves for their union mates. They will not take kindly to your suggestion that they lead those selfsame mates into a life of crime.'

'Crime, crime, we're kidnapping Monroe Hall, that's no crime, that's poetic justice.'

'Poetic justice is often a crime. But this one they won't do.'

'Then what's *your* suggestion,' Mark demanded.

'I never said I had one.'

'No, all you do is rain all over *my* ideas. The agreement with those three was, we would combine forces, and we would all work at coming up with something we could do together to get our hands on Monroe Hall, and then we would get back in touch. But you don't want to get back in touch, not with my idea. So why don't *you* come up with something?'

'Well, if I have to come up with something,' Os said, 'how about that green Subaru station wagon?'

Bewildered by the sudden change of topic, Mark said, 'What about it?'

'It's in and out of the estate all the time,' Os said. 'Where we can't go, it goes constantly.'

'So do the hired guards,' Mark pointed out. 'So what?'

'But that fellow in the Subaru isn't a hired guard,' Os said. 'Who is he? Why does he have such frequent access to the estate? And why couldn't he – think about this, Mark – why couldn't he fit a few extra people into that big station wagon of his once or twice, once going in, once coming out?'

'Subarus aren't that big,' Mark said.

'But could one be big enough?' Os did a maybe-so-maybe-not hand waggle. 'Why don't you and I,' he said, 'do a little window-shopping at a Subaru dealer?'

'You think—?'

'Well, I don't know yet, do I?'

Mark considered. 'It wouldn't fit *five* extra people,' he said.

Os smiled, a thing he didn't do all that often. 'Oh,' he said, 'agreements to one side, I don't believe we need bother our union friends with this concept just yet, do you?'

Mark returned the smile. Over his left shoulder, the central air-conditioning *thump*ed on.

14

'They won't do it,' Mac said.

Ace looked anguished, agonized, possibly seasick. 'But it's perfect for them,' he insisted. '*We* couldn't do it, but they could.'

'They won't,' Mac said.

'But why not?'

'Because,' Mac said, 'they'll say it's a harebrained idea.'

'Why would they say something like that?'

Mac was about to answer, because it *is* a harebrained idea, when he realized all he could do with that response was make Ace mad.

But he had to say something. He and Ace and Buddy were all gathered for late afternoon beers in Buddy's rec room, in which the finished parts were really quite comfortable, and the unfinished parts, like the bar and the paneling and mounting the dartboard, Buddy would be getting around to pretty soon. In the meantime, the cast-off living room furniture from various of Buddy's relatives made for a cozy little den that families were guaranteed not to enter, and that was pleasantly cool in the summer, and thoroughly warm – perhaps a tiny bit too warm, given the presence of the furnace three feet away – in the winter.

It was here that Mac had to find an alternative to the simple truth that what Ace had come up with was a harebrained idea. In its stead, he said, 'We don't even know if one of them can fly a plane.'

'They don't have to fly a plane,' Ace said. 'Did they drive that stretch limo? That's what gave me the idea. That limo wasn't theirs, they rented it, I saw the little sticker on the back.'

Mac said, 'I'm not denying that.'

'Look, Mac,' Ace said, 'these are guys lost a bundle to Monroe Hall, we know that, but these are *also* guys can go out and rent a stretch limo. You see what that means?'

'They still think rich,' Mac said.

'They're still connected, Mac,' Ace told him. 'You and me, we couldn't go rent a limo like that unless our daughter was getting married, and maybe not even then. These guys, they got corporate *accounts*, they got little companies and things they can use instead of money. Lines of credit. These guys could rent a plane.'

Buddy, who had not yet taken sides, said, 'They call it charter.'

'Fine,' Ace said. 'These guys could charter a plane.'

Mac said, 'But then what?'

'There's no way to get *through* that electric fence,' Ace said. 'But we could go over it, have the pilot land in a field far away from the houses, we go over, grab Hall, stick him in the plane, fly back out again.'

'Ace,' Mac said, 'if you make that suggestion to those two guys, they won't have anything else to do with us. And we're not getting anywhere on our own—'

'*I* am!'

'No, you're not.' Mac spread his hands. 'Follow this with me,' he said. 'You're over at Teterboro airport, you've got a airplane charter operation, these two upper-class guys come in, say we wanna charter a plane.'

'That's what I'm saying,' Ace said.

'The guy says, "And what's the flight plan, sir?" And these two upper-class guys, they say, "Oh, we just wanna fly over to Pennsylvania at night and land in a darkened field there, and then the plane waits there a little while, and then we'll come back with this other passenger in a burlap sack," and by that time the charter guy's already reaching for the phone.'

'They say they're going to Atlantic City,' Ace said. 'Once we're all in the sky, we tell the pilot, "There's this change of plans".'

'They have radios in the planes,' Mac said. Pointing a finger at Ace, he said, 'And don't tell me you're gonna point a gun at this pilot, you're gonna hijack this plane. The whole scheme you shouldn't tell our Harvard friends, but hijacking you shouldn't even tell *me*.'

Buddy, who still hadn't taken sides, sighed and got to his feet and said, 'More beer.'

'You're right,' Mac told him.

Buddy went over to the refrigerator, which still worked almost as well as when it had been made, sometime in the Korean War, and brought out three more cans of beer. Meanwhile, Ace had gone back to looking anguished and agonized and even more seasick. 'There's *gotta* be a way,' he said. 'You just cannot get through that electric fence, so how else you gonna do it but go *over* it?'

'Maybe you wanna charter a catapult,' Mac suggested.

'Jeesis, Mac,' Ace said. 'You don't have to insult me. I'm trying to come up with an idea here.'

'Yeah, I know you are,' Mac said. 'You're right, I shouldn't be a wise guy. I'm sorry.'

'Thank you.'

'You're welcome.'

'OK, then.' Ace folded his arms. 'So *you* come up with an idea,' he said.

'I've been trying to,' Mac assured him. 'So far, nada.'

Buddy, who maybe by now wasn't going to have to choose sides, delivered the beers, settled back into his very low armchair, and said, 'You know what I keep thinking about?'

They both gave him their full attention. Mac said, 'No, Buddy. What?'

'That green Subaru station wagon,' Buddy said.

They both considered that. Mac said, 'You mean, the one that the guy drives it looks like an action toy.'

'Like the hero of a video game,' Buddy agreed. 'Only shorter.'

Ace said, 'Shorter? How do you know he's shorter? You only seen him sitting down, inside his car.'

'All that chin of his,' Buddy said, 'it's the same level as the top of the steering wheel.'

Mac said, 'All right, he's probably short. So what? What about him?'

'He's in and out of there all the time,' Buddy said. 'It's almost every day he's in and out, just him and all that station wagon.'

'Hmm,' Mac said.

Ace said, 'Whadaya think he does? I mean, that he goes in and out all the time.'

'Maybe we should follow him,' Buddy said. 'Not goin in, we couldn't do that, I mean comin out. Find out who he is. Find out if he'd like some undercover passengers some day.'

'Buddy,' Mac said, 'you just might have an idea there.'

'And this one,' Ace said, 'we don't need to share with Harvard.'

'Ace,' Mac said, 'now *you're* right.'

Buddy said, 'You guys both think they're Harvard? They seemed more like Dartmouth to me.'

15

When the phone rang, Dortmunder was in the can, reading an illustrated book about classic cars. Apparently, some of these cars really were very valuable, but on the other hand, it seemed to Dortmunder, the people who valued these cars were maybe a little strange.

'John?'

'Yar?'

'It's Andy. Shall I tell him you'll call him back?'

'No, I'll be right there,' Dortmunder said, and was. Holding his place in the book with the first finger of his left hand, he took the phone in his right, said, 'Thanks, May,' then said, 'Yar.'

'Chester gave me the list,' Kelp said.

List. For a second, Dortmunder couldn't figure out what Kelp was talking about. A list of classic cars? He said, 'List?'

'Remember? You asked him for a list of the other things Hall collects, so we could find out what's useful to bring along as cargo.'

'Oh, right.'

'So he gave me the list, that you were gonna take to Arnie Albright.'

Dortmunder's heart sank. 'Oh, right,' he said, in tones of deepest gloom, because Arnie Albright, the fence with whom it was occasionally necessary for Dortmunder to deal, was a fellow with a distinct personality problem. His personality problem, in short, was his personality. He'd said so himself, one time: 'It's my personality. Don't tell me different, Dortmunder, I happen to know. I rub people the wrong way. Don't argue with me.'

This was the person, or the personality, that somebody was going to have to show Chester's list, and then stick around in order to discuss it.

Wait a minute; was there an out? 'Chester gave *you* the list,' Dortmunder said. 'So why don't you take it on over to Arnie.'

'John, he's your friend.'

'*Oh,* no,' Dortmunder said. 'Nobody is Arnie's friend. I'm his acquaintance, and so are you.'

'You're more of an acquaintance than I am,' Kelp said. 'Listen, you want me to drop the list off at your place, or would you rather pick it up over here?'

'Why me? You've got the list.'

'It was your idea.'

Dortmunder sighed. In his agitation, he now realized, his finger had slid out of the book and he'd lost his place. Would he ever get back to the right spot, in among all those cars? He said, 'I tell you what. I'll come over there—'

'Good, that'll work.'

'And we'll go see Arnie together.'

'John, it's just a piece of paper, it doesn't weigh that much.'

'Andy, that's the only way it's gonna happen.'

Now it was Kelp's turn to sigh. 'Misery loves company, huh?'

'I don't think so,' Dortmunder said. 'Arnie Albright is misery. *He* doesn't love company.'

So it was that, a little later that day, Dortmunder and Kelp both approached the apartment house on West Eighty-ninth Street, between Broadway and West End Avenue, where Arnie Albright lurked. Chester's list was now in Dortmunder's pocket, Kelp having insisted on making the transfer before he'd leave home, to remove himself, however slightly, from the center of the conversation to come.

There was a shopfront on the ground floor of Arnie's building, currently selling cell phones and yoga meditation tapes, with a tiny vestibule beside it. Entering the vestibule, Dortmunder said, 'He always yells my name out. Through the intercom. You can hear him in New Jersey. I hate it.'

'Put your hand over the grid,' Kelp suggested.

Surprised and grateful, Dortmunder said, 'I never thought of that.' Feeling slightly better about the situation, he pushed the button next to *Albright*, then pressed his palm against the metal grid where the squawking yelling voice would come out. They waited thirty seconds, and then a moderate voice said something that was muffled by Dortmunder's hand. Hurriedly removing the hand, he said, 'What?'

'I said,' said the voice, an ordinary plain moderate voice, 'who's there?'

This did not sound like Arnie. Dortmunder said, 'Arnie?'

'Arnie who?'

'No,' Dortmunder said. 'You. Isn't that Arnie Albright's place?'

'Oh, I get it,' said the voice. 'Would you be a customer?'

Dortmunder wasn't sure how to answer that. He looked helplessly at Kelp, who leaned closer to the grid and said, 'Would you be a cop?'

'Ha ha,' said the voice. 'That's funny. I'm a cousin.'

Dortmunder said, 'Whose cousin?'

'Arnie's. Oh, come on up, let's not shout at each other over the inter-com.'

As the buzzer sounded and Dortmunder pushed open the door, he said to Kelp, 'That sure doesn't sound like any cousin of Arnie's.'

'Well,' Kelp said, 'Cain and Abel were related, too.'

Inside, the narrow hall smelled, as always, of old newspapers, probably damp. The steep stairs led up to the second floor, where there was no one in sight, not Arnie, not a cousin, not a cop. Dortmunder and Kelp thud-ded up the stairs and at the top, on the right, there was Arnie's door open, and standing in the doorway with a friendly smile of greeting was a short skinny guy with a frizz of wiry pepper-and-salt hair draped over his ears below a round bald dome. He did have Arnie's treeroot nose, so maybe he truly was a cousin, but otherwise he looked completely human, dressed in tan polo shirt and jeans. 'Hi,' he said. 'I'm Archie Albright.'

'John.'

'Andy.'

'Well, come on in.'

The apartment looked different without Arnie's presence, like a place where a curse has been lifted. Small underfurnished rooms with big dirty windows with no views, the apartment was decorated mainly with Arnie's calendar collection, walls spread with many of the Januarys of history under illustrations variously patriotic, historical, winsome, and erotic, with here and there a May or November (incompletes).

Closing the door behind them, Archie Albright waved at the few uncomfortable chairs and said, 'Have a seat. John, huh? I bet John Dortmunder.'

Dortmunder, about to sit warily on an armless kitchen chair next to the last rabbit-eared television set in Manhattan, lurched and remained on his feet. 'Arnie told you about me?'

'Oh, sure,' Archie Albright said, still smiling, very much at his ease. 'The only way we let him come to the family get-togethers is if he'll tell us stories.' Nodding at Kelp, he said, 'I don't know which Andy you are, but I'll get it.'

Very quiet, Kelp said, 'We didn't know we were features in Arnie's stories.' They were all still on their feet.

'Come on, it's just in the family,' Archie assured them. 'And we're all in the business, one way or another.'

'Fencing?' Dortmunder asked.

'No, that's just Arnie. Siddown, siddown.'

So they all sat, and Archie said, 'Most of us, as a matter of fact, we're in counterfeiting. We got a big printing plant out in Bay Shore, Long Island.'

'Counterfeiting,' Dortmunder said.

Kelp said, 'What do you do mostly? Twenties?'

'Nah, we gave up on American paper,' Archie told him. 'Too many headaches. We mostly do South American stuff, sell it to drug dealers, ten cents on the dollar.'

'Drug dealers,' Dortmunder said.

'It's great for everybody,' Archie said. 'We get real greenbacks, they get bogus purplebacks good enough to pass. But if you guys are here, it's not for the funny papers, it's you got something to sell.'

'Well, this time,' Dortmunder said, 'what we got is something to discuss. When is Arnie gonna be back?'

'Nobody knows,' Archie said. 'The fact is, we did an intervention.'

Dortmunder said, 'Intervention?' He realized his conversation was consisting mainly of repeating things other people said, which irritated him but which he seemed unable to stop.

Kelp said, 'Intervention is where a guy is too much of a drunk, right? Then his family and friends get together and make him go off for rehab, and they won't like him any more if he doesn't shape up.'

'Well, Arnie doesn't have friends,' Archie pointed out, 'so it was just family.'

Kelp said, 'Arnie had a drinking problem? In addition to everything else? I didn't know that.'

'No,' Archie said, 'Arnie doesn't hardly drink much of anything at all. And absolutely no hard drugs.'

Dortmunder, happy to hear himself come up with an original sentence, said, 'Then how come you intervened?'

'For his obnoxiousness,' Archie said. 'You know Arnie, you know what he's like.'

'To see him,' Kelp said, 'is to wanna not see him.'

'Right.' Archie spread his hands. 'You know, you get to choose your friends, but your family chooses you, so we've all been stuck with Arnie all these years. So finally the family got together for a powwow, out at the printing plant, without Arnie, and we decided the time had come for an intervention. It took place right in this room.'

Dortmunder looked around the room, trying to imagine it full of an entire family that had had enough of Arnie Albright. 'That must have been something,' he said.

'Very emotional,' Archie agreed. 'Weeping and promises and even a threat here and there. But at last he agreed he had to do it, he had to go get his personality cleaned up.'

Dortmunder said, 'Where do you send a guy like Arnie to rehab?'

'Club Med,' Archie told him. 'He's down there right now, on one of them islands, and the deal is, he has to stay there until the manager says he's improved enough for the family to meet him without having to immediately put him to death. So nobody knows how long he's gonna be gone.'

'And the manager's in on it,' Kelp said.

Archie said, 'He says it's the first intervention like this he ever seen, but if it works out it could be a whole new market. He's very excited about it.'

Kelp shook his head. 'A rehabilitated Arnie. I can hardly wait.'

'Well, you'll have to,' Archie said. 'The manager agrees, Arnie's a tough case. That's how they know, if they can fix him, they got a market with legs. In the meantime, maybe I could do something for you guys myself.'

Feeling he had nothing to lose, Dortmunder pulled Chester's list out of his pocket and said, 'What we were gonna ask Arnie, which of these collections of collectibles would it be worth our while to bring him some?'

Archie accepted the list, glanced at it, and said, 'I'm not in that business myself, but I tell you what I could do. I could fax this to Arnie, he could fax back the answer.'

Dortmunder said, 'Isn't that a little open?'

'We got a code going,' Archie said. 'Phone and fax, both. Arnie's paying for his own intervention down there, because none of *us* would give a dime for the son of a bitch, so his business has to keep going. We take turns hanging out here for when the customers show up. I'll send him the list; tomorrow, the next day, you'll have your answer.'

'It's a funny way to do things,' Dortmunder said, 'but OK.'

They all stood, and Archie said, 'Phone here tomorrow afternoon, there'll be somebody from the family here, tell you did we get the answer yet.'

'Fine,' Dortmunder said.

As they walked to the door, Kelp said, 'Tell Arnie, don't give up. He's on the right path, at last.'

'I will,' Archie said. He opened the hall door, then grinned and pointed at Kelp. 'Kelp,' he said. 'That's which one you are.'

16

It was Chester's wife, Grace, who noticed the ad, in the local paper, the *Berwick Register*. When they were kicked out of the Eden of Monroe Hall's estate, Chester and Grace had found a small house in a little town called Shickshinny on the Susquehanna River, just north of Interstate 80, handy to most of North America. It wasn't as big or as nice a place as the house they'd had at Hall's, but it was cozy, and the smallness helped to keep Chester's rage on the boil. Grace always took an interest in wherever she was – Chester mostly took an interest in the roads – so she subscribed to the *Register*, and found the ad, in the Help Wanted column. 'Look at this, Chester,' she said, so he did.

WANTED DRIVER
Good pay, easy hours. No
priors. Discreet. 436–5151

'Grace,' Chester said, 'what are you showing me this for? You want me to *take* this job?'

Grace was a firm woman, firm in body and firm in attitude. 'Chester,' she said, 'I know you have faith in those dishonest friends of yours, but until they actually produce some swag for you to share in, yes, I think you oughta get a job. But what got my attention to *this* ad, it's got a funny word in it. You see it?'

Chester read the ad again. 'Discreet,' he said.

'And it doesn't ask for a chauffeur,' she pointed out, 'it asks for a driver. Why would they want a driver to be discreet?'

'Maybe it's a call girl,' Chester said.

'If it is,' Grace said, 'I don't want you to take the job. But if it isn't, who knows? Discreet. It might be interesting.'

So Chester made the call, and a guy with a slurry voice gave him directions to a house across the river past Mocanaqua, and Chester drove over to find a good-sized old stone house with woods between it and the neighbors on both sides. Not rich-rich, like Monroe Hall, but not scraping

71

along like Chester, either. So he stopped in front of the house, and as he walked toward it the door was opened by a guy with a glass in his hand. This was eleven in the morning.

'I'm Ches—'

'You couldn't be anybody else,' the guy said, sounding just as slurry as he had on the phone, but at least no worse. He was maybe fifty, with a big-boned shambly body and a thick head of wavy black hair and an amiable good-ole-boy grinning face. 'Comonin, I'm Hal Mellon,' he said, and switched the glass to his left so he could shake hands, then shut the door and waved generally at a large comfortable living room, saying, 'Let's sit down, get to know one another.'

So they sat down, and Hal Mellon said, 'I called this party, so I'll go first. I'm a salesman, I sell office machinery for the office, big firms, medium-size firms, I handle computers, copiers, faxes, shredders, you name it.'

'Uh huh,' Chester said.

'Well, I don't *handle* the products my own self,' Mellon said. 'I would-n't know how to operate one of those things if you held a gun to my head. What I do is, I schmooze the office manager. I explain to him how the thing I sold him last year is this year a piece of shit and he should let me sell him a new one. I'm the one convinces him he doesn't need one of this, he needs two of this, and probably one of that.'

'You must be good at it,' Chester said.

'I'm goddamn good at it,' Mellon told him, and swigged some of his drink. 'But I got one natural advantage.'

'Oh, yeah?'

'Yeah. My breath doesn't smell.'

Chester blinked. 'Yeah?'

'Yeah. I could be half in the bag – hell, I could be three-quarters in the bag – you wouldn't smell a goddamn thing on my breath.'

'Oh, I get it,' Chester said.

'You see, what it is,' Mellon explained, 'you can't do what I do sober. Before those miserable stinky rotten office managers can be my best friend, I gotta get tanked.'

'Sure,' Chester said.

Mellon nodded, and finished his drink. 'Anything for you?' he asked.

'Not when I got driving to do, thanks.'

Mellon burst into a huge grin. 'There, you see?' he said. 'There it is right there. In the offices, I can handle the situation. I don't weave, I don't slur more than I am right now, I can smooth it right on through. But behind the wheel? I got no reflexes, man.'

'Not good,' Chester said.

'My last DWI,' Mellon said, 'they took away my license *forever*. Never gonna drive again. And if I try to, they'll put me in jail. The judge said so, and I believed him.'

'So that's why you need a driver,' Chester said.

'I got a nice Buick in the garage here,' Mellon said. 'Maybe not the best car in the world, but it's what a salesman's got to drive.'

'Buicks can be good.'

'That's what we'd use,' Mellon said. 'Take me around to the offices, wait for me, keep his mouth shut.'

'Discreet.'

'That's it. I can't afford to have the word go around. Not to the managers, and not to my bosses.'

'I got it.'

Mellon sat back. 'Your turn.'

Chester said, 'Well, started out, I was a stunt driver in the movies—'

'No shit!'

'—then that job dried up so I drove for some bank robbers—'

'Holy shit!'

'—then I got put in jail—'

'Christamighty!'

'—then I got a job taking care of a valuable car collection for a rich guy, but then *he* got in trouble with the law, so now I'm looking for a job.'

Mellon stared at Chester as though he were a new kind of butterfly. Finally, he said, 'Would you do some stunt driving for me?'

'I don't think so.'

Mellon shrugged. 'Yeah, I can see that,' he said. Then he brightened again. 'Say, a guy with your background, you could be better than the radio in the car! We drive from appointment to appointment, you must have a whole *lot* of stories you could tell.'

'I'm sure we both do,' Chester said.

Mellon laughed. 'Yeah,' he said. 'But you'll remember yours.'

17

Monroe Hall, startled, looked up. 'What was that?' However, since he was alone in the library at the moment, there was no one to answer. Still, he was certain there'd been a . . . a . . . a something.

A sound? Squinting at his signed first editions, his collection of nineteenth-century leather-bounds, his assortment of privately printed early twentieth-century erotica (under lock and key and glass), Hall felt a sudden unease. There had been a . . . a what?

An absence. Yes? Yes. Some sort of absence. Something— The dog that didn't bark in the night. Yes, 'The Adventure of Silver Blaze' in *The Memoirs of Sherlock Holmes*, 1894. He had an excellent edition over there, very fine, no jacket or signature unfortunately, but still one of the more valuable bits of Sherlockiana.

What dog? There was no dog in this house, never had been, so if it did nothing that made perfect—

An absence of cuckoos.

That was it. Hall looked at his Rolex and it was nine past three, and yet no cuckoos had announced the hour, not one.

How long had this been going on, or not going on? Had he recently been only in other parts of the house, where he wouldn't have heard the clocks anyway, and so been unaware that they were falling off, or down? Here in the library, where he liked to stand and look at his possessions, but never read them – reading is so *bad* for a book – he was right next to the clock room. If the cuckoos had been on the job, he'd have known it.

Wanting to know the worst, Hall left the library, went down the corridor, and entered the clock room, where every single clock on all the walls and standing on all the shelves was absolutely still. Not a sign of movement. They'd run down at various hours, some with their doors and birds' mouths open, the rest shut down in mid-hour, like a medieval town under siege.

Hall was horrified. It was like looking at a massacre. 'Hubert!' he cried, Hubert being an upstairs servant one of whose jobs was to keep these clocks wound. 'Hubert?'

No answer. Hurrying to the wall phone, gleaming plastic among the dead wood, he pounded out Hubert's extension, which would activate the man's beeper no matter where on the grounds he might be. Then he hung up and waited, staring at the phone, because now it was Hubert's job to call him back.

Nothing. Where was the man? Where was Hubert? Why was there nothing in the world but all these dead cuckoo clocks?

'Alicia!' he screamed, needing her, needing her *now*. 'Alicia!'

He hurried back to the corridor, where his voice would carry farther. 'Alicia!' She had to be here! Where was she, off with one of those damned automobiles? 'Alicia!'

There was no one else, no one else in the world, who understood him and could give him solace at a time like this. With the rest of the world, no matter how awful things got, one had to go on pretending to be a grown-up. Only with Alicia could he relax into the baby he was.

'Alicia!'

No answer. No answer. They all failed you, sooner or later. No one to rely on.

He couldn't stand to look at the clocks any more, and he'd lost the spirit to go on gazing at his books. Pouting, lower lip stuck out, he trailed away down the corridor until he saw the open door of the gym, and went in there instead.

Ah, the gym. If only Flip Morriscone were here. Flip was a good fellow, one of the very few good fellows Hall had ever met. A good fellow, and an honest fellow, and a hardworking fellow, and the best thing of all, he *liked* Monroe Hall! If he were here now, he'd be supportive about the cuckoos, he'd know what to do next.

At loose ends – well, he was always at loose ends these days – Hall went over to the treadmill, set it at a very leisurely pace indeed, far more languid than Flip would ever allow, and went for a little walk.

A little walk to nowhere, that's what his life had come down to. He could walk, he could walk all he wanted, but he couldn't actually *go* anywhere.

Treadmill to Oblivion, 1954, Fred Allen's grim-titled memoir of his life writing and starring in a weekly radio show. Hall had a copy of it, of course, signed first edition with a dustjacket in almost perfect condition. He'd been told it was a very good book.

He didn't need to read those books. He didn't need to exercise on all these intimidating machines. He didn't need to drive all these cars. He needed to *have* them, that's all, have everything, have the complete set of everything ever made. *Then* he'd be happy.

It was almost two hours later that Alicia, back from her drive, found him there, still ambling in place on the treadmill, humming a mournful little tune. 'Why, Monroe,' she said.

'Oh, Alicia,' he said tragically. He stopped walking and bumped painfully into the front of the machine. 'Damn! Drat! Oh, *why* can't I—' He hopped off the treadmill, which ambled on without him. 'This is so *awful*.' he cried.

Switching off the machine, Alicia said, 'You're all upset, Monroe. What's happened?'

'The clocks,' he told her. 'They've all stopped.'

'Oh, dear,' she said.

'I called for Hubert, but no answer. Where is he? He doesn't have days off, does he?'

'Oh, Monroe,' Alicia said, 'I'm afraid Hubert has left us.'

'Left us? Why would he do a thing like that?'

'His family talked against us,' she said. 'They found him a different job, so he won't have to associate with us.'

'With you?' Hall cried. 'Everybody likes to associate with you!'

'Well, yes, dear,' she said. 'I didn't want to make too much of it, but yes, it was mostly you he was talking about. His family talking about.'

'So he's just gone off, and left the cuckoos to *die*. What a cruel heartless thing to do.'

'I tell you what, Monroe,' she said, 'why don't we go in and wind them up again? The two of us?'

'*We* can't wind all those clocks! Alicia, we need servants!'

'Well, I'm afraid we're having fewer . . . and fewer.'

'You go wind cuckoos if you want,' Hall told her. '*I'm* going to call Cooper.'

'I don't think Cooper can do much for us, Monroe.'

'He's an employment agent,' Hall pointed out. 'He's supposed to find employees for people who need employees, and God knows that's us. I'm going to call him now.'

Hall's office was farther down the corridor. Entering it, he made straight for the mid-nineteenth-century partners' desk with its green felt inserts on both sides. (He used both sides himself, of course.) Rolodexes were placed here and there, but he didn't need them. He well knew Cooper's number. He dialed it, gave his name to the receptionist, waited a very long time, and then the cheeky girl came back and said, 'Mr Cooper isn't in at the moment. Woodja like to leave your name and number?'

'Mr Cooper certainly *is* in,' Hall told her, 'and he already knows my name and number. He's ducking me. He's avoiding me. You can give him a message for me.'

'Sure thing. Shoot.'

'Monroe Hall needs staff. Did you get that? Did you write that down?'

'Monroe Hall needs staff,' she repeated, deadpan.

'Tell him,' Hall said, and slammed the phone down. Somewhere, a cuckoo rang.

18

When the doorbell rang, Kelp was seated at the kitchen table, reading a recent safe manufacturer's catalog, enjoying the full-color illustrations. He knew Anne Marie was somewhere else in the apartment, and figured the doorbell was for her anyway, because it was probably her friend Jim Green, come to talk about new identities. So he finished reading a 'burglar-proof' paragraph, smiling faintly to himself, then closed the catalog and was getting to his feet when Anne Marie called, 'Andy?'

'On my way.'

In the living room, Anne Marie smiled and said, 'Andy Kelp, this is Jim Green.'

'Whadaya say?' Kelp said, and stuck out his hand.

'How do you do,' Jim Green said. He had a gentle voice, a mild manner, a small smile, a soft handshake.

Looking Green over, Kelp decided he wasn't impressed. Anne Marie had been going on about how this was some kind of man of mystery or something, nobody knows his real name, he's the spook's spook, whatever. To Kelp, he just seemed like some average joe. Maybe even more average than most.

'Anne Marie tells me,' Green was saying, with a toothy smile in Anne Marie's direction, 'you and some pals are looking for new paper.'

'That's it,' Kelp agreed. 'You know, it doesn't have to hold up forever, only a few months.'

Still smiling, Green shook both his head and a hand, saying, 'No, excuse me, Andy, it doesn't work that way.'

'It doesn't?'

Anne Marie said, 'Why don't we sit? Jim, get you some coffee? A drink?'

'Nothing right now, Anne Marie,' Green told her, and Kelp again found himself wondering what impressed her so much about this guy. Anyway, they sat, and Green said, 'An identity isn't the same as like a counterfeit passport or something like that. An identity isn't really even something you carry around with you. Mostly, it's a new you we put into the files.'

'OK,' Kelp said.

'So it isn't a question,' Green went on, 'how long is this thing good for. It's good forever, unless you burn it. It won't burn itself. You get a new identity, it's always there waiting for you, it happens someday you can no longer go on being who you were before.'

'Sounds good,' Kelp said.

'And,' Green said, 'as with most things that sound good, it also sounds expensive.'

'That's why,' Kelp said, 'I was hoping for something maybe shorter term, because that might not be so expensive.'

Green nodded, frowning a little. Then he grinned at Anne Marie and said, 'You come up with a cute one this time, Anne Marie.'

'I know,' she said, grinning back.

'I tell you what, Anne Marie,' Green said, 'maybe I will take a cup of coffee.'

'Sure,' she said, rising. 'That was black no sugar, right?'

'What a memory,' Green said.

Kelp said, 'Anne Marie, while you're pouring, I might accept a beer.'

'Fine.'

She went away, and Green leaned back on the sofa and said, 'What can you tell me about what you need this for?'

'I can tell you a lot,' Kelp said, 'since Anne Marie says you're solid.'

'And I say the same for her. So what are we looking at?'

'Four guys,' Kelp told him, 'have to get employed by a guy that's under federal court observation and bankruptcy and ongoing investigations and all of this.'

'You're going to *work* for this guy?'

'It's the only way to get to where he is, and get what we want.'

'Interesting,' Green said.

'Because of this guy's situation,' Kelp said, 'he can't hire anybody with a record.'

'I can see that.'

'Because of *our* situation, we can't apply.'

'What you need,' Green said, 'is identities without felonies.'

'You got it.'

'Let me think about this.' Green nodded to himself, while Kelp's mind wandered. Then Green nodded more emphatically. 'I suspect,' he said, 'what we're also talking about here is short money up front, and a guaranteed big killing after it's all over.'

'Well,' Kelp said, 'there are no guarantees.'

Green looked surprised. 'Really? Usually, there's guarantees.'

'Well,' Kelp said, 'it isn't guaranteed to *not* work.'

'OK.' Green seemed to like to nod; he did some more of it, then said, 'Did you know Howard?'

'I've known *some* Howards,' Kelp admitted. 'You thinking of any one of them in particular?'

'Anne Marie's husband.'

'Oh, he was Howard? No, he cleared out two days before we met.'

'He was a jerk,' Green said. 'I only met him a couple times, but it only took a couple times.'

'Yeah, I understand that.'

'He was a jerk like her father, the Honorable, that I knew a lot better. If you never met Howard, then you never met the father, either, because he was dead by then.'

'You're right.'

'There's women like that,' Green said. 'They start out with a jerk for a father, they go find one just like him, get married. Some do it over and over, keep finding the same exact kind of jerk.'

'Doesn't sound like fun,' Kelp said.

'I was wondering, you see,' Green said, 'if Anne Marie would turn out like that.'

Kelp grinned. 'I think she changed her MO,' he said.

'I think so, too. She'll be back in a minute, so let me ask you. Is it OK we talk business in front of her?'

Kelp shrugged. 'Saves me repeating everything after you leave.'

'OK,' Green said. He did the nodding thing some more. 'Let me explain the problem,' he said, and Anne Marie came back in, with Green's coffee and Kelp's beer and a glass of pale stuff for herself, all on a little tray. 'Thanks,' Green said, and Kelp pointed at the glass of pale stuff. 'What's that?'

'Apple juice,' she said, and went back to her chair.

'Right,' Kelp said. 'That's one of your Midwest things.'

She said, 'Jim, do you know why I picked this guy up?'

Green said, 'You picked him up?'

'Sure.'

'I helped,' Kelp said.

Ignoring that, Anne Marie told Green, 'He didn't put anything in his bourbon.'

'Ahh,' Green said.

'I put an ice cube,' Kelp said.

'First man I ever met didn't want everything he drank to taste like Royal Crown Cola.' Giving Kelp a fond look, she said, 'You told me straight bourbon wouldn't make me drunk unless I had one of those funny chemistries.'

Kelp nodded. 'Yeah, but you didn't believe me.'

'No, of course not. But I liked you telling me. Women like a man who puts in the effort to attract her attention. Lies, inflates his part, acts cool. Women don't believe all the strutting around, but they like it, it's a compliment to them that he drags out his bag of tricks, just for her.'

It was Kelp's turn to show a fond look. 'You had a couple tricks in the bag, too, you know.'

'I thought you were worth it.'

They smiled at each other, and Jim Green cleared his throat and said, 'Uh, I'm still here, you know.'

They looked at him. 'Oh, hi, Jim,' Kelp said. 'How you doin?'

'Fine.'

'I forgot all about you over there.'

'Don't worry about it,' Jim said. 'Happens all the time.' Turning to Anne Marie, he said, 'I was just about to explain to Andy the problem.'

'I'm sorry there's a problem,' she said.

'Well, there would be,' he said, and said to Kelp, 'The identities I create are very tricky, and you need to find just the right little cranny in the system, and there's not a lot of them. So I can't use up *four* of them – in fact, not even one of them – for short money in front. Not even for a guy that I see is the right guy for Anne Marie.'

'Well,' Kelp said, 'it was a long shot. Thanks, anyway.'

Anne Marie said, 'Jim? You can't help? I was sure you could help.'

'Anne Marie, I don't *help*,' Green said. 'I do a professional job, and I get paid for it.'

Kelp said, 'Anne Marie, he's right. It was nice of him to come over here and listen, and if there was something he could do, you know he'd do it.'

'I been thinking,' Green said, 'sitting here, looking at you two, sorry I couldn't do what you want. I been thinking, and what I *do* have, I have the people that I worked with already, I know everything about who they are now because I made them who they are now.'

Anne Marie said, 'What about them?'

'Well,' Green said, 'every once in a while, not often, somebody stops being who I made them for one reason or another, inheritance, a general amnesty, death of an enemy. People go back to being who they started out as, maybe temporary, maybe forever. Now, I never done this before, I never even thought of doing it, but those identities are already in place, and I can get back at them again.'

Kelp said, 'You mean, we borrow them?'

'That's exactly it,' Green said. 'Now, you borrow, you could be borrowing trouble. I want you to know that. I'm not in touch with the *people*, just the identities, so for all I know somebody may suddenly have to go back to being Joe Blow all over again, and there *you* are, the cuckoo in his nest. The photo on his passport; you. The fingerprint on his top-secret clearance; yours. And who he gets mad at is you, not me, for hacking into his identity, and some of these people have no sense of humor at all.'

'I can see that,' Kelp said.

'Another possibility,' Green said, 'as long as we're considering what's the worst that could happen here, somebody *else* maybe cracked the new identity. The actual guy's gone back to who he used to be, and when the assassination team arrives, who they find is you.'

'Ugh,' Anne Marie said.

Kelp said, 'What are the odds, do you think?'

'Small,' Green said, 'or I wouldn't make the offer. Very very small, but possible. Like what you were telling me before, no guarantees. But you only want the identity for a month or two.'

'Maybe even less,' Kelp said. 'I hope even less,'

'I could see what I could do,' Green said. 'But first I got to meet your three friends, and take their pictures, and do stuff like that. Would you all like to come up to Connecticut?'

'We prefer to stay in the five boroughs, if we can,' Kelp said. 'But you're the one doing the favor, so it's up to you.'

'Come to think of it,' Green said, 'I probably couldn't fit all four of you in the trunk anyway. So could we think of a place here in town? I'd prefer someplace private within someplace public, if you could think of anything like that.'

'There's a bar I happen to know,' Kelp said, 'that I think you'll like.'

19

'Here it comes,' Mark said.

Os was driving today, even though Mark considered Os a bit too volatile to be a completely reliable driver in a tight spot. On the other hand, the little two-seater Porsche they were in, hiding behind its gleaming whiteness, actually belonged to Os, so Mark had only limited control over who would drive the beast.

At least they'd discussed strategy ahead of time, so that Os knew, the instant Mark said, in re the green Subaru station wagon, 'Here it comes,' that he should drive forward away from the compound entrance, in the direction the Subaru always took, already moving off when the Subaru made its turn onto the road behind them.

This had been Mark's idea; start out in *front* of the Subaru and then, at the first passing zone some three miles down the road, permit it to pass, so that the driver of that car would have no reason to suspect they were following him, not if he'd first seen them out in front. Mark was very pleased with himself for this clever bit of misdirection.

Looking over his shoulder, he saw the Subaru grow larger as it overtook them. But it seemed to him it was growing larger more slowly than it should. Their earlier sightings of the Subaru had suggested its driver liked to go fast, and so he did, but at the moment so did the Porsche, which was not the plan.

'Os,' Mark said, 'we're not in a race. You want him to pass, remember?'

'He'll pass. We're not there yet.'

Nevertheless, here came the passing zone, and Mark could see just how hard it was for Os to ease his foot on the accelerator, lose momentum, permit another human being to go on by him without a fight. Os's teeth were clenched, his eyes fixed on the road so he wouldn't even see that overtaking hunk of Japanese green, and it was Mark who watched the Subaru bustle by, its lantern-jawed driver just as intent as Os.

'That's fine, then,' Mark said, and at the very end of the passing zone, with in fact a big brown United Parcel truck thundering toward them the other way, a second car rushed past them, crowding Os to get itself back into lane before it would become a hood ornament on the United Parcel truck. The United Parcel truck bawled its outrage, the second car weaved but then got control of itself, and off it hurried after the Subaru.

Mark stared at that second car, now receding. That mud-colored Taurus. 'Os!' he cried, as outraged as the United Parcel driver. 'It's the union!'

'Well, goddamn them,' Os said. 'Almost put me in the ditch.'

'Os, they had the same idea *we* had!'

'Looks that way.'

'But they didn't *tell* us!'

Os, crowding up closer to the Taurus, said, 'We didn't tell them either, Mark.'

'It's not the same thing. Os, don't get so close.'

'I can't see the Subaru.'

'Forget the Subaru,' Mark told him. 'The union doesn't know about this car, so they won't recognize us. *They're* following the Subaru. You follow them. That way, you can stay farther back, and nobody's going to know we're here.'

'Not bad,' Os agreed, and slacked off.

For the next twenty minutes, their little caravan roamed rural Pennsylvania, farmland, woods, the occasional dorp, the green Subaru to lead the way, the mud-colored Taurus not far behind, the gleaming white Porsche some considerable way to the rear. It was all beginning to get boring when the Taurus's brake lights all of a sudden went on.

Mark sat up: 'Something's happening.'

'About time.'

The Taurus had slowed. Behind it, the Porsche slowed. Then, after a minute, the Taurus accelerated again, so the Porsche hurried to catch up.

Mark said, 'What was that all about?'

'False alarm.'

Another fifteen minutes on the road, and they approached a town, and this time it was the right turn signal the Taurus began to flash. Os obediently slowed, slowed even more, and they watched the Taurus turn in at a diner's parking lot, stop in a slot, and the three start to get out. The Subaru was nowhere in sight.

There was other traffic around them, light but insistent, so they had no choice but to drive on, Mark glaring furiously back at the diner parking lot, the three chunky men moving toward the entrance, gabbing together, obviously following nobody.

Mark turned his glare to the front. 'What happened?' he demanded. 'What happened?'

'We fucked up,' Os said, grimly looking at the road. They were deeper into the town now, with side streets, so Os took one.

Mark said, 'We? We fucked up? How? All we did was follow them.'

'Wrong them,' Os said, and pulled to the curb. There was no traffic on this little residential street. 'We were following the union guys. What we were supposed to follow was the Subaru.'

'They were following the Subaru.'

'Maybe.'

'Maybe? Os, they almost cut you off in that passing zone, almost got themselves creamed by that truck. They were trying to catch up with the Subaru.'

'Maybe,' Os said.

'Stop saying maybe,' Mark told him. 'They were following the Subaru. So what went wrong?'

Os didn't have an answer for that, any more than Mark did, so they sat in broody silence a few minutes, and then Os said, 'Brake lights.'

'Yes?'

'Their brake lights went on, back there somewhere,' Os said, and waved a hand generally at the world.

'You're right, they did.'

'So that's,' Os said, 'when the Subaru turned off.'

'But they didn't follow it.'

'Because it was going home.'

'Oh, my God,' Mark said. 'You're right! They see where he turns off, they mark the place, they keep going, we sail right on by.'

'Because,' Os said, with his infuriating doggedness, 'we were following the wrong car.'

Mark, choosing to ignore the implied criticism, said, 'Could we find that spot again?'

'Where they hit their brakes?'

'Of course. Could we backtrack, find it?'

'God knows,' Os said.

'I'm not doing anything else today,' Mark said, 'so let's try it.'

'By God, there it is.'

They'd driven, and driven, trying to stay on their backtrail even though all roads look different when traveled in the opposite direction, and trying to look at every house and drive and side road they passed, until Os declared they'd overshot somehow, they had to go back. So they did, discovering that they had in fact gotten briefly onto the wrong road, but then found the right road again, and there, on the left, in the blacktop area in front of what looked like a pretty large apartment house, very large for this backcountry neck of the woods, there was the Subaru. The same one, definitely, in front of a faux-Tudor building with a large sign on the weedy patch of lawn between parking lot and road: CARING ARMS ASSISTED LIVING.

Mark said, 'A nursing home? What the hell is he doing in a nursing home?'

'Let's see if it's the same car,' Os said, and turned in at the parking area. But as he did so, out of the building came the guy himself, bouncing along like a windup doll, a big gray canvas ditty bag thrown over his shoulder. So Os kept driving in a circle, back out to the road, as Mark twisted around to watch the guy's progress. Throw the ditty bag into the back of the Subaru, get behind the wheel.

'Os,' he said, 'this time we follow *him*.'

'A much better plan.' Os looked in the rearview mirror, 'Here he comes, and here's a gas station.'

So Os pulled in at the gas station, rolled very slowly past the people refueling there, and regained the road after the Subaru had already gone by. 'Now,' he said, 'we follow the right car, at last.'

'Not too close,' Mark said. 'This little white Porsche is a bit noticeable.'

'I know what I'm doing,' Os said, which might have been yet another implied criticism.

If it was, Mark ignored it, saying, 'I don't get it. Maybe three times a week, he goes and spends about an hour at Monroe Hall's place. Then from there he goes to a nursing home? What for?'

'They're customers,' Os suggested. 'It's some kind of inhome service. He's a . . . what? Religious adviser? Psychotherapist? Hairdresser?'

'*Physical* therapist?' Mark said. 'You saw the bag he carried, you saw how he's built, like every personal trainer you've ever seen in your life. Too muscular, and too short.'

'My mother,' Os said darkly, 'probably knows him.'

Mark said, 'I doubt he makes house calls in Boca Raton, but I know what you mean. And you know what I mean.'

Os said, as the unmindful Subaru scampered ahead of them across the rolling landscapes of Pennsylvania, 'You mean, we join him today on his rounds.'

'Sooner or later,' Mark said, 'this guy's day of kneebends and shoulder thumps must come to an end. Then he goes home. And we'll be there.'

'Leave it to the union,' Os said, 'to give up after one little try.'

20

'We couldn't just follow him around all day,' Buddy insisted. He was the driver, and the other two were disagreeing with his executive decisions.

Ace, for instance: 'We could have waited. How long's he gonna be? An hour?'

'And then on to somebody else,' Buddy said. 'It's the middle of the day, he could be seeing clients until six o'clock for all we know. Besides which, it's lunchtime.'

They were, in fact, seated at a window table in this diner in the middle of Somewhere, Pennsylvania, elbows on the Formica, waiting for various fried foods, and watching the occasional vehicle drive by out front. It was a timeless America they'd found, and the waitresses had a speed to match.

Mac, frowning deeply, said, 'Buddy, in a way I understand what you're talking about. Hanging around behind that guy could get boring after a while—'

'And he could notice,' Buddy pointed out, 'that same car behind him all the time.'

'That's also true,' Mac agreed. 'But, Buddy, we had a bird in hand.'

'We've figured out who the guy is, or at least what he is,' Buddy said. 'One of those rich-people personal trainers, your own gym coach. Hall can't get off the property, can't get much exercise, so this guy comes around to keep him in shape.'

Grudgingly, Ace said, 'OK. And the nursing home, that fits in.'

'Sure,' Buddy said.

Mac said, 'But so what? Buddy, what do you want us to do? Go through every Yellow Pages in central Pennsylvania, which has gotta be about a hundred—'

'More,' Ace said.

'More,' Mac agreed. 'Check out every personal trainer in every phone book?'

'We've got the guy's license number,' Buddy reminded them. 'And the make of the car. And we know what his business is. Mark, we've got over twenty-seven hundred members in ACWFFA. At least one of those people's got a cousin on a police force. We don't have to say what we want it for, a union brother will respect the need for privacy, but we do have a big spread-out powerful force out there, in the rank and file, and I think we should use it, and in no time at all, we'll have this guy's name and address and everything in the world that the law knows about him.'

Mac sighed. 'I didn't want to bring the membership in,' he said.

Buddy said, 'I know you didn't, and I agree, and I don't want to make anybody accessories or anything. But this is the quick and easy way, Mac, and sometimes, you just have to set your principles aside just a little bit and go for the way that works.'

Mac sighed agan. 'I suppose so,' he said. 'Just so this isn't the beginning of some slippery slope.'

21

When Dortmunder walked into the O. J. at four that afternoon, one of the daytime regulars down at the left end of the bar was fast beginning to work himself into a fulltime rant. 'Who come up with *this* great idea?' he demanded of the universe. 'That's what I wanna know. Whose idea was *this*, English is a second language?'

Rollo was at the right end of the bar, doing the crossword puzzle in the *Daily News*. Dortmunder headed straight for him.

'I was *born* in this country. I got English as a *first* language, and that's the way I like it!'

Rollo nodded a hello, and said, 'The other bourbon's got your glass in the back.'

Dortmunder said, 'Was there anybody else with him?'

Rollo looked confused. 'I'm not sure.'

'That'll be the guy,' Dortmunder said, 'from what I hear of him.'

'You're gonna have to come rip English out of my cold dead hand, that's what *you're* gonna have to do.'

Rollo said, 'You got more comin?'

'The vodka and red wine, and the beer and salt.'

'He's gonna push me into the profit margin, that beer and salt.'

'English was good enough for my father, and it was good enough for *his* father, and it would've been good enough for *his* father if he'd been here!'

Dortmunder headed down around the vocal end of the bar, where the regulars around the ranter had a fixed, glazed, genre painting look.

'English is a second language,' said in tones of deepest contempt and disgust. 'So whadawe supposeta do now, learn *Mexican* or something?'

'*Por favor*,' said a deceptively mild voice, as Dortmunder rounded the corner, headed down the hall, and entered the back room, where Kelp had naturally taken the best seat for himself, facing the door, with some nondescript guy to his left.

So Dortmunder went around the table the other way, to take the seat at Kelp's right, as Kelp said, 'Hey, John. John Dortmunder, this is Jim Green.'

Dortmunder said, 'So we're using our own names, are we?'

'Some of us are,' Kelp said.

Jim Green stood up to extend a hand past Kelp as he offered a bland smile and said, 'How are you today?'

'Terrific,' Dortmunder said, and shook the hand, which didn't do a whole lot of shaking back.

Kelp said, 'I'll explain things when the other two get here.'

'Sure.'

Dortmunder sat, then looked past Kelp to remind himself what Jim Green looked like. Oh, yeah, right. He poured himself a glass of 'bourbon' from the bottle on the tray at Kelp's right elbow, then leaned forward again to see what Green was drinking. Beer, no salt.

But here came the beer *with* salt, through the doorway, saying, 'I'd of been here sooner, only I started up Eleventh Avenue, and they got a whole shipment of BMWs comin in to the dealer there, nothin but trucks full of high-priced cars all over the place, backin into the windows, backin into each other, backin into the cabs all over there, so *then* I went over to the West Side Highway, and there's a cruise ship on strike at the docks there, pickets in Hawaiian shirts, handin out pink leaflets, whado *they* want with a livin wage, they got room and board on a ship, so I did a U-ey and went all the way down to Forty-second, and come up Tenth, and the way it's goin in midtown, I think next time, I'll take the Holland over to Jersey, up to the bridge, come *down* here. Either that or Staten Island.' By then, he was seated, beer and salt in front of him, to Dortmunder's right, and he nodded and said, 'Hi, John. Hi, Andy.'

Dortmunder said, 'Well, you made it, anyway.'

'Yeah, at the very least.'

Kelp said, 'Stan Murch, this is Jim Green.'

'Oh, hi,' Stan said. 'I didn't notice you over there.'

'How are you today,' Green said, and Tiny Bulcher came in, carrying a glass of red liquid and frowning at some personal dissatisfaction of his own. Green looked at him. 'Is he one of you?'

Kelp said, 'Tiny Bulcher, this is Jim Green.'

'Harya,' Tiny said.

'How are you today,' Green said, but more warily than before.

'*I'm* still OK,' Tiny said, and shut the door, then sat at the place in front of it, facing the rest of them.

'Now we're all here,' Kelp said, 'and Jim's gonna tell us what he can do to give us clean identities.'

'Right,' Green said, and could be seen to forcibly remove his attention from Tiny. 'Like I told Andy,' he said, 'a whole new identity, perfect and forever, is a very expensive proposition, and not easy, and I can't do it even once as a favor. But I got some lightly used identities that I can adjust for you guys if it's just short term, but there's the slight risk, and Andy says you'll chance it, that the real owner might show up. Or, worse, somebody that doesn't like the real owner could show up.'

Dortmunder said, 'I don't get that. How does that work?'

So Green explained it, and then Stan said, 'There's something I don't follow in there.'

So Green explained it again, and Tiny said, 'Are you talking about some bozo finds *us* or finds the paperwork?'

So Green explained it again, and Dortmunder said, 'If you say it works, it works, let's let it go at that.'

'Thank you,' Green said.

Kelp said, 'So what now?'

'Now,' Green said, and lifted from the floor beside his chair a big black squared-off leather case of the kind photographers use when they're away from home, 'we start assembling the identities.' And he placed the case on the table in front of himself, folded the top back, and it actually was, at least in part, a photographer's case, with a camera and some lenses and lights, but there were also other little dark machines in there, tucked together very neatly, that could have been intended to do anything from trim your toenails to encourage a confession.

Tiny, not sounding pleased, said, 'Whadawe got here?'

'I need stuff for your new identities,' Green explained. 'Photos, finger-prints, eye and palm scans, a swab for DNA.'

Stan said, 'Without even a phone call to my lawyer?'

Kelp said, 'It's OK, Stan, it just stays with him.'

Green said, 'Also, I'm gonna tape-record little bios from you, where you grew up, where you went to school, any jobs, specialties, scars or things like that I wouldn't see, stuff like that. The closer I can get the new you to the old you, the less you got to memorize.'

Tiny said, 'Dortmunder? This is what we're doing?'

'He's Andy's friend,' Dortmunder said.

'Well, he's Anne Marie's friend,' Kelp said, 'but he's OK, Tiny, I'm pretty sure.'

Green smiled, friendly with them all. 'You really can trust me,' he said.

Tiny considered him. 'No,' he decided. 'I don't have to trust you. I just have to find you, if I want to, and you got found once, so you could get found twice. If we want to. So go ahead.' Turning his massive head to the left, he said, 'This is my good profile.'

22

When Henry Cooper was a young man, he was a ne'er-do-well, a layabout, an idler, according to his father, Henry Sr., and it was true. He loafed through high school and much of college, collecting Fs and Incompletes as though they were merit badges, until when he was twenty, Henry Sr had had enough:

'You will *pass* your four courses this semester,' he announced, 'and I mean all four of them, or your allowance is stopped, your schooling is stopped, the lease on your automobile is stopped, the rent on your apartment is stopped, and all legal fees you incur for whatever reason will henceforward be paid by *you*. Is that understood?'

Well, in a way. The threat was understood right enough, but what to do about it was far from understood. Pass his courses, all four of them, the very first time? He was used to failing at least twice per subject before enough of the material could wedge itself into his inattentive brain so that he could eke out a D and move on to the next crop of failure. And yet, he couldn't survive a minute without Henry Sr.'s cash, and he damn well knew it. What to do?

At this time, Henry was enrolled in a huge Midwestern land grant university, thousands upon thousands of enrolled students, hundreds in every lecture hall, and all of it to cover for the school's football team, which was the actual product being manufactured there. The football team won games, the alumni therefore gave to the university endowment, and the school sailed sunnily on.

Henry was at this place instead of an Ivy League school closer to home, home being a well-off suburb outside Harrisburg, Pennsylvania, because (a) his father wasn't going to throw away *that* much money, and (b) no Ivy League school would have touched Henry Cooper with a rake.

So, given the general lack of rigor in this football factory, it shouldn't have been that hard for Henry to scrape along somehow, except that he could just never *pay attention*. He wasn't stupid; he was merely disengaged. He didn't have anything else in particular to do, but he also had not the slightest interest in what he found himself doing (but had to do, to keep supporting himself with Henry Sr.'s money), so how was he to survive this draconian threat?

The hugeness of the university is what saved him. Here and there among his fellow undergraduates were those who were both very good in a particular subject and also impecunious. Henry found four such who were willing to write his papers for him and take his exams for him in the large anonymous examination halls, in return for some small share of Henry Sr.'s cash. Every college student in America, prior to legal drinking age, learns how to manufacture fake ID, so it was nothing for Henry to provide his team with student passes featuring his name and their faces. 'Now, don't ace all this stuff,' he warned them. 'I want to be a C student; my father wouldn't believe anything better.'

And so it came about that Henry Cooper became a C student for the rest of his college career, finding new substitutes when necessary, that Henry Sr. became a happy or at least a somewhat less truculent man, and that Henry inadvertently stumbled upon his calling: he became an employment agent.

Bernice entered Henry's office, looking troubled and a little confused. 'I'm sorry, Mr Cooper,' she said.

'Don't be sorry, Bernice,' Henry told her. 'Just be sure you're right.'

A solid citizen of forty-two, a little puffy around the edges but kept in reasonably trim fit by regular golf and irregular fad diets, Henry Cooper held not the slightest memory of the sweaty subterfuges by which he'd managed to obtain his bachelor of arts degree and retain his father's subsidies. (Subsidies that were now reversed, Henry financing the old bastard's condo in Florida on the unstated agreement that Sr. would *stay* there and Henry would never visit.) All he remembered, really, of his college days were the football games and a few drinking chums.

Today Henry was a successful and respectable businessman who didn't cheat in any way at all, not even on his wife. (Who would have known, in any event, and would promptly have disemboweled him.) These days, the Cooper Placement Service provided him a comfortable living and a position of esteem in his community. He rooted for his alma mater's football team and donated to its fund drives. He was the perfect graduate.

He was also an excellent employer, known to be fair and calm, if a little hazy sometimes on details, so Bernice knew, when Henry told her merely to be sure she was right, to wipe away as much as possible the worried look, replace it with a tentative smile, and say, 'Yes, but, you remember, sir, you told me not to put through any calls from Mr Monroe Hall.'

'Oh, God, Monroe.' Henry touched the heel of his palm to his forehead. 'That poor son of a bitch,' he said. 'After all this time, there's finally something around him that isn't his fault. But there's really and truly nothing I can do about it.'

'I know that, sir.'

'I've *tried* to get him staff,' Henry said. 'We used to golf together. I've drunk the man's scotch, when it was still permissible to be seen with him. I am not averse to taking a commission from his employees.'

'Of course not, sir.'

'But there's simply nothing I can do,' Henry said. 'I hate to duck him, I'm not the sort to duck my responsibilities, *you* know that—'

'Yes, sir.'

'—but what could I say to the man? I can't bear to listen to him plead. What if he started to cry?'

'Oh, dear.'

'Exactly. So I don't care what sob story he told you, I'm not in the office.'

'Well, sir,' she said, 'this time he says he wants to buy the agency.'

Henry blinked. 'Buy the— Buy *my* agency? Cooper Placement Service?'

'Yes, sir.'

'That's absurd.'

'He says,' she said, then hesitated.

'Go on, go on,' he urged her. 'I know it isn't you saying it, it's Monroe saying it.'

'Yes, sir. He says, since you're no longer interested in the agency, he'll take it off your hands and find someone competent to run it.'

'Why, the gall!'

'He says, sir, name your price.'

Cooper was not tempted, not even for a second, though he knew Hall certainly had the money to back up the offer. But all at once, he was also no longer angry. A fitful empathy with his fellow man had made one of its unwelcome appearances. 'The poor bastard,' he said. 'He *must* be desperate.'

'For some time now, sir.'

'He's got all that money, they can't pin anything on him, and yet his life has gone to hell because he can't get staff.'

'I believe, sir,' she said, 'he doesn't actually leave his home. Or the estate.'

'No, he doesn't play golf any more,' Henry agreed. 'Too much likelihood some other player would remove his head with a four iron.'

'Ooh, sir.'

Henry sighed. 'I'll talk to him,' he said. 'Once.'

'Line two, sir. And thank you.'

She left, and with heavy heart Henry picked up his phone, punched 2, and said, 'Monroe, I'm doing my best.'

'Just name your price,' said Monroe's voice.

Henry had forgotten just how snotty Monroe habitually sounded. He held his irritation in check. 'Monroe, I always provided satisfactory service in the past. I'd be happy to go on staffing your estate, but *you've* made it impossible. It's your actions, Monroe, your notoriety, not any ineptitude or indifference on my part.'

'When are people going to get *over* it?'

'People don't get over it when you're a pariah, Monroe.'

'*Why do people keep using that word?*'

'Well, Monroe, think about it.'

'I don't want to.'

'Every day, Monroe,' Henry told him, 'I try to find people willing to go to work for you. Every day. Occasionally, I find someone.'

'Not for weeks!'

'Monroe,' Henry said, 'do you believe I'm doing my best for you?'

There was a long silence on the other end of the line, followed by a long sigh. During the silence and the sigh, Henry felt his empathy at last slipping away, like the tide going out, and grew stronger, more cheerful and relaxed. He did not think, 'There but for the grace of God go I,' because, having never faced the equivalent of Monroe's temptations (opportunities), he assumed he would not have fallen for them.

At last Monroe spoke, not directly answering the question. 'People don't want to talk to me,' he said. '*You* don't want to talk to me.'

'Only because I don't have good news.'

'Listen,' Monroe said, suddenly perking up. 'Why don't you and Gillian come out for dinner? When are you free? Tonight?'

'Oh, I don't think so, Monroe,' Henry said. 'Let me just go on trying to find people willing to work for you. Oops, my other phone.' And he slapped the plunger, to disconnect.

For a minute, Henry sat brooding, then he pushed the button to summon Bernice from her desk in the next office. When she came in, she was looking worried again. Good. Henry said, 'Bernice, would you like to go work for Monroe Hall?'

She was astonished, and then appalled. 'You're *selling*, sir?'

'Not a bit,' Henry said. 'I don't mean work here, I mean work there. At Monroe's place. Would you like that?'

'No, sir!'

'You're happier working for me?'

'Very happy here, sir.'

'The next time Monroe calls, I'm out.'

Bernice sighed. 'Yes, sir.'

23

When the phone rang, Dortmunder was making himself a mayonnaise and baloney sandwich on white. He heard the ring, looked at his incomplete sandwich laid open on the plate like a patient etherized upon a table, and thought, what if I don't answer? Then he replied to himself, it'll just keep ringing. So he plunged the knife into the mayo jar and marched to the living room where, as predicted, the phone was still ringing. He answered: 'Yeah?'

'*Dortmunder!*' rasped a voice so loud and irritating that Dortmunder automatically yanked the receiver out to arm's length, as though it had caught fire. From that distance, the rasp was less painful but just as repellent: '*Dortmunder! Where are you? You there?*'

Cautiously, Dortmunder approached the receiver to his head. 'Don't shout,' he said.

'*Dortmunder!*'

'Don't shout!'

'Am I shouting?' But then, of course, he wasn't. 'All these waves here, I can't hear a thing. Can you hear them? The waves?'

Then Dortmunder knew who it was; the same voice that used to rasp from the intercom on West Eighty-ninth street. 'Arnie? Is that you?'

'Who else?' Arnie Albright demanded.

'And you're still there? The Club Med?'

'Down in the islands,' Arnie snarled. 'Everything's sand, and everybody smiles all the time. I know you'll say it can't be that bad, John Dortmunder, but it is. Never get sent down to a place like this.'

'OK.'

'If you got the choice, you're sent up or you're sent down, take up. You don't have to take my word for it. Ignore me if you want, go your own way, whado I care?'

Dortmunder said, 'I thought the idea was, they were gonna modify your behavior.'

'I'm modified,' Arnie assured him. 'Trust me, I'm modified, but it doesn't do any good. The G.O.s won't eat with me.'

'The who?'

'The staff,' Arnie said. 'The help. Everything's democratic here, if you believe it, and the guests eat with the help. Everybody mixed up in the same tables. Only, after a few days, the G.O.s won't eat with me any more. They pretend like they're gonna, but then they don't. They go sit with the smiley people instead.'

'G.O.s,' Dortmunder said. 'That's what you've been saying.'

'They got their own language here,'Arnie said. 'Well, they do, anyway, they're French. But even beyond that. So G.O. is staff, and G.M. is the rest of us, the guests.'

'G.M.'

'Somebody told me,' Arnie said, 'it means Gentile Members, but that can't be right, can it?'

'I don't know,' Dortmunder said. 'I never been to a place like that.'

'Sunlight gives me a rash,' Arnie said. 'I hadda come here to find that out. But I got a little porch on my room, I can get air *and* shade, and this whole ocean is right here, it's practically in the place with me, and the waves *don't* sound like traffic, you know that?'

'No, I didn't know that,' Dortmunder said.

'You sure you can't hear them? Listen,' Arnie said, and apparently held his phone closer to the ocean because now Dortmunder could hear a faint slow repeated shushing sound that wasn't at all like traffic.

'Yeah, now I do,' he said.

A little silence, and then Arnie said, 'Did you hear it?'

'Yeah, then I did.'

'Well, you don't wanna talk to me,' Arnie said, 'so let's get to the subject matter.'

Dortmunder wanted to say, no, it's fine to talk to you, or no, it's good to hear your voice, but there are certain lies that just will not pass a person's lips, no matter how firm the intention, so what he did say was, 'Sure, the subject matter.'

'My cousin Archie tells me you wanna prepare a gift for when I get back there,' Arnie said, 'and I should tell you what kinda gift I'd like to see.'

Getting the idea, Dortmunder said, 'That's it exactly.'

'I'm not interested in clocks.'

'OK.'

'I am interested in music boxes.'

'Fine.'

'And I am interested in chess sets.'

'I'll make a note.'

'And I am interested in coins, but only if they're gold.'

'Good thinking.'

'But I am not interested in anything else. Well, yeah, I am.'

'You are?'

'I'm interested,' Arnie said, 'in a ticket outta here, but I don't think you got one of those.'

'No, I don't.'

'Well, I'm not gonna take up your time,' Arnie said, 'on the phone here, tell you *my* troubles. Whada you give a shit about *my* troubles? The fact is, you don't.'

'Uhhh,' Dortmunder said, and Arnie hung up.

It was amazing, really, how little effect Club Med had so far had on Arnie's personality. And it was also amazing how much of that personality could come through over the telephone.

It was a good ten minutes before Dortmunder got his appetite back enough so he could go finish making his sandwich.

24

Buddy said, 'I hate to say this, but we aren't getting anywhere.'

Ace looked up, his hands full of jockstraps. 'How can you say that? We're in the guy's house, aren't we?'

'Breaking and entering,' Buddy said, and shook his head. 'We never broke any laws before.'

'Stalking,' Mac suggested.

Buddy rejected that at once, 'Whadaya mean, stalking? We're just observing our former boss's habit patterns, that's all, nothing wrong with that. But this jock here—'

Ace dumped the jockstraps back into the dresser drawer and slammed it with his hip.

'—he isn't a boss of ours,' Buddy went on, 'he's nothing to do with us except Monroe Hall's a customer of his. What we're doing here, Mac, is breaking and entering, and it's against the law, and you know it.'

'To tell you the truth, Buddy,' Mac said, 'that part doesn't bother me so much. What bothers me so much, we aren't getting anywhere.'

Ace had another bureau drawer open. 'We're learning a lot about this guy,' he insisted, holding up a neatly rolled Ace bandage.

'What does it do for us?' Mac wanted to know. 'We broke in here, into the guy's house, three times now, and we're using information *and* equipment we got from a cop cousin in New Jersey that's an ACWFFA supporter—'

'Great guy,' Ace announced. 'Best cop I ever met.'

'But,' Mac said, 'he took a big chance with his own career, and for what? We keep searching the guy's house; nothing. We searched his car; nothing. Not even room for three of us to hide in it, by the way.'

'Well, maybe,' Buddy said.

Mac kept to his own thought. 'We made a copy of his address book and followed up on everybody he knows and they're all clients or doctors or other health freaks. We found nothing to help us, and all we're doing is spinning our wheels, and God knows what those Harvard boys are doing, but they aren't standing around not getting anywhere like us.'

'You notice,' Ace said, 'they haven't been in touch.'

'And we,' Mac said, 'haven't been in touch with them. Probably for the same reason.'

Alarmed, Buddy said, 'You think they're up to something?'

'Of course they're up to something,' Mac said. 'So are we. Why wouldn't they be up to something?' Looking at his watch, he said, 'We gotta get outa here. And *I* don't see any reason to break in here again.'

'Jeez . . .' Ace said, looking around the bedroom, once again restored by them to neatness.

'Forget it, Ace,' Mac advised him. 'We just aren't going to find any stuff in here we can use for blackmail.'

Looking hurt, Ace said, 'That's a nasty word, Mac.'

Riding over that, Mac said, 'No child pornography, no bigamy, no double identity, not even any overdue library books. Alphonse Morriscone is a Boy Scout, and I say we leave him alone from now on. Come on.'

As they walked toward the rear door, their usual route through Morriscone's house, Buddy said, 'I hate to invade this guy as much as you do, Mac, but what the heck else are we gonna do?'

'There's other things go in and outa that compound,' Mac said. 'The oil truck makes deliveries.'

Ace said, 'If you think I'm gonna hold my breath in an oil truck for forty minutes, you're crazy.'

Mac shook his head and opened the back door. 'That's not what I'm saying. Be sure it's locked, Buddy.'

'Right.'

'So what are you saying?' Ace demanded, as he followed Mac out to the small neat back porch while Buddy made sure the kitchen door was locked. From here it was a simple walk across a lawn flanked by privacy fencing in rough wood verticals – if Morriscone did nude sunbathing out here, he didn't take pictures of the fact – and through the hedge at the back to the unoccupied house on the next block with the For Sale sign out front. The way it was set up, they could get in and out of Alphonse Morriscone's home unseen any time they wanted. The only problem was, there was no reason to want to.

As they walked from Morriscone's house around the for-sale house and down the street to where they'd parked the Taurus, Mac said, 'It isn't just oil deliveries. They get food to that house, they send their dry cleaning out.'

Buddy said, 'You've watched their procedures, Mac. All those delivery trucks get completely searched by those rent-a-cops at the gate. Boy Scout Morriscone is the only one who just drives in.'

Ace said, 'Well, there's some employees. Staffers.'

'No use to us,' Mac said.

'And the wife does, too,' Ace said.

They looked at him. Buddy said, 'Now you wanna kidnap the *wife*? The three of us go into the estate hidden in one of those little dinky cars she drives?'

'I could hide under her skirt,' Ace offered with a big grin around at everybody, which fell away when he saw they didn't think that was funny.

Morosely, Mac said, 'Maybe we oughta try to find the Harvards.'

'Look at those capering apes,' Os said, binoculars to his eyes.

'You probably mean Ace,' Mark said, since he didn't have binoculars to his eyes. 'He's the worst of them.'

'God,' Os said. 'Not only proles, but useless.'

'I think it's our friend Morriscone who's useless.' Mark suggested. '*We* could find nothing in his background that we could use against the man, and by now, after three B and Es, it's becoming quite clear our friends in the labor movement haven't found anything in his foreground, either.'

'Time is going by,' Os said.

Across the way, the trio were getting into their Taurus. Watching them through the naked eye, Mark said, 'We have to *use* those people. Somehow use them. Use them somehow.'

'Good,' Os said.

25

Given her upbringing in Kansas and D.C., Anne Marie's automatic response to any gathering of individuals was to turn it into a social occasion – why miss an opportunity to work a room? But Andy absolutely refused to go along with the idea in re the upcoming three p.m. meeting in their apartment in which Jim Green would give Andy and the others their new identities. 'It isn't a party, Anne Marie,' he explained, not unkindly. 'It's more of a huddle-type thing, you know, informational.'

'I'm not saying a *party*,' she insisted, although she knew she was. 'Just a few hors d'oeuvres, maybe a glass of white wine. You can't drink beer and bourbon forever.'

Looking startled, he said, 'I can't?'

'I should think Jim would feel insulted,' Anne Marie said, 'when he's doing us this big favor, and he comes all the way down from Connecticut, and we don't even offer him a pâté.'

'We're not going to an *opening*, Anne Marie,' Andy said, 'and none of us is gonna want pâté on his new identity papers. Green is gonna bring the stuff down, hand it out, explain what he's gotta explain, and that's it. Everybody goes away.'

She shook her head. 'You want people to come into our home,' she said, 'and sit around and talk, and then just go away again, and nobody eats anything, and nobody chats about anything, and nobody drinks anything but beer.'

'Now you got it,' Andy said.

But she stuck around anyway, just in case a social aspect should happen to arise, in which case her hostessing abilities would be needed after all. And Stan Murch was the first to arrive. She greeted him at the door: 'Hi, Stan.'

'So now it's Brooklyn,' Stan said, coming in. 'I always figured, Canarsie's a convenient place to live, you got a lotta ways to get to Manhattan, you got Flatlands to Flatbush to the Manhattan Bridge, only Flatbush can get a little slow, so sometimes I do Rockaway Parkway to Eastern Parkway, and not Rockaway *Avenue*, that takes you to Bushwick, you don't wanna go to Bushwick.'

'No, I don't,' Anne Marie agreed. 'Would you like something to drink?'

But Stan wasn't done. 'So that's what I did today,' he said, 'only you got a mess at Grand Army Plaza, they're tearing everything up in front of the library there, you can't get through, so I eased around to Washington Avenue, up past the BQE to hang the left on Flushing, and again you can't get through. Why? A demonstration against the Naval Reserve Center, that's two blocks down to the right, the cops won't let the demonstrators any closer than Washington. I'm *backing* outa there, some guy pulls up on me and honks. I gotta get outa the car, explain to this bozo that all those yelling people and cops and picket signs he could see if he had working eyes and not just a working horn means you can't *go* that way. So he finally moves over to let me back up, then he jumps in where I was, cackling like an idiot, he put one over on me, he's probably still there.'

'A glass of wine?'

'So I come *under* the BQE on Park,' Stan told her, 'and Tillary, and did the Brooklyn Bridge instead, and after that Manhattan was a snap.'

'Stan,' Anne Marie said, 'you got here first.'

'So it could of been worse.'

'A beer?' she asked him.

'No, thanks,' he said. 'I still got some driving to do today,' and the door-bell rang.

This time, it was Tiny, and he had with him a small but lovely bouquet of pink roses. 'Here,' he said, and handed them over.

'Why, thank you, Tiny,' she said. 'That's very thoughtful.'

'Some girl on the street,' he told her, 'threw them at her boyfriend just before the cops showed up. I figured they shouldn't go to waste.'

'Oh. Well, thank you.'

'Any time.'

Tiny finished coming in, but before Anne Marie could shut the door Jim Green was there, smiling, saying, 'Hello, Anne Marie, how are you today?'

'Just fine,' she said, and would have closed the door but John was suddenly there. 'Oh,' she said. 'Did you two come together?'

John looked confused. Frowning toward Jim, he said, 'I don't think so.'

'No, we didn't,' Jim said, and at last Anne Marie could complete the closing of the door.

And here came Andy from deeper in the apartment, saying, 'Hey, we're all here. Anybody want a beer?'

'Not me,' Stan said.

'Maybe later,' John said.

'What we want,' Tiny said, looking at Jim, 'is to see who we are.'

'Coming up,' Jim said. He was carrying a hard-sided black attaché case, which he now put on the coffee table. He snapped open the catches, lifted the top, and inside Anne Marie saw several thick small manila envelopes, each with a name written on it in black ink. Taking these out of the case, Jim distributed them, saying, 'This is yours,' four times.

All four of the guys were immediately absorbed in the contents of their envelopes. Andy sat in his regular chair, Tiny took all of the sofa, Stan sat in the other armchair, and John perched on the radiator. As they started their study, Jim came over to say, 'Well, Anne Marie, you having more fun now than you used to?'

'A different kind of fun,' she said.

'Listen,' he said, 'if you ever need to disappear, let me know. For you I'll do a special job, not like these.'

'They seem happy with these,' Anne Marie said, and Jim grinned and turned to look at them.

They *were* happy with the contents of their envelopes, like children opening their presents under the tree, Christmas morning, every surprise a joyful one. 'A passport,' Andy said, in awe.

'Gotta have one of those,' Jim told him.

'John Howard Rumsey,' John said.

Andy said, 'Yeah? Who's that?'

'Me,' John told him.

'That ain't bad,' Andy allowed. Reading his passport, he said, 'I'm Fredric Eustace Blanchard. So I guess I'm Fred.'

'I'm still John,' John said. 'Easy to remember.'

His voice even lower than usual, Tiny rumbled, 'Judson Otto Swope.' Nodding around at the others, he said, 'I like that name. I didn't want a name I wasn't gonna like.'

Stan said, 'Says here, I'm Warren Peter Gillette. I don't suppose I have to remember the Peter.' He looked up to his left, as though out a car window: 'Hi, Officer, I'm Warren Gillette.'

'Yeah, here's my driver's license,' Andy said, and grinned at Jim. 'You take a better picture than Motor Vehicles.'

'Of course,' Jim said.

'I'm in securities,' Tiny said. 'What am I, a stockbroker?'

'You're in *security*,' Jim corrected him, though mildly. 'You worked for Securitech, an outfit that dealt with industrial espionage, helping companies keep their trade secrets.'

'How come I'm not there any more?'

'The company folded when both owners went to jail for insider trading.'

John said, 'I'm a butler?' He sounded as though he wasn't sure what he thought about that.

Jim said, 'You people need work histories that'll make your mark want to hire you, am I right?'

'I'm a chauffeur!' Stan said. He sounded very pleased.

'That's right,' Jim said. Pointing at Andy, he said, 'And you're a private secretary. In fact, you and John worked for the same man, Hildorg Chk, ambassador to the United States from Vostkojek, at their official residence in Georgetown.'

'We had dealings with that country once,' Tiny rumbled.

John said, 'What if they check with this ambassador?'

Smiling, Jim shook his head. 'Sadly,' he said, 'he was assassinated on a visit home over the holidays. That's why you and Andy are both looking for work.'

'I drove for a movie star,' Stan said, 'with a place on Central Park West. How come I'm not there any more?'

'His career tanked,' Jim said. 'He gave up New York, just kept his place in Pacific Palisades, drives himself these days, and is looking for interesting second-lead roles.'

Stan said, 'And if they check with *him*?'

'They'll get no further than his L.A. staff,' Jim told him, 'and they never knew the New York staff.'

John said, 'And the point is, am I right, this stuff is all real.'

'Those are real people,' Jim told him, 'as real as the paperwork can make them. All four of them *were* those people at one time, though it isn't who any of them were at birth, and now they're off being somebody else, the original or another new one. But you've got to remember, they can always come back.'

Andy said, 'Not all four of them.'

'No, but one could make trouble.'

Stan laughed. 'I can imagine some guy goes up to Tiny, and— What was your name?'

'Judson Otto Swope.'

'Right. Some guy shows up and says, Hey, *I'm* Judson Otto Swope.'

Tiny nodded. 'We could discuss it,' he said.

Andy said, 'We're not gonna worry about that. We just been christened brand-new guys, so let's relax and enjoy it.'

'Christen!' said Anne Marie, leaping to her feet. 'You're right, Andy, it's a christening. Wait right there, I'll get the champagne.'

26

'Tuesday,' Hal Mellon said, 'a man walks into a bar with a carrot stuck in his ear. You make the next right.' Chester made the next right. A lot of these Pennsylvania towns straddled rivers, and so did this one, so now Chester was driving across a small bridge.

'The bartender,' Mellon said, 'thinks to himself, oh, a wise guy, I'm supposed to ask how come you got a carrot in your ear, and he's got some smart-aleck answer. OK, he thinks, I'm not gonna be *his* patsy, I'm not gonna ask. And he doesn't. About two blocks down here, you'll see the big sign, Astro Solutions, that's where we're headed.'

'Right,' Chester said.

'So Wednesday,' Mellon said, 'the same guy comes in, with another carrot in his ear. The bartender thinks to himself, this guy doesn't give up easy, but I am *not* gonna ask him about that damn carrot. And he doesn't. Thursday, Friday, the guy comes back, always with a new carrot, the bartender's going nuts, he refuses to ask the question. Finally, Saturday, the guy comes in, he's got a stick of celery in his ear. The bartender's thrown completely off. Without thinking, he says, "How come you got a stick of celery in your ear?" and the guy says, "I couldn't find a carrot". We turn in here, visitor's parking.'

So they turned in, Chester parked facing the low light-green aluminum-bodied building, and Mellon said, 'I'll be back with my shield or on it.' But that's what he said every time he got out of the car, so Chester no longer made any response to the line. Mellon, who didn't need a response, got his sample case from the backseat and bounced toward the building, loping along on the balls of his feet.

Chester got out the book he was reading – *The Road to Oxiana*, by Robert Byron, a quirky recountal of a trip from England to Afghanistan in the early '30s, mostly by car, some of it by charcoal-burning car – and settled in for half an hour of peace.

Basically, this was a good job. Mellon paid him well, did no backseat driving, and Chester had plenty of time, like right now, to read, a habit he'd developed in prison. If it weren't for the jokes, it would be perfect.

It was salesman's jokes, that's what it was, and it just poured out of Mellon like cold water out of a spring. He didn't seem to have any control over it, and he didn't require any reaction from Chester, not a laugh, not a groan, nothing.

Chester did react, of course – he had to – but his reactions were silent. The jokes were tedious, and it hardly mattered if they contained any actual comedy or not. What Chester found himself concentrating on – unwillingly, but just as helplessly as Mellon himself telling the jokes – was the setups.

Why were that priest, that rabbi, and that minister walking down that street? Where were they headed? How had they happened to come together? What odd chance had put ex-presidents Bush, Clinton, and Carter on that same plane? Why do so many talking animals have nowhere to go except some bar?

The worst part of every day's driving was immediately after Mellon's return from an appointment. A salesman among office lugs, he would have sprayed his jokes on them like a male lion, and they would have sprayed a bunch of *their* jokes back at him. And when Mellon returned to the car, springs in his feet, sales in his salesbook, guess who'd get those jokes next?

Chester wasn't sure how much more of this he was going to be able to stand. He was *dreaming* some of those jokes, the stewardesses in the elevator, the astronaut in the men's room. When would Andy Kelp and his friends make their move against Monroe Hall? They were still going to do it, weren't they? But *when*? How much longer would they leave poor Chester all alone out here, at the mercy of Hal Mellon?

And here he came. Sample case into backseat, Mellon into the front seat, pointing: 'We keep on now the same direction, maybe twenty miles.'

'Right.'

'A Muslim, a Christian, and a Jew are on Mount Everest—'

It was twenty to six when he finally reached home in Shickshinny. He walked in, thinking a drink might be called for along about now, and Grace met him in the living room to say, 'Your friend Andy called.'

They decided not to do it! Heart in his throat, Chester said, 'What did he say?'

'Call him.'

'That's all?'

'What more do you need?'

'You're right, you're right.' He hurried across the room, picked up the phone, looked back at Grace. 'You're right,' he said.

'I'll get you a scotch,' she decided, and left the room. It was the girlfriend, Anne Marie, who answered, but when Chester identified himself she said, 'Oh, Andy wants to talk to you. Hold on.'

He held on. How could he convince them not to quit? Grace came in and stood with a short thick glass in her hand.

'Chester?'

'Listen, Andy—'

'Looks to me, Chester,' Andy said, 'we're gonna need housing out around you. Just till we get hired, right? But it's a hell of a commute from the city.'

'You're gonna do it?'

'Sure, whadya think? It's just we need billets.'

'Stay *here*,' Chester told him, happier than he'd been in a long time. (No more missionaries *and* no more cannibals.) 'We got plentya room.'

He and Andy chatted a little longer, while Grace gave him a skeptical look, and when he got off the phone she handed him his drink and said, '*We've* got plenty of room? Where?'

'It'll work out,' Chester said. 'They're gonna do it, that's all, that's all that matters.' He lifted the glass in a toast. 'Monroe Hall.'

She looked aghast. 'Monroe Hall?'

'May he rot,' Chester said, 'from the head down.'

'Oh,' she said. 'Right. Lemme get my own glass.'

27

Flip was furious; he was beside himself. How could Monroe Hall, who just last week had called himself Flip's 'pal,' have done such a thing? There wasn't even any profit in it for Hall; just loss, for poor Flip.

Driving toward the estate for today's session, he rehearsed in his mind just how he would tell the man off. 'Everybody *knows* you're the most self-ish man in the world, I mean that's what you're famous for, but why do *me* like this? What did *you* get out of it? Was it just for *fun?*'

Lips moving, mouthing the angry sentences, he turned in at the entrance and stopped at the guardshack. The sullen guard came out as usual, but today Flip didn't give him a friendly greeting. Today he didn't give him a greeting at all, or a word at all. Staring straight ahead, his telling-off of Monroe Hall still circling in his brain, he merely held his driver's license up where the troglodyte could read it, if he could read. The man took a long time, unmoving, standing beside the open window of the Subaru, but Flip didn't care. Take forever if you want, you creep. Ban me from the estate, I'll be just as happy to go home.

Whether or not the guard could read Flip's license, he could probably read Flip's face, because he finally stopped waiting for Flip to do or say something, but just turned around to lumber back into his cave, presum-ably to make the call to the Big House.

Flip put his license away, then glowered at the bar directly in front of him, waiting for it to lift. When it finally did start its upward arc, the guard came back out, leaned down close to the window, and said, 'You wanna be more friendly.'

Flip looked him up and down. 'To *you?*' Then he drove through and onto the estate.

Well, *that* made him feel a little better, for a minute anyway, until, as he approached the Big House, he saw the front door open and Hall step out into the sunlight to wave at him. Today's sweat-set was Day-Glo orange, so that Hall looked less like a Mafia subcapo and more like a weather balloon, slightly deflated.

I'll show you some weather, Flip mouthed, as he parked the Subaru in its usual place, got out, and threw his canvas bag over his shoulder with such force he hurt his back. Smarting even more, blaming Hall for this as well, he marched around to the front door, where Hall greeted him with his usual smarmy smile, saying, 'Right on time, Flip. As ever. Come in, come in. I did ask you one time if you rode horses, didn't I?'

Thrown off stride, Flip tried to work out that question and its answer while Hall shut the door and they started toward the central staircase. 'I don't,' he decided was the clearest response, then expanded on it: 'Ride horses.'

'Right, I remember,' Hall said. They moved up the stairs. 'You remember that, I told you I have these horses, beautiful beasts, but I can't find an instructor. This is a *perfect* time of year, Flip, perfect time of year. Up on that horse, ride over hill and dale, get an entirely new perspective.'

'I've never done it,' Flip said. *Now* I'll tell him off, he assured himself, but the instant didn't seem just right somehow.

Moving down the wide upstairs corridor, Hall said, 'I know you told me I shouldn't weigh myself every minute, but I *did* weigh myself this morning, and Flip, I'm down three pounds! From a month ago.'

'Very good,' Flip said, and somewhere a cuckoo commented threefold.

'Oh, there's that damn thing again,' Hall complained. 'Sometimes, Flip, I think I should just let it run down, not have it wound any more, not have to listen to it get things wrong all the time, but I don't know, I just can't do it. It would be like killing the poor little thing. I know, I know, you'll say I'm just a sentimental boob, but there it is. I've gotta let that clock do its thing.'

Sentimental! Following Hall into the gym, Flip gnashed his teeth, and made a dozen brutal crushing remarks that somehow never quite passed his lips.

It went on like that, an hour of fuming silence. He got minor revenges by pushing the treadmill beyond Hall's capacity, by overloading the weight machines, by being a bit more snappish and imperious than usual, so that by the end of the hour Hall was a sodden orange orange with all the juice on the outside. But the challenging of the man, the confronting him, the direct accusation, somehow that just never emerged. Flip boiled with it, he seethed with it, if he were a kettle his lid would be doing a polka, but it was just not possible for him to pour his fury all over Monroe Hall.

At the end, though, he did manage, though obliquely, to get to the subject of his distress: 'I won't be able to make our session Wednesday.'

Hall looked stricken; good. 'Oh, Flip,' he said. 'You have to.'

'No, what I *have* to do,' Flip told him, 'is go to Harrisburg to meet with somebody at the Internal Revenue office.'

'Oh, dear, Flip,' Hall said, looking as concerned as though he were an actual human being with actual human emotions, 'I hope you aren't in any trouble.'

'Turns out,' Flip said, packing his canvas bag, not looking at the rat, 'I am. Turns out, some cash income I received was reported to the IRS.'

'But, Flip, naturally,' Hall said.

Now Flip had to look at him, and the man was as innocent as a newborn. Into that perspiring baby face, Flip said, 'Do people report their cash income to the IRS?'

'Well, I certainly hope so,' Hall said. He paused briefly to wipe that face with a towel and pant a bit, then said,' It would be unpatriotic not to report your income, pay your taxes.'

'Unpa— Unpa—' Flip could only sputter at the outrageousness of this *felon*, this world-class *cheat*, this despicable *rotter*, telling Flip Morriscone he was unpatriotic! Unpatriotic!

'I certainly hope,' Hall was going on, as though Flip were not doing a meltdown directly in front of him, 'you declare what *I* pay you, because of course I report *all* my expenses. All my expenses, Flip, whether they're deductible or not. I believe in transparency, and you should, too.'

Flip slowly shook his head, unable to speak.

Hall lifted a chiding finger. 'Now, Flip,' he said, 'take it from one who knows, one who's been there. The best thing for you to do at this hearing is just come clean, pay whatever they want you to pay, and put it behind you.' The chiding finger waggled. 'And don't play fast and loose again, Flip, that's *my* advice.'

How he got out of that building without strangling Monroe Hall then and there Flip would never know. How he got out of there at *all* he couldn't understand, and had no memory of the corridor, the stairs, the front door or anything else until he found himself driving the Subaru past the sullen guard – whose look toward Flip was now reproachful, if you please – and out of the estate.

He made the turn. He drove away, toward his next appointment. At last, he spoke, through gritted teeth. 'Revenge,' he growled. 'Revenge.'

28

In a way, Marcie felt sorry for Monroe Hall. In the seventeen years she'd worked as an interviewer for Cooper Placement Service, she'd never seen an employer who was so thoroughly disliked. How bad could the man be?

Mostly, particularly in a rural area like this one, people just sucked it up and got on with it. 'What the heck, it's a job,' was the general opinion about almost anything. In her time, she'd placed personal maids with Iranian ex-wives, chauffeurs who were required to wear bulletproof vests when on the job for notorious drug dealers, gardeners for the weekend houses of top-level fashionistas out of New York, cooks for Ecuadorean aristocrats, dressers for rock stars, secretaries to disgraced politicians writing their truthless memoirs, and not one of those people had ever produced as negative a reaction in a prospective employee as almost everybody gave to the name Monroe Hall.

'Oh, no, not there, I don't need a job *that* bad.'

'But what's wrong with—'

'Let me put it this way, miss. I wouldn't go to work for that bastard if he paid me.'

'He *will* pay you, it's a job, you can—'

'Not for me. What else chu got?'

'Archivist for a professional wrestler called Ultra-Mud.'

'Oh, *I* heard a him! Sure! What the heck, it's a job.'

How many vacancies were there out to Monroe Hall's place by now? Attrition was just steadily eating into the workforce out there. Marcie believed, as of this morning, Tuesday, June 14, there were seventeen job slots unfilled out at the estate. Even two openings in security, and you were *never* supposed to run short on security applicants, particularly if you didn't worry too much about the prior-convictions check.

What it added up to, a girl could find herself feeling sorry for Monroe Hall. Oh, of course, only theoretically. She herself wouldn't work for the son of a bitch on a bet, the way he rode roughshod over family, friend, employee, and the government alike. She was perfectly happy right where she was at Cooper Placement Service, and even if she weren't, she'd rather

111

work at the Last Call coal mine over in Golgotha City, where filling out your last will and testament was part of the job application, than work for that—

'Don'tcha have anything else?'

The applicant's question snapped Marcie out of her woolgathering. She shouldn't be thinking about the dreadful if pathetic Monroe Hall; she should be thinking about a job for the gentleman across the desk from her in her cubicle, uh . . . Fred Blanchard, most recently a private secretary for a foreign diplomat down in Washington, D.C., now returning to her desk the list of current job availabilities she'd shown him.

Time to get down to business. 'Well, I'm surprised, Mr Blanchard,' she said, 'you haven't pursued your job search in the greater Washington area. We have fine people in this part of Pennsylvania, but not many international diplomats.'

'That's good,' Blanchard told her. He was a cheerful, sharp-featured guy with an easygoing manner. 'I've had enough of international intrigue for a while,' he told her. 'I got family up around here, I thought I'd like a little more laidback a setting. You've gotta have *some* rich people around here, need a private secretary, somebody to field the phone calls and the correspondence, deal with the press, take care of the archives.'

'Well, yes, but someone just at the moment in *need*—'

He watched her, bright-eyed as a bird. 'You thought of something?'

She leaned closer to him. As neutrally as she possibly could, she spoke the name: 'Monroe Hall.'

He didn't even blink. Still smiling, he said, 'Is that the kind of guy I'm talking about?'

'Oh, yes, he is,' she said, but then doubt scudded like a cloud across her features. 'Have you never heard of him? Monroe Hall?'

He thought, his smile turning quizzical, 'Should I?'

'His name was in the paper for a while.'

'Oh, the paper.' Blanchard brushed the fourth estate to one side. 'At the embassy,' he said, 'we only watched International CNN.'

'Would you – would you like me to set up an appointment?'

'Why not?' he said.

Talk about lightning strikes twice. Hardly was Marcie back from lunch, not two hours after sending Fred Blanchard up to talk to Monroe Hall – and *how* would that work out and did she hope he'd get the job or refuse it? – here came another one. His name was Warren Gillette, and the first thing she noticed about him was that he used to be the chauffeur for Jer Crumble, who just happened to be one of Marcie's most favorite movie stars. 'My goodness,' she said. 'You know Jer Crumble?'

'Mostly in the rearview mirror,' he said, 'Nice fella, though. Not one of your uppity types.'

She was very glad to hear that. 'I see he gives you a wonderful recommendation.'

'Yeah, I know.' Gillette chuckled. 'It couldn't of been better if I wrote it myself.'

'But why did you leave?'

'I didn't,' Gillette said, and shrugged. 'He left me. Gave up his New York place and went back to the Coast. For his career, you know.'

'Oh, I see.' She opened the lower right drawer of her desk and pulled a folder from it. 'We have a number of driver type openings. Not movie stars, though.'

Another chuckle. 'I guess I've had enough movie stars for a while.'

'Fine. Here's a delivery van, furniture store.'

He made a little grimace. 'I don't know,' he said. 'Maybe I'm spoiled or something, but I like to drive for one person, you know. And a good car. Jer always surrounded himself with very good cars.'

'Oh, my goodness,' she said, with sudden realization. 'We have someone, very local, who's famous for *wonderful* cars, and I know he's right now looking for a new chauffeur.'

'Well, this is my lucky day,' Gillette said. 'Who is he?'

Marcie squinched her eyes up, half in expectation of some sort of explosion. 'Monroe Hall,' she said.

'And he's a rich man with a lot of cars, you say.' Gillette nodded. 'What kinda business he in?'

Marcie said, 'You never heard of Monroe Hall?'

'Not another showbiz guy, I hope.'

'He was all over the newspapers,' Marcie told him, 'and the television.'

'At Jer's house,' Gillette said, 'all we ever looked at was the trades. Unless they're doing a TV docudrama on this guy's life, I doubt I've heard of him.'

'I bet they will,' Marcie said. 'He's a businessman, stole from his stockholders, stole from his employees, stole from his family, stole from the government.'

Gillette nodded through all this; then, 'Well, nobody's perfect,' he said.

Meanwhile, in another cubicle down the line, an applicant named Judson Swope, rather a fearsome large creature, was telling a wee little employee named Penelope, 'Yeah, sure, I know who he is. Monroe Hall. Put it over on everybody. Listen, I don't care what he done. If he pays me, I work for him. People don't like him, so somebody's gotta be there to bust heads. I like to bust heads, and I like it best when I get paid to do it. Sign me up.'

'Yes, sir,' whispered Penelope, while in the cubicle behind her a hang-dog sort of man with his hat in his hands was saying, 'I was a butler in my previous employment.'

Daisy, for this was Daisy's cubicle, looked at him in some surprise. 'You were?' It seemed so improbable.

'I open a mean door,' he assured her. 'Here's the form I filled out, and my references.'

Daisy studied the form first. John Rumsey, with a temporary address with friends over in Shickshinny. Good work history, excellent reference from the Honorable Hildorg Chk, Vostkojekian ambassador to the United States.

'A guy I worked with there, at the embassy,' Rumsey said, 'he come in here this morning, you got him a job, he said maybe you could get me one, too.'

'What name?'

'Fred Blanchard,'

'One of the other interviewers must have handled him. Where did we place Mr Blanchard?'

'With somebody called Monroe Hall.'

'Mon – His name is Blanchard?'

'Yeah.'

'One moment. Just— One moment.'

She hurried away and it didn't take long to find Marcie, and then it took no time at all to get John Rumsey signed up to apply for the job of butler out at the Hall estate. If John Rumsey didn't look to Daisy a heck of a lot like her idea of a butler, so what? He'd been good enough for Ambassador Chk. He'd be good enough for Monroe Hall.

'Monroe?'

A very guarded 'Yes.'

'This is Henry, Monroe.' Blank silence. 'Henry Cooper.'

'Ah! Reconsidered Henry? Ready to sell that agency, turn it over to fresh blood?'

'I just wanted you to know, I'm in the process of sending four new employees out to you today'

'Four?'

Expecting gratitude, possibly even fawning gratitude, Cooper enumerated them: 'Chauffeur, butler, private secretary, and a security man.'

'So,' Monroe said, even more snottily than usual, 'you *can* do it when I goose you a little, can't you?'

'What?'

'If I hadn't called, called your *bluff*, offered to take that do-nothing agency off your hands, get somebody *eager* in there, you *still* wouldn't be doing a goddamn thing but rest on your laurels.'

'Monroe—'

'Your problem, Henry, is, you spend too much time at the golf course and not enough time taking care of business. I'll be giving these fellas a very careful once-over, I want you to know that. We'll see if you're trying to palm anything off on us.'

'Mon—'

But he'd hung up, so Cooper did, too. Then he pushed the button to summon Bernice.

'Yes, sir?'

'Tell the girls, Bernice, we won't be sending people over to Monroe Hall's place any more.'

'No, sir?'

'No. Fuck him.'

'Yes, sir.'

29

Thank God, Alicia Hall thought, they still had Mrs Parsons to cook for them. Mrs Parsons detested Monroe – well, everybody detested Monroe, as she was sadly aware – but Alicia had brought Mrs Parsons into the marriage with her, Mrs Parsons having been Alicia's *mother's* cook, and Mrs Parsons had chosen to stay on where so many of the less steely had fallen by the wayside. Her decision, Alicia knew, had been based on the assumption that Alicia might well need protection, or at least moral support, in the long darkness of the marriage to come. That assumption was wrong, since Alicia was the one human being Monroe treated with unfailing gentleness and concern, but Alicia had been happy to play the part of a Brontë heroine if it meant she wouldn't have to learn how to cook.

Their dining room table was really wrong for their lifestyle, since it readily seated sixteen while these days there were never more than two places to be filled, at the end nearest the kitchen. The resulting long empty stretch of table made the two of them seem lonelier, somehow, than they really were. Or maybe it didn't; Alicia preferred, if possible, not to brood.

Mrs Parsons had been a wonderful cook for many years – the woman must be seventy, at least, stout, silent, and hatchet-faced – and her hand had not yet lost its skill. These days, given the servant problem in the house, she did most of her shopping on the Internet, which worked wonderfully well. The Internet really isn't the place to shop for peanut butter or cereal, but the more expensive, lush, esoteric reaches of the food world were born for Internet treatment. From FedEx or United Parcel to Mrs Parsons's kitchen for transmogrification, and finally to the two people seated in candlelight at one end of the very long table, her waddling figure bearing the platters and tureens, preceded by the best of all possible aromas. It made life as an outcast not so bad.

This evening, as they consumed a fine duck breast and baby new potatoes and haricots vert accompanied by an excellent St. Emilion, Monroe said, 'Darling, I have good news.'

116

Alicia had forgotten there might be such a thing. 'Really?'

'Henry Cooper, after just a little nudging from me, has come through at last. I knew I knew how to handle him.'

'Come through?'

'Tomorrow, we shall interview *four* prospective new employees,' Monroe told her, and he beamed when he saw how he'd astonished her.

Yes, he had astonished her. 'Four? Really, Monroe? All at once?'

'A new chauffeur, at last,' Monroe ticked them off. 'A new private secretary. A new butler. And an additional man to beef up security.'

'But that's fantastic,' Alicia said. 'How did Henry manage?'

'How did *I* manage Henry, is what you mean.' He chortled, pleased with himself. 'You'll never guess.'

'Tell.'

'I offered to buy the agency.'

'You what?' She stared at him. 'What would you want with an employment agency?'

'Nothing,' Monroe said. 'It was a bluff, of course. I simply told him I could see he wasn't on top of the business the way he should be, so I'd buy it from him and install someone really topnotch to run it for me.'

'But that's insulting,' Alicia pointed out. 'And Henry is our friend. Or was.'

'Insulting was the point, dear,' Monroe said. 'And don't worry about losing Henry Cooper. As I'd thought, my offer goaded him into finding fresh people for us right away.'

'Well, that's wonderful, of course.'

'They'll be coming by for their interviews tomorrow, and I really find it hard to believe I'll reject a one of them.'

'I certainly hope not.' Alicia looked at the food still on her plate. 'With a chauffeur,' she said, 'Mrs Parsons could do some farmstand shopping. The season's just beginning, Monroe.'

'Life is getting better,' he said, with his big smile. Then his smile turned into a laugh, as he said, 'Oh, I have to tell you, the most comic thing.'

'Comic?'

'You know,' he said, 'I must constantly make out tax returns, reports to the bankruptcy court, all of these things.'

'The accountants do, you mean.'

'Yes, of course, when I say "I" I don't mean literally "I". But the thing is, my instructions have always been, overload them. Give them every detail, no matter how irrelevant. If I buy a newspaper, put it down. Put everything down.'

'But, Monroe, why?'

'Two reasons,' he said. 'They want reports, I'll give them reports, I'll give them so many reports they'll choke on them, they'll go blind trying to keep up with all my reports, I'll bore them into an early grave with the volume of my reports. And the second thing, connected to that, if it ever *does* become necessary, and you know I hope it never does—'

'Oh, dear.'

'Yes, I know. But if it ever does become necessary to tuck a little something naughty in there, I can reasonably hope, with all the mass of detail over such a long period of time, no one will notice.'

'I hope it never has to happen,' Alicia said. 'We've had all the trouble we need, my dear.'

'Oh, exactly so,' he said. 'But here's the comical thing, I found this out yesterday. The trouble that descended this time was not on me but on that personal trainer fellow of mine, Flip.'

'Flip?' She didn't understand. 'How can *he* be in trouble?'

'Because I reported to the IRS that I'd paid him so much and so much,' Monroe said, 'as I report everything. But I paid him in cash, and *he* never reported it.' Monroe's laugh was hearty indeed. 'One of the little people,' he said, 'he's not supposed to get away without paying taxes. *We're* supposed to get away with that sort of thing. *He's* supposed to pay his little mite, to take up our slack.'

With a little moue of distaste, Alicia said, 'Monroe, don't joke like that.'

He looked briefly sober, but the laugh was still back there. 'Oh. Yes. In any event, he got caught. He wanted to complain about it, I could see it in his eyes, but he didn't have the guts for it.'

Alicia said, 'Did you ever tell him you were going to report those payments?'

'It never occurred to me,' Monroe said. He shrugged, drank wine, patted his lips, said, 'It will be a good lesson to him.'

30

Dortmunder was never happy outside the five boroughs. There was always something wrong with the rest of the world, some way it had figured out to make him uncomfortable. For instance, at the moment, in the uncharted middle of Pennsylvania, he had to sleep on the kitchen floor.

Chester and his jolly wife, Grace, lived in a very small house in a very small town. Because Tiny and Stan, in their new persons from Jim Green, didn't know each other or any body else in this area, they could stay at nice motels along the Susquehanna River while waiting to be employed by Monroe Hall, but Kelp had given the employment agency Chester as his kinsman and local contact, and Kelp and Dortmunder had to already know each other because they'd both allegedly worked at the same embassy down in Washington, D.C., so they both had to stay with Kelp's 'relative' at least the one night, and even before the coin toss Dortmunder had known which of them was going to get the living room sofa. So it was on some folded blankets on the kitchen floor that Dortmunder was expected to get his night's rest, and fat chance.

The problems were many. The floor, to begin with, but beyond that the very fact of *kitchen*. Even a small kitchen in a small house in a small town, like this one, is as full of gleaming machinery as that inside the villain's mountain in a James Bond movie. The stove, the microwave, and the clock radio all had sharply bright numbers to tell you the time, in two shades of green and one shade of red, and of course they were all a minute apart except for a few seconds every now and then when two of them pretended to agree. So they were irritating, and they were also bright.

Then there was the refrigerator. At least it didn't have any shiny numbers glaring off it, but that was about the only good thing you could say about it. Occasionally it was silent, but that in a way was the worst, because that meant the victim had to wait, never knowing when the motor would suddenly *thrug*-ug-ug-ug . . . And then also the icemaker, from time to time, with a muffled crash like somebody disposing of a skeleton in a Hefty bag, would spit out another strip of ice cubes onto the previously existing cubes below.

A very busy place, all in all, this kitchen, at the bottom of which, like at the bottom of a well, Dortmunder lay in discomfort and tried to grab a little sleep before morning, when he was supposed to be bright and rested enough to go play butler, an impersonation he'd never tried before.

Well, he'd gone into training for it, with May's help. May was a movie fan, which meant she went to movies and remembered them, and which also meant she had recently added a time-flashing machine to their own lives, a DVD player, in the living room. Which was all right, because Dortmunder never slept in the living room anyway, except in front of the six o'clock news.

Once this butler task had arisen, May said, 'I *told* you that would come in handy,' and rented disks of *Ruggles of Red Gap* and *My Man Godfrey* and *The Remains of the Day*. He watched them all, parts of them more than once, and gradually felt he'd got the idea. He wouldn't be able to work the accent, but other than that he thought he could handle the assignment. A lot of it, he'd decided, was in the clothes.

Which could have been another problem, but in the end it turned out OK. When you do your shopping after midnight, what you bring home has got to be ready-to-wear, because you can't very well ask for alterations. Dortmunder's new black suit, picked up with Kelp's guidance and assistance, bagged a little bit here and there, but was, generally speaking, fine.

But now, lying all night in this very active kitchen, looking at the brightly lit if equivocal numbers, listening to the symphony of the refrigerator, thinking about butlers, all while he was supposed to be asleep, he did make a pretty long night of it. On the other hand, when Grace Fallon walked in at seven that morning to start twice her usual number of breakfasts, Dortmunder actually was asleep. Her arrival startled him awake, and for just a minute he couldn't figure out *what* he was doing lying on a kitchen floor or who was that woman in the blue jeans and pink sweater and gray hair walking around, reaching for the coffeemaker.

'Morning,' she said, as cheerful as anybody who'd spent the night in their own bed. 'Sleep well?'

Memory returned. Dortmunder sat up, aching all over. 'Just fine,' he said.

Well, according to his research, butlers did tend to have bags under their eyes.

31

It was the most jam-packed day in Monroe Hall's life since all the trials and depositions and press conferences and hearings had wound down, leaving him free but not exonerated, loose but unable to move. And this was even without Flip's usual Wednesday session, the silly sod being off to Harrisburg to pay his pittance to the IRS. Teach *him* to emulate his betters.

Well, in any event, there were four prospective employee interviews scheduled for today, which was four more employee interviews than most days, and Hall couldn't help it, he had to just keep looking at that list, as though he hadn't already memorized the thing, down to the last parenthesis:

TIME	NAME	POSITION	LAST EMPLOYER
10:30	Warren Gillette	chauffeur	Jer Crumble (actor)
11:00	Judson Swope	security	Securitech
11:30	John Rumsey	butler	Vostkojek embassy
12:00	Fredric Blanchard	secretary	Vostkojek embassy

'I know all about you,' Warren Gillette said.

Not knowing how to take that, Hall said, 'You do?'

'Jer just loved your cars,' Gillette told him.

'Oh! My cars! The actor!'

'That's it.'

'He knew about my collection, did he?' Hall was very pleased at that idea.

'Oh, sure,' Gillette said. An open-faced cheerful man with a shock of red hair, Gillette somehow *looked* like a chauffeur, even without the cloth cap he held folded in one hand. 'Jer always said,' he told Hall, 'the bad thing about living on Central Park West, you didn't have any room to keep some cars around you. Jer just *loves* cars.'

'Yes, of course.'

'That's one of the reasons he moved back to the Coast,' Gillette said, 'so he could have enough land to have some cars around him.'

'Wise man.'

'Not a great collection like *yours*, though, he knew, he'd never catch up to that.'

I'm loving this interview, Hall thought. 'I might,' he said, 'be able to give him advice, from time to time.'

'Oh, he'd love that,' Gillette said. Leaning forward, confidential, he said, 'What I was hoping was, part of this job, do you think I'd ever get to *drive* one of those babies every once in a while?'

Hall beamed on him. 'You can count on it,' he said.

When Hall got one look at Judson Swope, he thought, I want him on *my* side. A great mound of muscle topped by an artillery shell head, Swope didn't stomp in as though he were here to move the furniture, he stomped in as though he *was* the furniture.

'Sit down,' Hall invited, mostly because Swope was rather too intimidating a figure on his feet.

Swope sat – the chair wailed in complaint, but didn't dare crumble – and said, 'I see you already got a bunch of security here.'

'Well, I have to,' Hall explained. 'I have all these valuable collections, music boxes—'

'I know what you done.'

'Ah.' Hall tried to read that mountainous face, but it wasn't exactly rich with expression. 'The previous fellow,' he said, 'the driver, he didn't seem to know, so I thought, perhaps . . .'

'Drivers don't know nothing.'

'Well, that's true, if you've ever had to take a long drive with one. But my, uh, my history, doesn't bother you?'

'You didn't do nothin to me.'

Perish the thought. With a shaky smile, Hall said, 'That's good then. Now, uh, now let me, uh, let me see . . .' He fiddled around among the papers on his desk mostly because Swope made him nervous, then did stumble across the packet of papers concerning Swope forwarded by Henry Cooper's agency: the FBI clearance, the bankruptcy judge's approval, the Pennsylvania State Police clean bill of health, and Mr Judson Swope's recent work history. Why, come to think of it, was he available, a man like this?

Ah, Securitech. 'I knew Danny and Peter,' he said, tapping the papers.

Swope nodded, agreeing with him.

Hall spent a moment in Memory Lane, then said, 'Skated a bit close to the wind, I'm afraid.'

'That's what the wind's for,' Swope said.

Surprised, Hall said, 'It is, isn't it? We'll get along, Judson. I may call you Judson?'

'Why not?'

'Why not indeed?' Hall leaned forward, enjoying both the hint of intimacy and the hint of superiority in the use of the name. 'All of the hiring details were worked out at Cooper's, salary, health benefits, all of that.'

'They're all fine,' Swope said.

'Good, good. Now, housing. Have you something local?'

'In a motel till I get a job.'

'There's a house available on the estate,' Hall told him. 'Saves going in and out through security all the time.'

Swope looked interested. 'A house?'

'I'm taking on four new staff today,' Hall said, feeling expansive as he heard himself say it. 'I thought all four of you might like to bunk in there. Separate rooms, of course, completely furnished. My new chauffeur's already agreed to move in.'

'Sounds OK,' Swope agreed.

With a happy smile – this really *was* an excellent day! – Hall said, 'Oddly enough, that's where my old chauffeur used to live, with his family. He was happy there.'

'Oh yeah?'

'And I was happy with him, yes, I was. Then it turned out, there were things in his background . . .'

'People make mistakes,' Swope suggested.

'Ah,' Hall said, 'but then they can't be around *me*. The court is very clear on that. In any event, you'll love the house. And I'm sure you'll get along with the others living there.'

Swope nodded. 'Everybody gets along with me,' he said.

John Rumsey was somehow not what Hall had expected in a butler. The black suit was fine, though it suggested Rumsey might have lost a pound or two here and there in recent days. The stiff-collared white shirt, the knife-thin black neck-tie, the gleaming black oxford shoes as big as gunboats, all filled the bill.

But was it right for a butler to look *hangdog*? How could he ever order Christmas carolers to clear out, run along there, that'll be quite enough of *that*?

On the other hand, when was the next time Monroe Hall would be in a position to be irritated by Christmas carolers? Many snows from now, according to the signs.

The man's defeated look to one side, his history was excellent. Clean police check, excellent former employment with an eastern European embassy in Washington. Even though only eastern, if a European embassy in Washington had found this fellow Rumsey adequate as a butler, then why shouldn't Monroe Hall?

Hall looked again at the records. Reason job ended: employer slain. 'What?'

Rumsey looked guilty. 'I didn't say anything.'

'No, I know. I did. Employer *slain?*'

'Oh, yeah,' Rumsey said. 'That's what happened.'

'But – why?'

'He went home for the holidays.'

Which wasn't precisely an answer to the question, but Hall let it go. He said, 'So when he didn't come back, you quit?'

'Fired,' Rumsey said. 'We were all fired, in case anybody was loyal to Chk.'

'I'm sorry?'

'In case we were loyal to Chk.'

'I'm sorry?'

'The ambassador,' Rumsey explained. 'Hildorg Chk. In case we were loyal to him, they threw us all out.'

'*Were* you loyal to him?'

Rumsey shrugged. 'While he was there.'

'Yes, of course.' Looking down at his paperwork again, Hall said, 'I see I have another former employee of Ambassador Um here.'

'Yeah, Fred.'

'Fredric Blanchard.'

'I'm staying with him and a cousin of his,' Rumsey said, 'until I find a thing.'

Which led Hall to offer the house where Gillette and Swope were already billeted, which was accepted at once. After that, he reassured himself that Rumsey, like the others, was content with his terms of employment, then said, 'So I'll expect you at eight in the morning, show you your pantry, where the callbells are located, internal telephone, all that. Introduce you to my wife and what's left of the staff.'

'That's good,' Rumsey said. 'Only, shouldn't your wife say I'm OK first? I wouldn't wanna think I got a thing here and then your wife says, "Listen, I don't want that guy" I mean, it can kinda happen, that kinda thing.'

'I know exactly what you mean,' Hall said, pleased and surprised by the man's sensitivity. 'But my wife and I discussed it, and our situation is so, shall we say, unusual here, unless it's a maid for herself, for instance, or something like that, she'll be guided completely by me.'

Rumsey nodded. 'So if you say I'm in, I'm in.'

'Exactly. So you can move into the house any time today, the guards at the gate will know to let you through, and I'll see you in the morning.'

'See you then,' Rumsey said, and came very close to smiling, Hall caught him at it. He should smile more often, Hall thought, it makes him look a trifle less pessimistic.

Rumsey got to his feet and sloped across the office. Hall watched him carefully, and it seemed to him Rumsey did a very creditable handling of the door.

The last of the four, Fredric Blanchard, the private secretary, was the most difficult of the interviews because, on sober reflection, Hall finally admitted to himself he no longer *needed* a private secretary. There are people one needs at one stage of life – a nanny, say, a tutor, a drug dealer, a bookie, a bail bondsman – that one simply doesn't need at some other stage of life. Has no use for, no call upon.

In a word, 'I'm sorry,' Hall told the bright-eyed, sharpnosed attentive fellow across the desk, 'but I'm afraid I've wasted your time. I shouldn't have had you come out here.'

Fred Blanchard cocked his head, like a particularly attentive crow, without losing the welcoming smile he'd brought in here. 'Sorry to hear that,' he said. 'Can I ask how I come up short?'

'It isn't you, you know,' Hall told him. 'It's me. You're overqualified. I don't need a private secretary anymore.'

'I have trouble believing that,' Blanchard told him.

'Oh, I *used* to need a private secretary,' Hall said, with a little nostalgic sigh. 'Two, in fact. They were always at each other's throats, that was part of the fun of it. But, you see, I don't have that kind of life any more, I'm not flying off here, skiing off there, board of directors meetings, chairman of symphony board, all that's behind me now. I barely – you know, legally I *could* leave this property, if not the state, but I just don't feel like it any more. The fire's gone out. I just stay *here*.'

'Mr Hall,' Blanchard said, 'if I may say so, sir, you need me more than ever. *Now*, is the time you need me, sir.'

'Need you?' Hall didn't understand. 'For what?'

'Rehabilitation!' Blanchard cried, and pointed a stern finger at the ceiling. 'It's time,' he declared, in ringing tones, 'to get your story out there!'

'My story *is* out there,' Hall said, 'that's the trouble.'

'Your old story is out there,' Blanchard insisted. 'It's time for a new story, and that's why you need *me*. A personal. Private. Secretary.'

'Yes, but—'

But Blanchard was unstoppable. 'Now, if I were PR, you'd be wrong to say yes. The evils PR do would be hard to assess. That starts with "P", and

it rhymes with "T", and that means trouble. But a private secretary does-
n't have that commercial hypocritical taint. A private secretary can get the
new you out there!'

'The new me?'

'It's time,' declared Blanchard, 'that everybody just got *over* it!'

'Yes!' cried Hall. 'Just myself, I—'

'You're chastened,' Hall told him. 'You're human after all. You regret
the effects of what you've done, but that's the past. That's yesterday, when
all your troubles—'

'Would I have to give back the money?'

'Never!' Blanchard's eyes flashed. 'You're explaining your common
humanity, you're not feeding the multitudes!'

'No, no, I see.'

'We'll start small,' Blanchard said. Somehow, he was halfway across
Hall's desk, staring into his eyes. 'Church social egg rolls on the lawn. Boy
Scout groups meeting *here*. Have your photo taken at the wheel of one of
Mr Hall's famous cars.'

'Not driving it!'

'*Sitting* in it.' Blanchard beamed, his arms spread wide. 'The squire of
Pennsylvania,' he announced. 'How bad a fella could he be?'

'You're hired!' Hall cried.

32

Mac said, 'Buddy? Wha'd we stop here for?'

Here was the road along the periphery of Monroe Hall's estate. Everything to the left of the road belonged to Hall. The guardshack entrance was about a mile and a half behind them. Buddy had pulled off where the shoulder was wide, and across the way was the end of the former tomato farm, now reverted to weeds, with the untouched woods just starting to its right.

Buddy said, '*Look* at that place. Not a gate around. You could just walk in there.'

'The wire,' Mac said.

Buddy, sounding bedeviled, said, '*I know, I know.*'

As usual, Buddy drove, Mac in back. Now Ace, beside Buddy, frowned at him and said, 'Buddy? You got an idea?'

'I don't know.' Buddy glared at the peaceful empty field over there as though trying to read too-small print. 'The wires are too close together,' he said.

Mac said, 'We know that.'

'We don't have a plane,' Buddy said, and nodded. 'And we can't get one, I know that.'

'Good,' Mac said.

Buddy said, 'Could we pole-vault over it?'

'Not me,' Ace said.

Mac said, 'Buddy, did you do pole vault in high school?'

'I don't think we had pole vault,' Buddy admitted.

Mac said, 'You wanna try to learn pole vault now, at your weight—'

'Whadaya mean, my weight?'

'You know what I mean. Any of our weight, but you're the one wants to pole-vault. You figure you'll get *over* that electric wire and not fly *into* it three feet off the ground like the Wright brothers—'

'I could train,' Buddy said. 'We could all train.'

'Tonto go home now,' Ace said.

Mac said, 'I could hold your coat, Buddy. And I could take you to the

127

emergency room after you land.'

Buddy, exasperated, said, 'Now, who the hell is this?'

'It's me, Buddy, Mac, your friend, and I'm trying to—'

'No, this little white car behind us.'

So Mac twisted around, and behind them, just off the road, had parked a little white two-seater Porsche. As Mac focused on it, both doors opened, and Mark and Os stepped out, dressed in their usual suits and sunglasses and supercilious expressions. 'Hey, it's Harvard,' he said.

Buddy said, 'I still say Dartmouth.'

'Anyway,' Mac said, as their two alleged coconspirators approached their Taurus, 'we know they're not Oklahoma Normal.'

This time, without an invitation, Mark and Os simply joined them, opening both rear doors, Mark sliding in on Mac's right, Os on his left. Fortunately, the new arrivals were both slender, so it wasn't too crowded back there. 'We've had a thought,' Mark said, by way of greeting.

'We've had a lot of thoughts,' Mac told him.

'Oh, really?'

'We were here now goin over the last of them. Pole vault.'

'Ah,' Mark said. 'We considered that one, as well. But it's not so good on the follow-through.'

'Follow-through?'

'Let us say,' Mark suggested, 'that one of us, or for that matter all of us, are athletic enough to pole-vault over the fence, landing in absolute safety on the far side. Do you know what happens next?'

'Something bad we didn't think about,' Mac guessed.

Os said, 'The pole keeps going. It hits the fence. It breaks the wire.'

Mark shook his head. 'No way to stop it.'

Ace said, 'How do you like that, Mac? Your catapult idea was better after all.'

'Catapult?' Surprised, Mark said, 'No, that's one we didn't think of. On the other hand, you'd hit the ground at rather an unacceptable speed, wouldn't you?'

'We rejected it already,' Mac said,

'Quite sensibly. In fact,' Mark said, 'we've noticed that you haven't come up with anything consistently except to keep very close tabs on our friend the personal trainer.'

Mac said, 'You've *noticed*?'

Excited, Buddy said, 'I've *seen* that white car, Mac! They been following us.'

'In reality' Mark said, unruffled, 'we've all been following the personal trainer, at a loss for anything else to do. You three have been in his home so often you ought to pay rent. We've all searched his car. Through sources

I can't reveal, we've gone into his background and found nothing useful to blackmail him with.'

'Same with us,' Mac said. 'Through sources *we* can't reveal, we came up with the same nothing.'

'So we now,' Mark said, 'have a suggestion.'

Sounding suspicious, the way he always did, Ace said, 'Yeah? What?'

'The approach direct,' Mark said.

33

'Knock, knock.'

'Who's there?' Chester asked hopelessly.

'O.J.,' Mellon said.

'O.J. who?'

'Orange juice sorry now?'

'Yes,' Chester said truthfully.

'Time for lunch,' Mellon said. 'Turn in up there, the restaurant in there's good and it's always empty.'

Having left the town of Mellon's last appointment, they were now out in the country again, driving past a mall where the tallest and most impressive construction was the sign out by the road: MIDPOINT MALL. Which, come to think of it, was probably the goal for every mall, wasn't it?

Turning in at that giant sign, seeing in truth acres of parking lot with only a few dusty vehicles, mostly pickups, huddled close to the glass fronts of the line of stores, Chester said, 'How come it's so empty?'

'They lost their anchor store. What we want is down at the end, past where it used to be.'

Driving straight ahead, ignoring the white parking-space lines painted all over the blacktop, Chester said, 'How come they lost it?'

'Went bust,' Mellon said. 'It was one of those big box housewares places, but there was an even bigger one about ten miles farther on. Killed them. Now there's nothing in here but the little satellites, the photo developer, the liquor store, cell phone store, restaurant. It's just past where the anchor used to be.'

Driving by the onetime anchor store, Chester slowed to look at the place. Large windows were blankly open, but showed little of the cavernous interior because there were no lights on in there. A chain was looped through the six door handles and padlocked. Above the entrance, the faint ghosts could be seen where the letters of the store's name had been removed: SPEEDSHOP.

Making out those letters, Chester said, 'They've got other stores, don't they?'

'Oh, sure,' Mellon said. 'These big chains, if they make a mistake where they put one of their places, they just walk away from it, cut their losses.'

The restaurant was next, and last. Chester said, 'Would you mind, before we go in, we drive around and take a look at the back?'

'The back? Whadaya want the back for?'

At the corner of the building, where the large restaurant windows showed mostly empty booths, the blacktop continued on around, and Chester continued with it as he said, 'Some friends of mine and me, we're gonna steal some very big things pretty soon, and we'll need a place to stash them. If there's a big enough back door, this place could be fine.'

Mellon looked at him, a half-smile on his lips. 'Chester,' he said, 'you've got one dry sense of humor.'

'Yeah, I been told that.'

Chester took the next corner, and here was a lot more blacktop, because deliveries were made at the rear of the stores. Three big wide segmented iron garage doors were closed in the area where the Speedshop must have been. The doors stopped about three feet up from the ground, at the level of the floor of a big tractor-trailer, but that shouldn't pose too much of problem.

'Yeah,' Chester said, looking it over. 'That'll do just fine.' And he made a U-turn to go back around to the restaurant. Mellon's look had turned quizzical.' It *is* a gag,' he said, not as though it were a question; but it was a question.

Chester grinned at him. 'Sure. You think you're the only one can tell a joke?'

Mellon laughed like a fool, all the way to the booth.

34

When you spent last night night on a kitchen floor, you don't have that much to pack today. Dortmunder was packing it when Kelp came by to say, 'I'll go promote us a car now.'

Dortmunder said, 'You can't take one with MD plates, you know.'

Kelp looked stricken. 'Why not?'

'You're a private secretary, not a doctor. You got guards at the gate there, they're gonna have your license number on their list.'

'Gee, I'm glad you thought of that,' Kelp said. 'I'll grab a couple extra plates, too.'

He would have left then, but Chester came in and said, 'I got it. You wanna see it?'

Kelp said, 'You got what?'

Dortmunder said, 'Why would I wanna see it?'

'Pretty soon,' Chester pointed out, 'you're gonna have a bunch of hot cars on your hands. You're gonna want to stash them. I think I got the place. You wanna see it? I'll drive you there.'

Kelp said, 'Great. And then you can drop me at a mall, I gotta shop for a car.'

'It *is* a mall,' Chester said.

'OK,' Dortmunder said. 'In that case, I gotta see it.'

It took most of an hour to get there across trackless Pennsylvania. They arrived just before six in the evening, still full daylight at this time of year, though the little anchorless mall somehow seemed darker than the rest of the world. Chester had explained about the loss of the anchor, so Dortmunder was prepared for a mostly empty parking lot, but the reality was still grim. It was like a medieval village after the plague.

As Chester drove the length of the mall building, the proprietors of most of the satellite shops were just closing after another day of rotten business, leaving only the restaurant and video store open at opposite ends. Chester said, 'The restaurant stops serving at nine, so everybody's outa there before eleven. And the video place shuts at eight.'

Dortmunder said, 'Good. We don't know yet exactly how it's gonna go down, but probably at night.'

'Late at night,' Kelp said.

'That's right,' Chester said, as he made the turn around the restaurant. 'Most of the cops around here know those cars, because Mrs Hall drives them a lot, and people like to look at Mrs Hall. Including the cops. There it is.'

The rear wall of the building was very blank. The only vehicles in sight were two cars parked together down at the far end, not next to the building but out by the chain-link fence that separated the pavement from the scrubby woods beyond.

Chester pulled to a stop by the middle of Speedshop's three loading bay doors, and they got out to see what was what. Immediately, Kelp pointed up at a rectangle of unpainted cinder block wall above the door. 'That's where the alarm used to be.'

'One of them,' Dortmunder said.

'No, John,' Kelp said, 'I don't think there's power in there. Let's see.' He tugged at the door handle. 'Locked, but this is nothing.'

Dortmunder came over to look. 'Can you open it without busting anything?'

'Sure.'

Chester said, 'What if there *is* another alarm?'

'Maybe,' Dortmunder told him, 'you should be in the car with the engine running and a couple doors open. Just in case.'

'Right,' Chester said, and went to do that while Kelp took two thin metal spatulas from his shirt pocket and bent over the keyhole in the door handle.

Watching him, Dortmunder said, 'I never broke into an empty store before.'

'Think of it as practice. There we are.'

The door slid up a foot. They cocked their heads, listening, and heard nothing but Chester's car engine. Kelp leaned down, stuck his head in through the opening, listened some more, then brought his head out to say, 'It's ours,' and signal to Chester to cut the engine.

With the door lifted a couple more feet, they climbed up and inside. Kelp lowered the door almost all the way, and they moved forward into the dimness.

All of the shelving and wall dividers had been removed, but the space wasn't entirely empty. A few broken clothes racks and a couple wooden chairs and some other miscellany were shoved against one side wall, and the store pattern was still visible on the floor, where the pale rubberized squares marked the main aisles, with different flooring for the different departments, some bare wood, some composition, some industrial carpet. From the inside, they could see that the windows across the front were very dusty. Near the front right corner, two electric panels stood open, their main switches set to OFF.

The only interior walls still in place were around the rest rooms, at the rear left. Dortmunder went into MEN, turned the faucet at the nearest sink, and nothing happened. Going back out to the others, he said, 'They really shut this thing down.'

'Sure,' Kelp said. 'They don't want electric fires, and they don't want leaks.'

Dortmunder looked around the big dusty empty space. 'I wish there was something we could use for a ramp.'

'We'll need something,' Kelp assured him. 'And I'll leave that door unlocked.'

Chester, very pleased with himself, said, 'I knew this was the place.'

'It is,' Kelp agreed.

They went back outside, closing the unlocked door, and Kelp looked over at the parked cars at the other end of the area. 'Let's take a look at those,' he said.

So they drove over to the parked cars, and both were very dusty, though they were locked. Kelp said, 'Chester, tell me you have a couple screwdrivers in the car.'

'I got a couple screwdrivers in the car,' Chester said.

'Good, we can take off two plates at a time.'

'I got one regular screwdriver,' Chester said, 'and one Phillips. Which do we need?'

'Oh.' Kelp looked at the license plate. 'Regular.'

'I'll get it.'

As Chester headed for his trunk, Kelp shrugged and said, 'So I'll take off one at a time.'

Dortmunder looked over toward the building. There were only gray metal fire doors to the different shops back here, no windows. 'If somebody opens a door and looks out,' he said, 'they might notice no plate on the back of one of the cars.'

'So we'll do three, one at a time,' Kelp said, 'and move the one I don't need from the front of one car to the back of the other. Nobody's gonna notice both cars have the same plate number.'

Chester came around with the screwdriver. 'Here you go.'

'Great.' Taking the screwdriver, Kelp said, 'Just gimme a minute here, and then take me to the hospital.'

35

Tiny didn't like to drive. He didn't so much sit in an automobile as wear it, and that made it difficult to do things like turn the steering wheel and switch the high beams on and off. Fortunately, there are taxi companies everywhere, so when he got back to the motel after being hired by Monroe Hall, he used the local phone book to make contact with Keystone Kab. 'I want a taxi,' he told the dispatcher, 'and I need legroom.'

'We got a station wagon, you want that?'

'I don't wanna lie in the back, I want legroom where I'm gonna sit.'

'Oh, it's got legroom.'

'Run it over, then.'

They did, and it was a huge old relic, manufactured long long ago in a previous century, and driven by a wizened old cracker even older. But it had legroom. And in the back, there was also room for Tiny's suitcase.

It wasn't a long drive to Hall's compound, but when they got there some confusion and delay developed, because the guards on duty didn't know what to do about the unauthorized person at the wheel of the cab. Phone calls were made to the main house, and finally it was decided one of the guards would ride along for the round-trip. He thought at first he might get into the back with Tiny, but when he saw how much seat was left he decided to ride with the driver instead.

The road split when it got past the gate, one part going straight up to the main house while the second spur went off to the right. The guard directed the cabby to take that turn, then twisted around to say, 'You been hired for security, right?'

'Right.'

The guard, a rangy man with a sour weather-beaten face, stuck his hand out toward Tiny: 'Mort Pessle.'

'Judson Swope.'

They shook hands, and Pessle took his back quickly, nestling it in his armpit as he said, 'When you get settled in, come on back to the gate, we can work out your schedule, arrange for your uniform.'

The guard's uniform was brown. Tiny nodded at it. 'I like how I look in brown.'

The house, when they got to it, was green and rather small, though not as small as where Chester lived now, off there in Shickshinny. It was about half a mile from the gate, with a lot of untended lawn around it, than other small houses. To the right, past the electric fence, the county road and its traffic could be seen but not heard.

'See you later,' Pessle said, and Tiny agreed that's what would happen, then carried his bag into the house.

He was the first arrival, so he had his choice of rooms, though in fact he would have had his choice of rooms anyway. There were three bedrooms and one bathroom upstairs, one bedroom with its own bathroom downstairs, so Tiny took the one downstairs. The whole place was furnished sparely but neatly. He sat on the bed, which complained loudly, but it was comfortable enough. Comfortable enough for as long as he figured to use it.

He had unpacked and was inspecting the food that had been put into the kitchen for them – not enough, but not bad – when Dortmunder and Kelp arrived, lugging their luggage. 'We found a place for the cars,' Kelp said. 'Just came from there, it's perfect.'

'Good,' Tiny said. 'And you got wheels of your own.'

'Sure.'

'You can drive me back to the gate,' Tiny told him, 'and I'm in the downstairs bedroom.'

'Right.' Kelp still hefted his suitcase. 'I'll just pick a room, then take you—'

'Why not take me now,' Tiny suggested. 'Get it over with.'

'Oh, yeah, OK.'

So Kelp put his suitcase down while Dortmunder went up to choose the best of the upstairs bedrooms. He and Tiny went out, and here in front of the house was parked a silver Yukon XL, one of the larger General Motors SUVs, approximately the size of a sperm whale.

'I can always count on you, Kelp,' Tiny said, as he climbed into the roomy rear seat.

'And I always count on doctors.'

Back at the gate, Mort Pessle introduced Tiny to the other guard on duty, a heavy-browed sullen-looking guy named Heck Fiedler, then said, 'Come on over and meet the boss.'

The boss, in his own office in the building to one side of the entrance, was an older man, big and bulky, with a completely bald head and a stiff white beard like a clothesbrush. His name was Chuck Yancey, and his handshake was almost as good as Tiny's. Mort Pessle went away after the introductions, and Yancey said, 'You done any policin?'

'No,' Tiny said, 'mostly I bust heads.'

Yancey chuckled, approving of that. 'You may get an opportunity along those lines,' he said. 'I'm not promising. Now, in that room through the door there you've got a whole rack of uniforms. Somethin oughta fit you. I know you're a big fellow, but we've had a lot of big fellows here. If you don't find anything good enough, pick out whatever's the nearest and you'll take it to our tailor in town.'

'Good,' Tiny said. 'I like to be neat.'

'I know the feelin. One other thing.'

Tiny looked alert.

'The new man,' Yancey said, 'which is you, gets the graveyard duty.'

'Graveyard? You got a graveyard here?'

'No,' Yancey said, with another chuckle, 'I mean the late shift on the gate, midnight to eight in the morning. If you're a reader, you can bring a book, or listen to the radio. We'd rather you didn't watch TV.'

'That's OK,' Tiny said.

'There's nothing ever happens at night,' Yancey told him, 'so it's just you on the gate. You'll have that the first two weeks, then we'll switch you into the regular rotation. It's boring there all night on your own, but you'll get through it.'

He would be on duty all by himself at the entrance every night for two weeks, from midnight till eight in the morning. Nobody was ever around, and nothing ever happened. 'I'll make it work for me,' Tiny said, and went off to find a uniform.

36

When Hall came down his main staircase to the main floor on Thursday morning, not yet sure how he felt about the day – his digestion, the weather, his level of irritation, how much his assets had appreciated during the night in their quiet seedbeds in foreign lands – somebody he'd never seen before came striding out of a side door, said, 'Murnen,' and opened the front door.

Hall gaped. The man simply stood there, in profile, like one of the royal guards at Buckminster Palace, at what his sloping body apparently took to be attention, and continued to hold the knob of the wide-open door as he glared straight across the open doorway. He wore an ill-fitting but expensive black suit, narrow black tie, white dress shirt, and black shoes like gunboats. He was some lunatic who had—

The butler! The new servants. One of *four* new servants, the incredible beginning of a new era, a new and much much better era.

And his name was ... Rumpled, Rambo, Rasputin, er, Rumsey! 'Ah, good morning, Rumsey!'

'Murnen, Mr Hall.' Rumsey went on glaring across the doorway, and went on holding the open door.

'Very good, Rumsey,' Hall said, 'but actually, I wasn't going out.'

Rumsey took a second to digest that. Then, with a robotic nod so brisk it was a miracle he didn't break his neck, he efficiently slammed the door. 'Sur.'

'Actually,' Hall said, feeling obscurely he had an ongoing part to play in this conversation, 'I was on my way to the breakfast room.'

'Sur.'

'That's where I usually have breakfast.'

'Sur.'

'Well...' Hall would have turned away, but then he thought of something. Two somethings. 'When Mrs Hall comes down, in a few minutes,' he said, 'she won't want to go out, either.'

'She'll be off to the breakfast room, sur.'

'Exactly so. And would you send Blanchard and Gillette to see me in my office, just to the left there, at ten?'

There was a blankness in Rumsey's blinking. 'Sur?'

'Blanchard and Gillette.'

'Blan . . .' The man was completely at a loss.

'For heaven's sake, man,' Hall said, 'you and Fred Blanchard have worked together for years!'

'Oh, *Fred*!' Rumsey cried. 'Fred *Blan*chard. Oh, sorry, right about that.' Now, leaning unexpectedly close as for a confidence, he said, 'Out of context, you see what I mean?'

'Yes, well,' Hall said, automatically taking a backward step that bumped him into the staircase he'd just left, 'this is rather new for us all.'

'Blanchard and Gillette,' Rumsey said, morphing back to near-erectness. 'He'll be the driver. The other one. Ten o'clock. Will do, sur.'

'Well, my dear,' Alicia said, over crustless toast and coddled eggs and strawberry jam and well-creamed coffee, 'what do you think of our new people?'

'They're perfect,' Hall told her. 'Of course, I've barely seen them so far, and I must say Rumsey the butler's an odd duck. But then, so many servants are, really.'

'America doesn't know how to breed servants,' Alicia said.

'That's perfectly true.'

'The problem,' she suggested, 'is that the Inquisition had ended, or at least its really active years had ended, before the founding of the United States, so on this side of the Atlantic there was never that drilled-in terror over generations to make people eager to obey orders.'

'I like your insights, Alicia,' Hall said, patting his lips with damask, 'but now I must go have a word with two more of our new acquisitions.'

Monroe Hall's office, in the front right corner of the main floor, with large windows that offered ego-supportive views down toward his guardhouse and leftward toward his village and outbuildings, had been designed and furnished by one of the finest teams of nostalgic re-creators in America. Did you want a keeping room? Did you want a bread oven? Did you want gaslight to supplement your electric bulbs? Did you want, along a waist-high dado cap around the room, to tastefully display your collection of iron nineteenth-century mechanical banks? Call Pioton & Fone, and watch your dreams come true. Monroe Hall had, and he couldn't enter his office, as a result, without smiling. Didn't it look just like Gentleman Johnny Burgoyne's office, just before Yorktown? Yes, it did. Mm, it did.

Today, entering the office, Hall saw Blanchard and Gillette already present, which made sense, because Hall was deliberately ten minutes late.

Both were studying the iron banks on the little rail around the room, Blanchard leaning close over the one of a fisherman on a boat. Place a coin on the flat plate at the end of the fishing line and the weight causes the machinery inside to move the fisherman's arm, and the fishing line, until the coin falls into the open mouth of the creel at the stern of the boat, and thus into the bank.

Looking around when Hall made his entrance, Blanchard said, 'Morning, sir.'

'Morning.'

'Oh, yeah, morning. Sir,' Gillette the driver said.

'Morning,' Hall repeated. He was so pleased to have these people.

Blanchard dabbed a thumb over his shoulder at the fisherman. 'How do I get my quarter back?'

'Ha ha.' Got another one. With a big broad grin, Hall said, 'You don't, Fred. Sorry about that. Ho ho. Now come on, you two, let's work out our day.'

They obediently moved over toward the genuine nineteenth-century partners' desk, built at a time when lawyers trusted one another. As Hall took a seat there, the other two remaining standing, Blanchard frowned back at that fisherman as though wanting to remember exactly where to find him, some other time, but then he joined Hall and Gillette and didn't seem troubled at all.

37

Flip Morriscone was nowhere to be found, all day Wednesday. He didn't make his three o'clock appointment with Monroe Hall or, so far as they could tell, any other of his appointments. To be certain the man had neither overslept nor died in his sleep, the union team of the conspiracy trooped through the Morriscone house one last time, then came back out to report to capital, 'Not there.'

Now that they'd finally made their decision, and had finally accepted the need and utility of cooperation between the two groups, it was frustrating that their very first decision couldn't be acted upon. Before parting for the day, all five gathered in their usual places in Buddy's Taurus, where Buddy said, 'We're *still* not getting anywhere.'

'One day,' Mark pointed out. 'Maybe he had food poisoning, went to the hospital. Maybe his uncle came to town, he took the day off, they went to the races.'

Buddy, looking confused, said, 'Races. Oh, the track, you mean.'

Mac said, 'There's no point giving up after just one day.'

'Exactly,' Mark said.

Ace said, 'How much longer you wanna go spinning your wheels?'

'We'll give it the rest of this week,' Mac said. 'Two working days, and Saturday. If we don't find him before, and if he isn't home Saturday, we'll try to think of something else.'

Os said, 'I know some people in the Army Reserves.'

They looked at him. Even Mark seemed a little nervous, when he said, 'Os? And?'

'If it goes into next week,' Os said, 'I borrow a tank.'

Fortunately, it didn't come to that. They did find him, late Thursday morning. Following what they knew of his schedule, they drove along, packed together into the Taurus – Mark and Os were truly sacrificing for this job – and there he was at last, Flip Morriscone, coming out of the well-appointed home of one of his clients. His green Subaru was parked at the curb of the public street, as they pulled to a stop farther along.

141

Here he came, long canvas bag bouncing on his shoulder, the satisfied look of the successful torturer in his eye. Mark and Mac, as representatives of the combined team, approached him as he reached for the rear door of the Subaru to toss the bag in, Mark saying, 'Mr Morriscone. If we could have a moment?'

It had been decided that an Ivy League accent would be more reassuring than a union accent for the initial approach, and that Mark was just naturally less scary than Os. In the Sancho Panza role, Mac was deemed by all to be the most acceptable.

Morriscone continued his movement of tossing the bag into the back of the wagon, then slammed the door and turned to them, seeming not at all worried to be accosted by strangers. 'Yes?'

'There's a certain someone that you and we know,' Mark began, smooth and calm, 'that we have a dislike for.'

Morriscone looked baffled. 'There's somebody I know that you don't like?'

'Exactly. Now, we want to do something to this fellow—'

'Hey,' Morriscone said, taking a step backward. 'Keep me out of this.'

'Not to kill him or anything like that,' Mark assured him, 'but to, let us say, cost him something.'

'Good God!' Morriscone was getting more and more agitated. 'What are you, gangsters?'

'Not at all,' Mark said, 'we are perfectly respectable people, as I'm sure you can see for yourself. All we ask is a little assistance from you, for which you will be well reimbursed as soon as—'

'Bribery!' Morriscone was actually shouting by now. 'Get away from me!' he shouted. 'I've got trouble enough, I can't be— Do you want me to call the police?'

Mac could see that Mark's oil was not smoothing the waters the way they'd hoped. They'd agreed beforehand not to mention the target's name until they had Morriscone convinced to help them, just in case he'd feel the need to go warn Monroe Hall, but maybe all in all that strategy hadn't been such a good one. Taking a deep breath, speaking forcefully into Morriscone's agitated reddening face, Mac announced, 'Monroe Hall!'

'Mon—' Morriscone's jaw dropped. He stared at them both like long-lost brothers. 'You want to get even with that son of a bitch, too?' A broad grin creased his features. 'Why didn't you say so?'

38

What Stan Murch had been looking forward to driving was, maybe, a 1958 Studebaker Golden Hawk two-door roadster, or another two-door, the 1932 Packard model 900, or a 1955 Mercedes Gullwing Custom, in which the doors swing out and upward, or a four-door 1937 twelve-cylinder Pierce-Arrow limousine, all of which he happened to know were in Monroe Hall's antique car collection, because he'd researched this job with loving care. He'd gotten lists of Hall's holdings from newspaper reports and then discussed them with Chester who, after all, was also a driver, though privately Stan thought probably not of the very highest rank.

What he hadn't expected was to be making supermarket runs at the wheel of a black Suzuki Vitara, a kind of pocket SUV that drove like a jeep; the original jeep, that is, from World War Two, and probably under fire. Nor was that the worst of it, because he *really* hadn't expected to be steering a no-pedigree wire-cage shopping cart up and down supermarket aisles in the wake of a harridan named Mrs Parsons.

Mrs Parsons was some piece of work. She was to the manner born, and she wanted you to know it. When, at the post-breakfast meeting in Monroe Hall's office at the main house, Hall had said, 'Here's your cap, Gillette, and I hope you have a tie and a dark jacket to wear on duty. Good. Get them, and then you'll drive the cook to the supermarket,' Stan had thought he understood all the words in that last sentence, including 'cook,' but apparently he'd been wrong.

This was Stan's first experience as a member of the servant class, and already he could see why it had been necessary to invent electricity, so you wouldn't need so many servants as before, and that way you might be able to hold them off when they turned on you. Hall himself was enough of a pain in the ass, calling him 'Gillette' all the time. He'd never been addressed in quite that last-name style before, and the fact that it wasn't actually his own last name only took the sting out a little.

And there was also the other fact that the chauffeur's cap he was supposed to wear dropped down to block his eyes unless he padded the inner rim with newspaper, so that what he looked mostly like, with this black-beaked oversize hat on his head, was a ventriloquist's dummy. And not one of the smart ones.

But then, there's Mrs Parsons! Apparently, the way it worked, not all servants were born equal, and *definitely* chauffeurs weren't born equal to cooks. Or at least this chauffeur, this Gillette here, wasn't born equal to Mrs Parsons, who even got an honorific in front of her name.

And who, when Stan stopped the bucking Vitara at the side door per Hall's instructions, came out from the house there, marched over to the vehicle, and stopped next to the left rear door. Stan waited for her to get in, but she didn't; she simply stood there, a stout old woman with a face like a bald eagle with a headache, wearing a black cloth coat, black beret-type hat on iron-gray curls, and black lace-up boots. In her left claw she clutched the black leather handle of a black leather handbag.

When she didn't move, and didn't move, he finally got the idea, and stepped out to open her door for her, with an ironic bow she either didn't see or didn't choose to see. 'Thank you, Gillette,' she said. 'I am Mrs Parsons.'

'Think of that,' Stan said, as she climbed in. Already he hated her, though not quite enough to slam the door on her ankle.

Later, he would be sorry he'd missed that chance. The entire drive to the supermarket, between her barked directions to the place, she told him in great detail and with much repetition just how dreadful a marriage her poor 'Miss Alicia' had made with 'that man.' Not having a name at all, Stan supposed, was even worse than being Gillette all the time.

At the supermarket, he'd assumed he would sit at the wheel with a newspaper while she did her thing. First, of course, as he already knew, he would have to get out and open the door for her. But then, having done so, he was not pleased to hear her say, 'Well, come along, Gillette.'

He went along. It turned out to be his job to push the shopping cart along behind her and fetch the items from the grocery list she'd dragged out of her purse. Up and down the aisles they went, him with his funny-ha-ha hat, her with her imperious manner and her list.

At the end, he was to follow her – she definitely was to go first – out of the store and across the parking lot. He considered speeding up, as though it were an accident, but how much damage can you do with a shopping cart?

Later, Stan promised himself: Before we're done around here.

39

Flip met his new coconspirators at his office-gym, a deep narrow store-front in a suburban mall between nowhere and nothing. Almost all of his contacts with his clients were in their own residences or, occasionally, offices, but every once in a while it was necessary to provide a place for the sessions, as when a client's marriage had ended with more than the usual fallout and flak, and it would be some time before he would have his own exercise mat again. Also, Flip needed his own gym, to keep himself in peak condition. Therefore, Flip's Hustle House, which consisted of an ordinary office in front, a gym almost as extensive as Monroe Hall's behind it, and a smallish changing room and shower behind that, all at the rear of this Meandering Bypaths Mall, tucked away where only the most determined could find it.

Which included this new group of five. Although, as Flip had noticed from the very beginning, they weren't a group of five after all, were they? They were a group of two, a pair of snotty silver-spoon-in-the-mouth sorts, supplemented by a group of three, baggy out-of-shape heart-attack-to-come working stiffs. It was amazing, Flip reflected, as he watched his new team troop into the office, how Monroe Hall could bring disparate people together.

The snot called Mark seemed to be the spokesman. Once they were all seated, either comfortably on one of the three chairs or uncomfortably on the floor, Mark said, 'Let me put our cards on the table,' which, in Flip's experience, meant wool was now headed toward one's eyes. 'We have reasons,' Mark went on, 'to feel that Monroe Hall owes us something.'

'So do we!' announced the sack of guts introduced as Ace.

Mark nodded at him patiently, as though he'd learned a long time ago to make the nodding patiently at Ace an automatic reaction to the sound of the man's voice. 'I was including *you* in *us*,' he said.

Mac, the brains of the sagging team, said, 'Ace, we're all in this together.'

At the moment, Flip thought, and watched and listened.

Mark, the interruption over, went back to laying his cards on the table.

145

'We've studied Monroe Hall's estate,' he said, 'all of us,' with a glance at Ace, 'for some time. His defenses unfortunately are excellent.'

Flip nodded. 'All that money can buy,' he said.

Os, the usually quiet one, growled. It was an actual growl, the sort of thing that usually emanates from something on a leash. While Flip looked at him in some surprise, Mark patted Os's knee – Os was chaired, Mark floored near him – and said, 'Yes, Os, we know, some of that money is ours.'

'And some,' the jack-in-the-box, Ace, also on the floor, put in, 'belongs to the ACWFFA.'

'Agreed,' Mark told him, leaving Flip in the dark, and turned back to say, 'We had all noticed that the only person in this wide world with unquestioned access to that compound, apart from Hall's wife, is yourself.'

'He needs a personal trainer,' Flip explained. 'Stuck in that place, he gets no exercise at all.'

'We studied you,' Mark said. 'I admit it. We even broke in and entered your house.'

Flip stared in astonishment. This *was* cards on the table. Trying to think what might be in his house of an embarrassing nature that they might have stumbled across, he said, 'You did?'

'Finding nothing of use,' Mark said, to Flip's great relief. 'The same with your car.'

'My car?'

'That Subaru. We wondered how many people we could hide in it, or one like it. Possibly have one of us disguise himself as you, hide others in the vehicle—'

'No, no,' Flip said, and had to smile, looking at them. 'I'm sorry, I don't mean to be rude, but I really don't think a one of you could disguise yourself as me, not for a second.'

'There were these problems,' Mark agreed. 'They appeared to be insurmountable. But then, my friends and I—' He paused here, surprisingly, to smile in amiable fashion toward the flab called Mac, and to say, 'Particularly my friend Mac.'

'It was all of us,' Mac assured him.

'In any event,' Mark said, 'it occurred to us that, since Monroe Hall famously alienates everyone who comes within even the slightest contact with him, why wouldn't he have alienated *you?*'

'Why, indeed?' said Flip, furious all over again, thinking grimly of the three hundred forty-seven dollars he'd just this afternoon mailed to the feds. 'What he did to *me*, the no-muscle-tone son of a bitch,' he said, 'is turn me in to the IRS.'

'The IRS?' They were all astonished, but none more so than Os, who said, 'Forgive me, but what about you could possibly interest the IRS?'

'My money,' Flip said simply. 'There's nothing too small for those people to go after, now that we're at war.'

'War?' More general astonishment, this time summed up by Buddy: 'What war?'

Now Flip too was astonished. 'What?' he said. 'Don't you know there's a war on?'

They didn't. So involved were they in their own concerns that an entire war had slipped beneath their radar.

Mark, as though questioning this war's pedigree and bona fides, said, 'What war is this?'

'They're calling it,' Flip said, 'Project Everlasting Watchfulness and Prosperity Under God.'

Mac said, 'That's the name of the war?'

'Apparently,' Flip said, 'they worked it out with focus groups and ad agencies and everything, and that was the name that sold best.'

'That isn't how they *used* to name wars,' Mark protested. 'They used to name wars with some gravitas to them. The Civil War. The French and Indian War.'

'The Thirty Years' War,' suggested Mac.

'The Napoleonic Wars,' Buddy offered.

'The War of Jenkins' Ear,' Os tossed in.

'Well, all right,' Mark conceded, 'they weren't *always* mature and dignified, but mostly they were.'

'Say it again,' Ace urged Flip.

'Project Everlasting Watchfulness and Prosperity Under God.'

'It sounds,' Buddy mused, 'like one of those religious tracts they put in your screen door.'

'They did the most up-to-date branding,' Flip assured him. 'It's all very modern.'

Os said, 'So's carpal tunnel syndrome.'

Mark said, 'Never mind this war and these namings.' Gazing intently, openly, *honestly* at Flip, he said, 'We have come to see if your entrée to Hall's property, plus our manpower and motivation, might help us get our hands on the bastard.'

Flip said, 'What do you want to do with him?' He wasn't sure he was ready to go along with murder, but felt at least he should hear them out.

It was Os who answered: 'We want his money.'

'*Our* money,' Buddy said.

Mark said, 'The idea is, we get him off that compound. We get him to a computer, possibly that one there on your desk.'

'I don't think so,' Flip said.

'Somewhere,' Mark agreed. 'We force him to access his offshore accounts, and transfer large pieces of his money to *us*, to our friends here, and now to you. Once the transfer is complete and irreversible, and once we have our alibis in place, just in case he recognizes some of us through the masks we'll naturally wear, we'll release him, considerably poorer.'

'And serve him right,' Buddy said.

Flip said, 'Mmm, I don't know.'

'The money transfer?' Mark shrugged. 'Trust me, I know how to make those work.'

'No,' Flip said, 'I'm talking about getting him *out* of there. I don't know how many of you I could even get into the place, but to then get all of us and a trussed-up Monroe Hall back *out* again, I just don't—'

And then he saw it. His eyes opened wide, and so did his mouth. He gazed at a vision in the middle distance. Flabby Mac said, 'You got something, I saw it hit you.'

Mark said, 'I saw it, too. Between the eyes.'

'Horses,' breathed Flip.

They all frowned at him. Buddy, dubious as could be, said, 'Horses?'

'He's got a couple horses,' Flip told them, 'but his trainer quit. He doesn't know how to ride, and he wants to learn.'

Ace said, 'What good does—'

Mark said, 'Let him tell us, Ace,' and Ace looked surprised at the interruption and on the brink of being offended when Mac quietly said, 'OK, Ace,' and Ace subsided.

So then Flip said, 'Twice he asked me if I knew a horseriding trainer, but I don't. But now I could.'

Os said, 'Flip, that's very nice, but that electric fence is too high. Even if you *knew* how to ride, you couldn't jump that fence.'

'I'm not talking about jumping any fences,' Flip told him. 'Think about horses. How do they get anywhere? Do they *walk*? Never. Horses ride!'

Mac said, 'Say, you're right.'

'We've all seen them,' Flip said, 'the horse carriers, the trailers, high solid sides, you can never see into them, except a horse's tail at the window at the back.'

'And one of these days,' Mac said, 'if I get your meaning, Flip, that horse's tail is going to be Monroe Hall.'

40

Hall was very pleased with the additions to his staff. Far from being third-raters, lummoxes that Henry Cooper would palm off on him because he knew he could – what, in fact, Hall himself would have done if the positions were reversed – these four newcomers were just fine.

Swope, for instance, the new security man. According to Yancey, chief of that section, he was going to be a solid addition down there. 'Very handy if we should have an incident,' is the way Yancey had put it.

As for the driver, Gillette, even the awful Mrs Parsons gave him high marks, 'a very agreeable young man,' and Mrs Parsons, in Monroe Hall's experience, had never liked anything on this earth except Alicia. He well knew she hated him personally and would talk against him to Alicia if Alicia would permit it, but she would not. She wouldn't fire the old shrew, but at least she wouldn't let the woman poison her mind. Hall could do nothing but keep out of the old bat's way, eat her food – surprisingly delicious, coming from such a sour source – and wait for some friendly pneumonia to take her away.

Of the newcomers, the butler, Rumsey, was the most problematic, but that was only because, as Hall had to keep reminding himself, he just didn't *look* like a butler. What he mostly looked like to Hall was a second-story man, someone whose slouching shoulders and hangdog expression would show in their best light at a police lineup. On the other hand, he certainly showed willing enough, and was Johnny-on-the-spot if needed, which he really hadn't been yet.

In any event, the best of the addition was the private secretary, Fred Blanchard. And to think he'd almost failed to hire the man. He was a dynamo, Blanchard, and he was worth his salary if all he did was remind Monroe Hall what his life used to be like.

There was a second, smaller desk in Hall's office, with less of a view, for the use of a secretary, empty ever since he'd immured himself on this property. That desk had been occupied in the old days by a series of impersonally efficient middle-aged women who'd handled his mail, his telephone, and his appointments without ever making much impact on him.

149

Blanchard wasn't like that. He was *active* over there. The first thing he'd done was dig out the phone book and order a subscription to the local newspaper, the *Argosy-Bee*. When Hall had objected that he'd never felt a need to know what might be in the pages of the *Argosy-Bee*, Blanchard had cheerfully said, 'We need to know our neighborhood, Mr Hall, because it's the springboard for our return to society.'

'*Are* we returning to society?'

'Absolutely! You've made your mistakes, but who hasn't? You've suffered, you've repented. The world *wants* to welcome you back, it just doesn't know it yet. But it will, it will.'

More phone calls followed: a subscription to a clipping service, 'because we need to know what they're saying about us, so we can correct it,' calls to the local offices of national charities to offer the possibility of money and space for future events, calls to hospitals, volunteer fire departments, Boy and Girl Scouts, on and on.

What Hall was seeing here was community outreach with a vengeance, a thing he could never have done on his own, but which, as he watched Blanchard schmooze his way through the good people, gave him at last hope for the future.

The problem was, the only thing he was really good at was fleecing his fellow man. He'd been born rich, so it might have seemed redundant, but he'd also been born with this peculiar skill. It was his only skill, and also his main pleasure.

But once you've become publicly successful as a voracious cheat, as unfortunately Monroe Hall had, you could never ply your skill again, because now everybody was alert. He was retired now, despite himself, and like many retirees, he had absolutely no idea what to do with himself. He had everything he'd ever worked for, except the work itself.

Wait. In a pause in Blanchard's phoning, here came an incoming call, which Blanchard took with smooth proficiency: 'Hall residence, Blanchard speaking. Who may I say? One moment, please.' He put his hand over the mouthpiece, turned to Hall, and said, 'We'll want the phone company to give us a phone with a hold button.'

'Fred? Who is it?'

'Oh. Somebody called Morriscone, Flip Morriscone. Yes? No?'

'What, is he not coming tomorrow, too? Let's see what the excuse is this time.' Snatching up the phone on his own desk, he snapped, 'Hall here,' as Blanchard hung up.

Flip's tone was as happy as ever; apparently, the IRS visit hadn't been overly painful, after all. 'Hi, Mr Hall. Guess what?'

'I'm no good at guessing, Flip.'

'I found you a riding instructor!'

Astonished, Hall said, 'You mean horses?'

'Well, I don't know what else you're going to ride, Mr Hall. Sure, horses. His name is Jay Gilly, and he wants to know if he can come by tomorrow afternoon. Around two?'

'That would be perfect, Flip.'

'Here's the thing, though,' Flip said. 'Since you're a beginner, he wants to bring his own horses.'

'I have horses, Flip.'

'He knows that. But these are special, trained to be gentle with new riders. He'll bring them in his own horse trailer, and take them away again after the lesson. OK?'

'Well, if that's what he wants to do. And I suppose he'll talk about fees when he gets here.'

'Oh, sure. Be sure to leave his name at the gate, Mr Hall. Jay Gilly, with a horse trailer. Two tomorrow.'

'I'll call the gate right now,' Hall promised. 'Thank you, Flip.'

'My pleasure, Mr Hall.'

Hanging up, Hall said, 'Fred, call the gate. There'll be somebody coming through at two tomorrow afternoon. His name is Jay Gilly, and he'll be bringing horses in a trailer.'

'Right away,' Blanchard said, and did it, and then Hall said to him, 'Ever ride horseback, Fred?'

'I bet on them a couple times,' Blanchard said, 'so now I don't trust them.'

41

It was falling apart, because nobody wanted to play Jay Gilly. Mac could see the way things were trending, and he just didn't like it at all.

They were all gathered in Flip Morriscone's office, all except Flip, who'd had to go off to tend to another client. 'Just pull the door shut when you go,' he'd told his new best friends. They'd assured him they would, and he'd grinned around at them all, said, 'Revenge *is* sweet,' and left.

But revenge wasn't being sweet at the moment. Right now, it was turning more sour by the second, and all because nobody was willing to be Jay Gilly. We should have worked this out before Flip made the call, Mac told himself. But in that case, he pointed out to himself, he still wouldn't have made it, would he?

It was Buddy's contention that Mark Sterling was the ideal Jay Gilly, vociferously backed up by Ace. Their argument was class: 'It has to be one of you guys,' Buddy said. 'We don't look like horse people, us three, we look like what we are, which is working stiffs.'

'That's right,' Ace agreed. 'We couldn't hoity-toity if you held a gun to our head.'

'Well, I'm not quite sure what "hoity-toity" might be,' Mark snipped, giving a perfect example of the thing itself, 'but neither Os nor I could portray this Gilly fellow for a very good reason. Monroe Hall *knows* us.'

'Exactly,' Os said. 'We were in business together, worse luck.'

That stopped everybody for a second, but then Ace said, 'He *knows* you. You're buddies all the time now? Or were you in an office here and there with a bunch of other guys, sittin around a table, robbin the widows and orphans together, ten guys in a room for an hour, he's gonna *remember* you?'

'Yes,' Mark said.

Os said, 'He'll certainly remember *me*. Last time I saw him, I threw a golf trophy at him. If he hadn't ducked, I'd have shot that upraised golf club straight into his left eye.'

'Well, that's you,' Ace said. 'What about your pal here? What's to make *him* stand out in Hall's memory?'

THE ROAD TO RUIN

'I'm the one,' Mark said, 'who wrestled Os to the ground, then wasted two or three minutes apologizing to the bastard.'

'Never apologize,' Os said.

Ace said, 'You could go in disguise.'

Mark looked revolted. 'Disguise? Some Santa Claus beards? Those false spectacles with the eyebrows and the nose?'

'Well, a better disguise than that,' Ace said. 'Like they do in the movies.'

'We can contribute the horse trailer,' Mark reminded them, 'and one horse, but that's the extent of our contribution.'

It was true. It turned out that Mark had some cousin over in New Jersey who was connected with horse people, and had arranged for the loan of a horse trailer with horse. Tomorrow morning, Mark and Os would drive to New Jersey to get the thing. But in the afternoon, who would drive it to Monroe Hall's place?

Mac said, 'Mark, I see the problem, we all do really see the problem. Monroe Hall would recognize you. But Buddy's right, we three don't look like horse people.'

'Well, now, there you're wrong,' Mark told him. 'Yes, it's true, there are some upper-crust horse people. The Windsors come to mind. But mostly, you know, they're arrivistes. And in any case, a riding instructor isn't part of the horsey set, any more than a trainer or a groom. These are people standing in horseshit every day of their lives, the ones who actually work with the beasts. The owners are well away somewhere, only to appear when it's time to grace the winner's circle. Mac, you *know* what you have to do.'

This was the bad place where it had all been trending, and now here it was. Knowing there was no way out, no one else to whom he could hand off this intimidating task, he sighed, long and deep, and said, 'Mark, tell me you know enough about those people so you can teach me how to pass.'

'Done,' Mark said.

Os, deadpan, said, 'Mac, you will look smashing in jodhpurs.'

42

'Are they still behind us?' Mark asked. No matter how he crunched down, he couldn't get a useful image from the mirror outside his passenger door.

'Of course they're still behind us,' Os said. He was not in the best of tempers. 'If they weren't still behind us, would I still be driving?'

Mark resisted the desire to say, 'God knows.' Instead, deciding it was time to placate his partner, he said, 'I know you'd rather we didn't have to do this.'

'And how right you are.'

'But there's just no alternative. I've thought and thought—'

'*I've* thought and thought,' Os assured him, 'and if there were any alternative at all, some dotty absent relation of your own, for instance, we would be hotfooting in *that* direction this instant.'

Of course. Mark knew, from long experience of Os, it was time now to let it go, permit Os to fume in silence and gradually come to accommodate the situation. It was only when he was argued with, or even merely talked with, that Os would move on from disgruntled to ominous.

The problem was what to do with Monroe Hall once they got their hands on him. They would certainly have to hold him for a few days at least, while they pressured him to do their bidding and reassured themselves the money transfers had actually been made. The *place* to hold him would have to be isolated, yet Internet-linked, and anonymous enough that Hall wouldn't be able to find or identify it afterward. The three union members in the Taurus behind them were totally useless when it came to such a place, and Mark had to admit he was useless as well. The only answer, which Os was reluctantly forced to admit, was his aunt Elfreda's lodge up in the mountains. Thither they were going now; to be certain it could accommodate them.

This lodge had been in Os's family since the family's income was based on coal and railroads, built by some ancestor of his as a manly midwinter retreat for hunting and poker, no wives allowed. As time moved on, and customs changed, the lodge became more of a family location, with skiing for the most part to replace the hunting. But the lodge was still only used in the depths of the winter, the family having other places to go and other things to do the rest of the year.

Aunt Elfreda, a much-married lady of innumerable offspring, had inherited the lodge years ago and used it now mostly for vast holiday get-togethers, followed by smaller more ad hoc ski weekends. The lodge had become Internet-connected some years ago, because many of Elfreda's children and their spouses were in commerce and wouldn't have been able to participate in the jollity if their umbilical to the office were disconnected.

Off-season, such as now, the lodge was shut up tight, protected by alarm systems with which Os was of course familiar. The next legitimate human presence in or around the lodge would be in early December, when the caretaker family from the town twenty miles away would come to clean and tidy and stock the place with provisions for the new season.

The roads northeastward toward the lodge were increasingly narrow, winding, and hilly, as they moved up into the Allegheny mountains. Towns were few and far between, and Mark was surprised, when they approached one of them, to be greeted by a sign that read GRISSLE. As they passed among the hamlet's six houses, one church, and combination post office/gas station/convenience store, he said, 'Grissle? The town is called Grissle?'

'It's where the caretakers live,' Os said. 'We'll be there very soon now.'

Well, not *very* soon. It was another twenty miles, higher into the heavily forested mountains, with the occasional dirt road wandering off to left or right, but at last Os took one of those side roads, leftward, and now it *really* got steep. 'They're having a little trouble back there,' Os said, smiling at the rearview mirror. 'But they'll be along.'

Up, up, and all at once the lodge appeared. At first there was a pair of elaborate stone gateposts to the sides of the road, but without a gate. Beyond them, the forest had been thinned somewhat but not entirely cleared, and the road curved up to a stop in front of what looked like the world's biggest log cabin, girdled all around with broad porches and featuring massive stone chimneys at both ends. All the windows were covered with sheets of plywood. Separate outbuildings, also of logs, seemed to be garages and storage sheds.

Os stopped the Porsche just before the gateposts. 'First line of defense,' he announced, shifted into park, and got out of the car.

Twisting around, Mark saw the Taurus slowly make its way up the road. Turning instead to watch Os, he saw him open what had appeared to be just another stone in the lefthand gatepost, but which now turned out to be a fake, with a hinge. Inside was an alarm keypad, on which Os rapidly punched out a number, then closed the fake stone and came back to the car. Pausing beside it, he called down to the Taurus occupants, '*Courage, mes amis!*' then got chuckling behind the wheel and drove on up to the house.

Here, it turned out the keypad was behind a concealed panel on a support post of the porch roof, just at the top of the four-step stoop. Os played another brief étude on it, then turned to the front door as the Taurus stopped below, just behind the Porsche. The three union men got out and were clearly suitably impressed, staring around in awe. 'And this,' Buddy said, 'is the house they *don't* use.'

As they came up the stoop, it was Ace, naturally, who said, 'How come there's no windows? Afraid of snipers?'

'They're covered in the off-season,' Mark explained.

Os, who'd taken a key from a niche in the log wall and was using it to open the door, said, 'Rodents will eat through the wood between the windowpanes, when the house isn't occupied. They like the grout.'

'And the plywood makes it perfect for us,' Mark said.

Os opened the door and they all trooped into a very dark room. 'One mo,' Os said, marched into the darkness, and a minute later he switched on a table lamp beside a sofa. A very large room sprang into existence, more like the lobby of a fake-rustic hotel than somebody's living room.

Buddy said, 'They leave the electricity on? All year round?'

'Of course,' Os said, and it was left to Mark to explain, 'For the alarms, and you have to have some heat in the place.'

'And,' Os added, 'one must maintain the temperature and humidity in the wine cellar.'

'Oh, yeah,' Buddy said. 'I didn't thinka that.'

Mac said, 'Mark, what did you mean, the plywood makes it perfect for us?'

'Hall won't be able to see out,' Mark told him. 'He won't be able to identify a thing.'

Os said, 'A couple of laptops are kept here, with the phone number installed for local Internet access. When the family's here, anyone who needs to log on can take a laptop to his bedroom, plug it into the phone line there, and do whatever he wants. So that means we can put Hall in any of the bedrooms. They all have attached baths, and they all have doors that lock.'

Ace said, 'You got a small one? With a lumpy bed?'

'I like your thinking,' Os told him. 'Come along, let's choose.'

As they started across the lengthy living room – wooden walls, massive stone fireplace, layers of huge wool rugs – Mac said, 'You know, this place is about the size of our houses.'

Surprised, Mark said, 'Really? You live in a house this size?'

'No, *our* houses,' Mac told him. 'All three of them, put together.'

'Ah,' Mark said.

'Come along,' Os said, and kept switching on more lights as they moved deeper into the windowless, cavernous lodge.

43

Of course Stan Murch was the *driver*, but when it came to just driving around from place to place, that was usually Kelp. Tiny wasn't physically suited to the task, and nobody was eager to see John behind the wheel. So, a little after five that first full day on the job, Thursday, June 16, it was Kelp who slid into the driver's seat of his recently acquired Yukon, with Stan in the copilot's seat and John in back; but not back the way he'd been back in the monster station wagon. This time, if he wanted, he could lean forward and rest an elbow on top of the front seat and partake in the conversation.

Except, this time, there wasn't any conversation. It was a short run from Hall's big white house across the compound past mostly empty buildings, and they all spent that time with their own thoughts, reacting to a full day of more or less honest employment.

For Kelp, the experience had been an eerie one. He'd expected to show up, have to bear with some kind of over-bearing guy, and just hunker down and wait for the auto removal. Instead of which, he'd been thrown off from the very beginning by the guy's decision not to hire him after all.

He couldn't have *that*; he needed to be here with the crew. So it meant he first had to convince Hall that he really did need a secretary, and then by God *act* like one, persuade Hall of his value by doing things that Hall would like.

And that led to the second surprise; he didn't find Monroe Hall a bad guy at all. The exact opposite, in fact. Hall was so surprised and pleased and grateful that Kelp was actually going to restore his good name – as though by now Monroe Hall had a good name to restore – that he was like a puppy getting his first bone. His admiration and gratitude were so intense it made Kelp redouble his efforts, reach out to the surrounding community, stay calm and resilient through all the rebuffs from the people he phoned – and you'd think people working for charities would be more charitable, somehow, but no – and actually work to make an opening here and there that a contrite Monroe Hall might somehow someday be able to crawl through.

In fact, by the end of the day, Kelp found himself a little sorry he wouldn't be able to stick around long enough to finish the job. (The finish, of course, the spectacular finish, would be the Monroe Hall Cup, added to some national pro-am golf tourney. Sure he could do it. Every golfer in the country paying his club dues from his corporate account would look at Hall and say, 'What the hell, forgive and forget. Mighta been me.' And it mighta been.)

So Kelp was silent because he didn't have anything negative to say about Monroe Hall, and he had the feeling positive statements about the guy wouldn't go over so well with this crowd. So what he did, he followed the old folk wisdom: If you've got nothing bad to say about someone, don't say anything at all.

The run to the green house where Chester had once lived was a short one, and when they walked in there was a smell in the house that might have meant the furniture was being refinished but was actually Tiny in the kitchen, making everybody's dinner. They all trooped in, to view the unprecedented sight of Tiny in two aprons, overlapping, with a meat cleaver in one hand and a long wooden spoon in the other, with a lot of big pots and pans hissing and snarling on the stove. What he looked mostly like was some darker version of Maurice Sendak's *In the Night Kitchen*. 'Soup's on at six,' he told them.

Looking doubtful, John said, 'We're having soup?'

'No,' Tiny told him. 'It's what you say. "Soup's on". It means food. Don't talk to me now, I don't want no distraction. I'll talk to you when we eat. I got good news and better news.'

Kelp said, 'I figured, if you wanted a ride from the guardshack, you'd a called me.'

'My shift didn't start yet,' Tiny said. 'That's parta the news. Outa my kitchen.'

So they got out of the kitchen, and went to the living room, where Stan said, in a very quiet voice, 'Suppose we could go out to eat?'

'No,' Kelp said. 'Nobody refuses Tiny's hospitality.'

'I think I'll take some Pepto-Bismol ahead of time,' John decided.

And then it was good. It wasn't your ordinary stuff, but it was good. Real tastes, but not too sweet, not too sour. There was lamb, in chunks; there was bacon, not too crisp; there were home-fried potatoes, with some kind of tasty oil on them; there was swiss chard, boiled up and spread with some kind of sauce that tasted sort of like chutney; there were biscuits, so light and fluffy you had to put butter on them to keep them from floating away. And there was not just beer, but stout, to tie it all together.

There was no talk at the table for quite some time. It was Kelp who first came up for air, saying, 'Tiny, this is great. What is this? This is great.'

'It's Tsergovian,' Tiny told him. 'It's from the old country. It's how my people used to eat in the old days, when they had food.'

John said, through a full mouth, 'Then I'm surprised they ever left.'

'Well, there were a lotta days,' Tiny said, 'when they didn't have food. So that's why they come here, before my time. The food wasn't as good over here, but it was around every day.'

Stan said, '*I* wouldn't mind this food every day.'

'Which brings up the question,' John said, through another mouthful of food, 'when do we do what we come here for.'

'Which is the good news and the better news,' Tiny said, 'I told you I got. I didn't want to disturb you from your eating.'

'Well, I'm done now,' Kelp said. 'Whoo.'

'Save a little room,' Tiny advised him, 'I got pumpkin pecan pie for dessert.'

Everybody moaned, and Kelp said, 'Tiny. Tell me that isn't the good news.'

'No,' Tiny said. 'But we gotta eat this pie.'

'Maybe for breakfast,' Stan suggested.

Tiny considered that and, to everyone's relief, nodded. 'That could work,' he said. 'OK, the news and the news. The good news is, the new hire in security gets the shit detail.'

They looked at him. Kelp said, 'That's the good news?'

'The shit detail,' Tiny said, 'is guard duty at the main gate, midnight till eight in the morning. All by myself until six a.m., when a couple day guys show up.'

'Wait a minute,' John said. 'You're gonna be *alone* on the *gate* all *night*?'

'Midnight to six.'

Stan said, 'Then we're outa here,' and Kelp felt a little pang. He'd thought he'd have a few days anyway to get Hall shaped up for his comeback.

But Tiny said, 'Not right away. Tonight, clear sky, big moon, all the stars. *Tomorrow* night, heavy cloud cover. No rain, but also no moonlight, no starlight.'

John said, 'So tomorrow night. Good. But first we gotta find the cars.'

'That's my better news,' Tiny said. 'While I was down there today, picking out my uniform – a very nice brown, a little tight in the shoulders, but for two nights I can live with it – I come across a map they got there of the compound. On that map is marked where every one of Hall's cars is stashed. And on a big board in the office there are the keys to every one of those buildings, each one with a tag on it, says which building it is.' He looked around at them. 'You sure nobody wants a little pie?'

44

Pumpkin pecan pie for breakfast is only good at first. When Dortmunder followed Kelp and Murch out of the house Friday morning to start their second day on the job, he noticed he wasn't the only one burping.

Riding back to the main house, Dortmunder reflected on how surprised he'd been by Monroe Hall. He'd expected a real bastard, but the guy had been easygoing, even kind of shy. Dortmunder couldn't see why everybody hated him so much. He didn't voice this opinion, though, because he knew it wouldn't be understood by the rest of the crew, and so, like them, he remained silent.

At the house, Hall himself greeted them just inside the front door. 'Ah, Fred,' he said to Kelp, with a big smile, 'go on in the office, I'll be right with you.'

'Check,' Kelp said, and went off.

Dortmunder planned to go off, too, to his position in the butler's pantry, a cross between a smallish windowless office and largish closet off the kitchen where the bells to summon him were mounted on the side wall, but as he took a step, Hall gave him an icy look and said, 'Wait right there, Rumsey.'

Oops. That was *exactly* the tone of a tier guard in a state pen; once heard, not easily forgotten. What was wrong now?

Hall was willing to let him wait for the answer, turning instead to Murch, switching on the big friendly act again, saying, 'Gillette, Mrs Parsons wants to visit some farm markets this morning.'

'Will do,' Murch said, which was probably not what a real Gillette would have said, but Hall's concentration was actually still on Dortmunder, i.e., Rumsey.

As Murch headed for the kitchen and Mrs Parsons, Hall lowered a look of utter contempt in Dortmunder's direction, and said, 'Do you call yourself a butler?'

At the moment, there was only one answer to that: 'Yes, sur.'

'They must have quite a lax view of butlers in eastern Europe,' Hall suggested.

'I don't know, sur.'

'All those years of the workers of the world running things, and we see how well *that* panned out. And you're still one of them, are you, Rumsey?'

Dortmunder had no idea what they were talking about. 'Oi'm Amurrican, sur,' he pointed out.

'Perhaps a little too American,' Hall said. 'I suggest you take a look at the upstairs corridor, Rumsey, and try to see, do *try* to see, in what tiny way you have been remiss.'

'Yes, sur,' Dortmunder told Hall's back, as the man marched off to convene with Kelp, who was a *good* boy.

Upstairs corridor. Dortmunder had already noticed that you never call a corridor a hall in a house owned by somebody named Hall. But what was the upstairs corridor – or hall, dammit – to do with Dortmunder? He hadn't yet even *been* up there, so what could he have done wrong?

Well, it was time to go see how he'd managed to get himself in the doghouse in a location he'd never even visited. Feeling ill used, he climbed the broad stairs, and here was an upstairs hall, very wide, with closed doors. Dortmunder started down it, looking for clues, and a cuckoo spoke eight times, seven minutes late.

The corridor was almost empty. Here an antique three-legged table with an elaborately shaded lamp on it; there a pair of black oxford shoes less gunboaty than his own, placed neatly side by side next to a closed door; here a big painting on the wall of mountains and clouds and sunset. Or sunrise.

Dortmunder walked down one side of the corridor and back up the other. No dog crap on the floor, no spilled glasses, no overflowing ashtrays. What's going on here? He stood finally near the stairs, gazing at the corridor, scratching his head, until one of those doors opened and Mrs Hall came out, looking fresh and beautiful and, when she spied Dortmunder, bewildered.

'Yes, Rumsey?'

'Mr Hall sent me up here, mum.'

'What for?'

'I dunno. He got mad about somethin and said I was supposed to come up here.'

'Hmm.' She too looked up and down the corridor, but when she turned back to him her expression was oh-please. 'Oh, Rumsey' she said. 'Do you call yourself a butler?'

Which was what the husband had asked, and which Dortmunder didn't like to hear at all. Everybody was threatening to blow his cover. He was beginning to think there was something about buttling he'd missed in those training films. 'I do my best, mum,' he said.

'The *shoes*, Rumsey.'

He blinked at them. There they were, neatly placed on the floor, midway down the corridor on the right. 'I didn't do that, mum.'

'Well, of *course* not, Rumsey.' Now she clearly didn't know what to think. 'Mr *Hall* put them out there.'

'Oh.'

'Don't you know *why*, Rumsey?'

'Take them to the shoe repair?'

'Rumsey, I can't believe you have been a butler for—'

'We never had nothing about shoes at the embassy, mum.'

She looked skeptical. 'Who polished the ambassador's shoes?'

In that instant, he got it. The boss puts the shoes in the corridor; the butler mouses through, later at night, to take them away to his pantry and polish them; then the butler brings them back and puts them where he found them, only now gleaming like bowling balls.

So why hadn't he known that? And who *did* polish the ambassador's shoes? 'His orderly, mum,' Dortmunder said, floundering for the word. 'Military orderly. All that sort of thing. Tie bow ties, polish shoes, all that. Specialist, mum.'

'Well, that's certainly a different way to do things,' she said. 'But we may never understand the eastern Europeans. Somehow, it's all Transylvania, all the time.'

'Yes, mum.'

'Well, do them now,' she said, with a graceful gesture shoeward. 'And assure Mr Hall you'll understand your duties much better from this point forward.'

'I will, mum,' Dortmunder said.

You'd think that would be the end of it, but no. When he carried the damn shoes – not that dirty, anyway – down the stairs to the first floor, there was Hall hanging around down there, obviously waiting for him, to give him a nasty spiteful smirk when he saw the shoes hanging from Dortmunder's fingers. 'Well, we are full of the old initiative, aren't we?'

'Sorry, sur,' Dortmunder said, while in his mind's eye he held one shoe in each hand and slapped their soles smartly up against both sides of the son of a bitch's head. 'Done differently in the embassy, sur,' he explained. 'Be better from now.'

'How encouraging,' Hall mocked, and then, as Dortmunder turned away toward his pantry (come to think of it, he *had* noticed shoe-polishing equipment in there), called after him, 'Former boss assassinated, eh? For wearing *filthy shoes*, do you suppose?'

'No, sur,' Dortmunder muttered – the best he could do.

Raising his voice even further, Hall ordered, 'Bring them to me in my office when they're *clean*.'

Well, he knew what that meant: white-glove inspection. 'Sur,' he said, and plodded on.

In the event, he only had to go back twice to buff the shoes some more, even though he could see his reflection in them the first time he'd whacked them around. But three trips was all it took. While Kelp sat smug and amused in his little corner of the office, Hall gave each shoe a long and critical once-over, and at last grudgingly said,' I suppose they'll do. And do you know what to do with them *next*, Rumsey?'

'Put em outside your door, sur. Where I got um.'

'*Very* good,' Hall told him. 'We may make a third-rate butler of you yet.'

'Thank you, sur.'

Dortmunder turned away, the gleaming shoes in his hand, but Hall said, cold as ice, 'I'm not finished.'

Oh. So Dortmunder turned back, lifted his head and his eyebrows, and said, 'Sur?'

'A riding instructor is coming with horses this afternoon at two,' Hall said. 'The gate will ring you in your pantry. You will go to the door to await his arrival. When he reaches the house, you will instruct him to wait outside, then come in here and inform me of his presence.'

'Yes, sur.'

'That's all. Dismissed.'

Dortmunder thudded up the stairs to return the shoes to where he'd found them. Horse, with trainer. Now, in his mind's eye, he saw Hall, atop a horse, turn to listen to an instruction from the trainer, oblivious of that oncoming tree branch. Very thick tree branch.

45

Mac didn't know which part of the enterprise frightened him the most – all of it, probably. All he knew is, it was the most scared he'd ever been in his life. More scared than the first time he'd had sex with the girl who would soon become his wife; hell, more scared than the first time he'd had sex with *anybody*. More scared than when they put him in charge of the K-type showerhead assembly line. More scared than the first time he'd gotten off a ski lift at the top of a mountain and looked down.

Well, that time, he'd ridden the ski lift back *down* the mountain again, and had been firmly après-ski ever since. But he didn't have that choice this time. There was only one way off this particular mountain.

And it was worse than the mountain, because the mountain was just one thing. With the mountain, you've got this steep bank of white with trees and boulders on it, and the job is to get from the top to the bottom without ricocheting too much. Simple, straightforward. But this horse thing was all *details*, and every detail was scarier than every other detail.

Take the mustache. It was a thick mustache, like a push broom, and it felt very insecure glued to his upper lip. Also, it tickled his nose. But the worst, the most scary part, was how horribly Os had smirked in amusement while gluing the thing onto him.

You took one look at Os, you knew he was a mean practical joker. But this was too important to him, wasn't it? He wouldn't arrange for Mac's mustache to fall off his face at just the wrong instant for a *gag*, would he? Would he?

All right, say he wouldn't. The thing could nevertheless fall off anyway, without underhanded scheming from Os.

So that was one thing to be scared of. Then there was the horse. No, that was scary enough, but before the horse was the horse *trailer*. It was attached at the rear of a very big pickup truck with four wheels across the back axle, and it wasn't until Mac really closed with the idea that *he* was the one who would have to drive it that he saw just how *big* the damn combination was.

The truck was bad enough, but the trailer was big as a house, built for

166

four horses, two across and then another two across, with a side door on the forward left to feed and look after the front pair. In it at the moment was one horse, at the back, with a big blanket suspended from the roof in front of it to block off the front half, which was where everybody else would hide while Mac drove to Monroe Hall's compound.

Which was another thing to be scared about. Were they really gonna buy it, those suspicious professional sentries at the entrance to Hall's compound? Were they really *not* going to search the trailer from one end to the other and find the four hidden men and all that rope, but just be contented to look at the rear end of one horse? Would they really believe this stupid mustache, and this stupid four-color jockey's hat, and this stupid green cable-knit sweater with stupid gray leather elbow patches, and these stupid jodhpurs? (Mac had never heard of jodhpurs before, and now that he had, he wished he hadn't.)

And then the horse. No, forget it, let's not even think about the horse. Because everybody else is ready, whether Mac is ready or not. They're all going through the side door into the concealed part of the trailer. Os, entering last, pauses to give one last word of advice: 'Try not to have to back up.' But even that he says with a kind of snotty chuckle and a twinkle in his eye.

Sheesh. Where did he go wrong?

And yet it worked like a charm. The thirty-mile drive was long enough for Mac to get used to that blunt gray metal box tailgating him, forever up close and personal in the mirror. He never had to back up, thank God, but he did have to learn to brake gently, or the trailer would buck and weave and threaten to take matters into its own hands. And best of all, the mustache didn't fall off.

He actually got to the compound ten minutes early, and when he said to the brown-uniformed tough guy at the gate, 'Jay Gilly, I'm expected,' all the fellow did was make a checkmark on his clipboard and say, 'I got to call the house.'

'Sure.'

While the guard was calling the house, a second guard walked around the pickup and horse trailer, more out of curiosity than suspicion. Then the first guard nodded at him through his guardshack window and the bar lifted in front of him, and by golly, after *months* of trying he just drove onto Monroe Hall's property and up the long blacktop road to the big white house.

And here he wouldn't have to back up either, because the road made a little loop past the front door of the house before angling off to a parking area on the right. Mac did the loop so that the left side of the pickup was toward the house, so no one down by the gate would be able to see what was going on up here. Leaving the engine on and the gearshift in park, he got out of the pickup, touched fingertips to the mustache for luck, and walked up to the front door.

Which opened just before he got there, and a sad sack in a black suit looked out at him as though waiting to hear his parole had been denied. 'Sur?'

'Jay Gilly,' Mac said, though he wished Flip had given him some other name. He didn't feel like a Jay Gilly, and was glad he wouldn't have to pretend to be Jay Gilly for very long.

'One moment, sur,' the gloomy fellow said, and shut the door again. Butler, he must have been, and gloomy because he worked for Monroe Hall.

Mac had acted in high school, mostly because his sister Beth had acted in high school, expecting to be a movie star any minute. (She was now a wife and mother, married to a bus driver.) The drama department at Mac's high school had all the girl actors they could need, and then some, but it was tough to get boys to come fill in the boy parts in the plays. Beth had dragged Mac along, saying it was because she sensed his massive talent, but he knew her real reason was that she was sucking up to Ms Mandelstam the drama teacher in hopes of better roles. Mac had parts in *Romeo and Juliet* and *Teahouse of the August Moon* and *Major Barbara*, and felt pretty good about it, though he knew darn well he did not have massive talent, and once high school was over he never thought about acting again.

But here it was, wasn't it? A new play and a new role: Jay Gilly, horse-riding instructor. He didn't have any written lines – sides, they were called, he remembered that – but he did have a character to play, and would have to play that character from this front door all the way down to the side door of the trailer. And then briefly again at the gate, on the way out. But his main period on stage was to begin here, right now.

And here it was. The door opened again, and the sad-sack butler stepped back to hold it open and stare into space as out came Monroe Hall himself, recognizable from all those newspaper photos and the few perp walks he'd done when the feds still thought they could pin something on him. He was dressed in what he must think appropriate for climbing on a horse, being tailored blue jeans and expensive leather cowboy boots with pictures of cactus plants on the sides and a redcheck flannel shirt. He also had a big smile on his face as he said, 'Jay Gilly?'

'Yes, I am,' Mac said, and thought, yes, I am! I can do this. 'How do you do, Mr Hall?' he said, and stuck out his hand.

'Just fine,' Hall said, though he had a rather limp handshake. Waving at the sky with the same hand, he said, 'What a beautiful day to go riding, eh?'

'Yes, sir, it is.'

'Let's see what this horseflesh looks like, shall we?'

'Certainly, sir. Just walk this way.'

'Come along, Rumsey.'

Come along? They didn't want the butler; they didn't need the butler in this scene; this was supposed to be just themselves and Monroe Hall.

But what could Mac do about it? Here came the butler, slope-shouldered and heavy-browed, and here came Hall, and there was nothing for it but to walk ahead of them down the path from house to pickup and along the side of the pickup and the trailer, where in fact he did have a previously prepared line to deliver, as a signal to the group inside the trailer: 'This way, Mr Hall.'

Well, he did have to say it, butler or no butler, and so he said it, and then, all according to plan (except for the butler), that door in the side of the trailer popped open and out jumped four people in a variety of masks with Buddy (paper bag with eyeholes cut in it) carrying the burlap sack meant to go over Hall's head.

And Hall couldn't have played his part better. His reaction was stunned astonishment. He didn't try to run; he didn't bob and weave; he didn't even holler; he just froze.

Buddy leaped forward, raising the sack, as Mark (green ski mask, with elks) and Ace (Lone Ranger mask) jumped to grab Hall's arms, while Os (rubber Frankenstein head), who was supposed to grab Hall's ankles, pointed instead at the butler and cried, 'Who's that?'

'The butler,' Mac said, apologetic even though it wasn't his fault.

'Grab him!' Mark yelled, he already having his hands full with the belatedly struggling Hall, Mark and Buddy and Ace now tugging the sacked Hall toward the trailer.

Up to this point, the butler had just been watching events unfold, interested but not involved; as though he thought of himself as merely a bystander. But now, when Os lunged at him, shouting, 'Come on, Mac!' the butler backed away, putting his hands up as he cried, 'Hey, don't call *me* Mac, I'm the butler, I'm not in this.'

'He'll raise the alarm!' Mark shouted from halfway into the trailer.

Mac, having already figured that out, leaped forward to join Os in grabbing the butler by both arms and dragging him in his employer's wake.

The butler struggled like mad: 'What are you doing? I got *work* here! I got things to do!'

What, was he crazy? Mark on one side, Os on the other, they lifted the butler by his elbows, ran him forward, tossed him through the trailer door onto the fallen cluster inside, Os jumped on top of the scrum, Mac slammed the door, and three minutes later the guards were waving bye-bye as he drove out the gate.

46

'Of course,' Kelp said into the phone, 'Mr Hall would expect to contribute to the orphans' picnic, other than merely providing the grounds and the staff to cater the affair.'

The child welfare woman had not yet thawed. Nor had she yet agreed to provide orphans to assist in Monroe Hall's rehabilitation. Icily, she said, 'Contribute. He'd want to supply milk and cookies, would he?'

'Well, beyond that. Mr Hall was thinking,' Kelp said, making it up as he went along, 'of contributing a bus.'

'A . . . I'm sorry?'

'A bus,' Kelp repeated. 'A large vehicle for conveying fifty-four seated persons, and twelve standees.'

'I know what a bus is,' she snipped.

Kelp waited. Let the penny drop. Well, more than a penny.

Thud. 'A bus?' There was a new squeak in her voice. 'He would – he'd – he'd contribute a *bus*? Oh, I see, you mean, he'd pay the rental.'

'No,' Kelp said, 'he'd pay for the bus. Surely there are other times you'd like to take the kiddies on excursions. You'd have to come up with your own driver, though.'

'Excuse me, Mr . . . ?'

'Blanchard, Fred Blanchard.'

'Mr Blanchard, are—'

'Fred, please.'

'*Are* you,' she insisted, 'saying that Mr Hall would *buy* and *donate* to *us* a bus?'

'He's been impressed by the work you're doing over there.'

'Mr—'

'Fred, please. And you're?'

'Alice Turner.'

'Alice, why don't we work out a date here, agreeable to both of us, so Mr Hall can be sure to have the bus ready in time to bring the kiddies to the picnic?'

'Well . . .'

'Sunday after next, would that be good?'

171

No, as it turned out, that would be a little too soon, as Kelp had expected. Alice had board members to consult, and so on, and so on, but by the end of the conversation all ice was gone, and it was pretty clear that Monroe Hall was in one picnic with sixty kiddies and out one bus.

Kelp was just hanging up, pleased with himself – charitable work is always satisfying, particularly with somebody else's money – when Mrs Hall walked in, for the second time in ten minutes, but this time looking worried. 'Fred,' she said, 'have you seen Mr Hall?'

'He's out riding a horse,' Kelp told her. 'They left about fifteen minutes ago.'

'Well, no, he's not,' she said.

Kelp said, 'The instructor drove in with his own horse, fifteen minutes ago.'

'And left, just a few minutes later,' Mrs Hall said. 'When I couldn't find Monroe, and I didn't see any horse transporter out front, I called the gate, and they said the horse transporter left not five minutes after it arrived. They thought it was merely somebody bringing a horse on approval, for Monroe to possibly buy.'

'No, it was to learn to ride.'

'I know that,' Mrs Hall agreed. 'But the gate didn't know that. Nobody thought it necessary to tell the gate *why* a horse transporter was coming into the compound, so when it went right back out, they assumed it was merely a horse that Monroe had decided not to buy.'

Frowning, Kelp got up and went over to look out the front window. No horse transporter in front of the house. Nothing in front of the house, all the way down to the guardshack. 'Maybe,' he said, and turned around to look at Mrs Hall's worried face, 'he decided he wasn't ready to ride a horse after all, and sent the guy away. Or just didn't like the guy.'

'Then where did he go? Fred, where did my husband go?'

Kelp looked out the window. 'Well, he wouldn't leave the compound.'

'Not willingly.'

Kelp studied that worried face again, and this time he suspected his own face showed a little worry as well. 'Mrs Hall,' he said, 'nothing's *happened*, everything's *OK*.'

'Then where is Monroe?' she said. 'I've called all the other places around the compound where he might be, and no one's seen him. Not since the horse transporter came in and went right back out again.'

'But—' Kelp didn't like what Mrs Hall was thinking, because he knew it was the same as what he was thinking, and he wasn't ready for what they both were thinking. He was too *busy* for what they both were thinking.

Mrs Hall said, 'There are people who would like to get their hands on Monroe.'

This was true. Their hands and probably also their feet. Feeling discombobulated, not himself, not even Fred Blanchard, Kelp said, 'Couldn't he, uh, couldn't he be, uh . . .'

She was shaking her head. 'He isn't on the compound,' she said. 'He wouldn't leave, but he isn't here.'

'Uh . . .'

'Fred,' she said, 'call the police.'

What Kelp thought was, Wait a minute, you've got this backwards here! *I* don't call the police, *other* people call the police about *me*! What he said was, 'Yes, Mrs Hall.'

47

Dortmunder was furious. He was so mad he forgot to be surprised. A bunch of clowns in funny faces boil out of a horse carrier and lay rough hands on Dortmunder (and also on whatsisname, Hall) and throw him *into* the horse carrier, which smells exactly like a horse carrier, and he doesn't even take a second out to marvel, to say, Wow, looka that! Guys jumping out of a horse carrier, with weird stuff on their heads!

No. From instant one, he knew what was going on, and it made him so mad he could bite through a phone book. What he was thinking, and what he wanted to shout, was, 'Geddada here! This is *my* heist! You're busting into the middle of a serious operation here! Stand in line, take a check, wait your turn! I'm not the butler, I'm the car thief? Take a hike, will ya?'

Fortunately, he didn't shout any of that, because it might have queered the deal if he did, if the deal wasn't queered already. But even if he'd so forgotten himself as to voice his perfectly justified grievances, these people probably wouldn't have heard him, because they were all shouting already:

'Tie him up! Tie him up!'

'He is tied up!'

'The other one!'

'Oh, for God's—'

Rough hands grasped Dortmunder, followed by rough rope. It wasn't pitch black in here, but it was dim, and crowded, and filled with confusion. Also, the vehicle now bolted forward, which didn't help.

'Put a blindfold on him!'

'We didn't bring another one!'

'Who knew we were gonna get a *butler*?'

'I'm not—'

'Cover his mouth, we're coming to the guardshack! No, I've got this one, the other one!'

Rough hands spread over most of Dortmunder's head. He felt the trailer go over the speed bump at the guardshack, and then it swung leftward, throwing everybody around, and the *oofs* and *ows* this led to were

174

music to Dortmunder's ears. Also, it meant all those hands left his head in order to try to break various falls in various directions.

'We gotta *blindfold* this guy!'

'Bu – uhh – uhh, put that paper bag over his head.'

'He'll see me when I take it off!'

'Turn him around. Turn him around!'

Several people in this crowded dark space with the horse blanket wafting gently and odoriferously at the back, like the curtain before a very bad play will start, grabbed Dortmunder's arms and neck and rib cage and turned him to face away from the curtain. Now he couldn't see anybody clearly, not that he wanted to, but only the blank front wall, beyond which the truck would be rolling along through Pennsylvania.

A paper bag came down over his head. All the hands let him go. He started to turn.

'Put the eyeholes at the *back*!'

'Oh! Right!'

Hands grabbed him again, turned him again, the paper bag was turned – now they're gonna give me a paper cut on the neck, he thought, but they didn't – and then he was released again, just in time to go flying when the trailer took another sharp turn.

Apparently everybody went flying; more satisfying *oofs* and *ows*. Dortmunder hit more people than wall, which was also good. Then one of the calmer voices said, 'We have to sit down. Everybody sit down. Help those two sit down.'

More hands, encouraging him downward. Thump, he sat on a floor he doubted he'd want to sit on if he could see it. Somebody shoved him and poked him, and there he was with a wall behind him. He braced his back against it.

They were all settling down now, calming down. The voice that had suggested they get off their feet now said, 'We've got about two hours' drive ahead of us, so you two try to get comfortable, but don't think you're going to pull anything, because you're not.'

'I know that voice.' That was Monroe Hall talking.

Absolute silence. Dortmunder listened, and then heard whispering, and then another voice said, 'No, you don't.'

'Not you,' Hall said. 'The other one.'

'There is no other one,' the new voice said. 'There's only me.'

Clowns, Dortmunder thought. I knew they were clowns to begin with. And here they are messing up something I had put together and planned and worked for and even learned how to be a butler so I could pull it off, and *these* bozos come along.

I'm gonna get them for this, Dortmunder promised himself. He didn't care what happened to Hall, they'd planned on dealing with the insurance company anyway and still would, but these guys couldn't just waltz into a perfectly planned and smoothly functioning heist and expect to get away with it. I'm gonna get them, he vowed. Just as soon as we get somewhere and I'm not all tied up and no paper bag over my head and it's not five against one, whenever that happens, and it's gonna happen, I'm gonna get them. Just wait.

48

Tiny wasn't supposed to be on duty till midnight, but now everything was out of whack. Chuck Yancey phoned him at two twenty-five and said, 'We got an emergency here. Put on your uniform and come on down.'

'I need transport.'

Sigh. 'Mort'll be there in five minutes.'

So five minutes later, when Mort Pessle arrived at Chester's old house, Tiny was in the brown uniform, in which he looked mostly like a bungalow. He got into the backseat, and along the way Mort told him the situation: 'They got Mr Hall.'

'Who got Mr Hall?'

'Don't know yet. They were in a horse trailer.'

Tiny wasn't loving this conversation. '*Who* was in a horse trailer?'

'Whoever took Mr Hall,' Mort said. 'That's how they got him off the compound.'

'In a horse trailer.'

'Chuck's really mad,' Mort said, meaning Chuck Yancey, the boss of security.

And that was true enough. When Tiny walked into the office, Mort having gone back to duty on the gate, Heck Fiedler stood to one side, looking scared and trying to look invisible, while Chuck Yancey paced back and forth like a very irritated tiger. Glaring at Tiny, he said, 'This happened on *my* watch.'

Tiny nodded. 'Mort says they used a horse trailer.'

'Goddamn horse trailer.' Yancey punched the air and kept on pacing. 'Nobody *looked* inside it.'

Sounding as scared as he looked, Heck said, 'There was a horse in it. You could see the horse.'

'You could see the horse's ass,' Chuck snarled at him. 'You could see *that*, could you? Recognize *that*, did you? Old home week, huh? Like looking in a mirror, was it?'

To maybe take a little heat off Heck, who probably shouldn't have spoken up, Tiny said, 'What's a horse trailer doing in here?'

177

Chuck turned his glare on Tiny, who didn't mind. 'Hall *asked* for it,' he announced. 'Called down yesterday, says a horse is coming, in a trailer, with a guy named—' Glare at Heck again. 'What was that name?'

'Jay Gilly,' Heck said, and blinked a lot.

'*That'll* turn out to be a fake,' Chuck snarled, and said to Tiny, 'Hall says it's coming, let it through. It came, it was let through. It went back out again. Fifteen minutes later, *Mrs* Hall calls down, "Where's my husband?" Nobody knows. Guess who didn't look in the horse trailer, going in *or* out.'

'We never search anything going out,' Heck said, not yet having learned the wisdom of silence.

He got the full Yancey glare this time. 'Some of us,' Chuck said, spacing his words, 'don't bother to search things going *in* either.'

Tiny said, 'What do you think they'd of found?'

'Men,' Chuck said. 'There had to be people hidden in the trailer, to grab Hall when he came out to look at the horse, and hold him down while they drove past Heck here. Did you *wave*, Heck?'

Heck might actually have answered that question, but Tiny said, 'Well, if they took him away, that means at least they didn't wanna kill him.'

'Or maybe,' Chuck said, 'they wanted time to torture him first.'

'That's a possibility.'

'On *my* watch,' Chuck said. 'I thought I was better than that.'

'You *are*, Chief,' the unquenchable Heck said. 'It was my screw-up, and I feel awful about it.'

Chuck gave him a long smoldering look. 'I'm thinking,' he said, 'of some way to make you feel worse.'

Tiny said, 'You wanted me down here. What am I supposed to do?'

'We're waiting,' Chuck told him, 'for the cops to get here.'

'Oh,' Tiny said. 'You called the cops?'

Chuck gave him the kind of look he'd been giving Heck. 'Who else you gonna call?' he demanded. 'Miss Marple?'

'Not unless we find a body,' Tiny said, and Chuck could be seen to gather himself for an intemperate response when Kelp walked in.

Which took Tiny a few seconds to realize. Somehow, this was a different Kelp. The suit and tie were part of it, but there was something in the stance as well, and the look in his eye. This was a Kelp who'd received a battlefield commission, who was suddenly an officer and a gentleman, and who was feeling pretty good about the fact.

'Well, Captain Yancey,' Kelp said, 'this is a fine mess, isn't it?'

'Not captain any more, Mr Blanchard,' Chuck said, though it was clear he liked the title. 'Those were my army days.'

'You earned the rank, Captain,' Kelp assured him. 'It's yours forever.'

'Well, thank you, Mr Blanchard,' Chuck said. All his fury seemed to have drained away. Even Heck was looking less scared. 'What's the word from the main house?'

'Well,' Kelp said, in his blandest and most deadpan manner, 'it seems they took Rumsey, too.'

Chuck looked quizzical. 'Rumsey?'

'The butler,' Kelp explained.

Tiny couldn't help it; he laughed. Everybody looked at him in surprise. Chuck, as though he might get angry again, said, 'Swope? You find something funny?'

'The butler,' Tiny said, and did not wipe the smirk off his face. 'He's gonna be mad,' he said.

49

'The question is,' Lieutenant Orville said, 'is the butler in on it?'

Lieutenant Wooster cocked his head, like a very bright spaniel: 'You think the butler did it?'

'It's been known to happen.' Liking the phrase, Lieutenant Orville said it again: 'Known to happen.'

The two lieutenants had taken over the missing Monroe Hall's office as their investigation HQ, since obviously Monroe Hall had no present need of it. Orville and Wooster were CID, Criminal Investigation Division, and this case was their baby, nor were they unmindful of the potential in it for themselves. Hall after all was a very famous man, some might even say a very infamous man. Clustered outside the compound already, partially blocking traffic on the county road, barely an hour after the event, were a dozen TV vans, just itching to broadcast Lieutenant Orville's manly face and professional manner worldwide via satellite as he reported on progress in the case (Wooster was the sidekick, and knew it), which Orville would do just as soon as he had the merest sliver of progress, or something that could be made to look like progress, to report.

In the meantime, forces were gathering, positions were being manned (or more likely personed), and the parameters of the situation were being – you know it – staked out. Lieutenant Orville was a fellow with a literary bent, which meant he'd read a lot of Sherlock Holmes and Perry Mason and *87th Precinct* (damn, those boys were good), and which *also* meant he had trained himself to have a keen and analytical mind, and to leap on every anomaly that reared its head, of which, in the present case, the anomaly was the butler.

Why kidnap Hall? That much was obvious. Hall was incredibly wealthy, and would be worth a lot in ransom. A fortune in ransom. But what the hell was the butler worth? Why snatch the butler?

This question had led Lieutenant Orville to a further thought. What if the butler had *not* been snatched? What if the butler had gone willingly? What if, in fact, the butler had been a coconspirator from the very beginning? What if he were not a victim but a perpetrator? That would put a different light on the situation, would it not? It would.

'Mmm,' Lieutenant Orville said. 'What do we know about this butler?'

It is the sidekick's job to assemble the data and lay it before his chief. Now Lieutenant Wooster withdrew his notebook from his jacket pocket, flipped a few pages, and read, 'John Howard Rumsey. Hired day before yesterday.'

'Oh *ho*. The plot,' Orville said, 'thickens.'

'There's a funny little cluster of hiring two days ago, in fact,' Lieutenant Wooster said. 'The butler. A chauffeur. A private secretary. A—'

'Private secretary,' Lieutenant Orville said. 'Is that the geek we threw outa this room?'

'Fredric Eustace Blanchard,' Lieutenant Wooster read. 'Yep, that's him. And the fourth one was a new guard for the security team here.'

'Security, eh?' Lieutenant Orville permitted himself a little pitying smile. 'And I suppose none of these people had ever laid eyes on one another before two days ago.'

'Well, a couple of them,' Lieutenant Wooster agreed. 'But the butler and the secretary, Blanchard, they'd both worked together at the Vostkojek embassy before this.'

'At the what?'

'Vostkojek embassy. It's a country in Europe, it's an embassy in Washington.'

'Well, which is it?'

Lieutenant Wooster thought that over. 'An embassy in Washington.'

'And these two worked there, did they? How come they left?'

'The story is, the ambassador was assassinated.'

Lieutenant Orville sat up straighter. 'What? Murdered?'

'That's right.' Lieutenant Wooster consulted his notebook. 'Apparently, the new ambassador fired everybody and brought all new people in. So Rumsey and Blanchard came to work here.'

'Pretty long way from Washington.'

'Yes, sir.'

'How'd they happen to wind up here, do we know?'

'They were both sent over by an employment agency, Cooper Placement Service. In fact, all four were.'

'Oh, were they? Bob, I think it might profit us to take a little look at this Cooper Placement Service.'

'Check.'

'Shake the tree a little,' Lieutenant Orville said, doing a tree-shaking gesture. 'See what falls out.'

'Check.'

'In the meantime,' Lieutenant Orville said, 'let's bring this faggot Blanchard in, see what he's got to say for himself and his pal the butler.'

'Check.'

Lieutenant Orville had taken an instinctive dislike to the secretary, Blanchard. He trusted his instincts, mostly because they were all he had, and when Lieutenant Wooster brought the fellow in to be questioned, Orville felt it again, that immediate distrust.

Look at him, in his natty suit and tie, that shit-eating grin, that politeness that was just a little too polite, so that it was more like an insult than real politeness. There were criminals Lieutenant Orville had met who had that same slick surface, smooth and oily, covering something completely different underneath. It was as though Fredric Eustace Blanchard were not Fredric Eustace Blanchard at all, not a private secretary, not in any way the person he seemed to be, as though there were another person hidden down inside there, who would be very interesting for Lieutenant Orville if he could only winkle him out.

Well, that was unlikely, and probably not useful to the investigation at hand, so once Blanchard was settled at his ease beside Monroe Hall's big double-sided desk, with Lieutenant Orville in Hall's seat behind it and Lieutenant Wooster ready to take copious notes at what had been Blanchard's desk, Orville went directly to what he thought was the point: 'Tell me about the butler.'

'John Rumsey,' Blanchard agreed, and smiled for no reason Lieutenant Orville could see, and said, 'Worked with him down in D.C.'

'Where your employer was murdered,' Lieutenant Orville pointed out. 'Yours and Rumsey's.'

'That was sad,' Blanchard said, but went on grinning.

'Were you and Rumsey questioned in the case?'

'Not us,' Blanchard said.

'Oh?' Lieutenant Orville registered surprise. 'Why's that?'

'Well,' Blanchard said, 'Ambassador Chk was killed in Novi Glad.'

'And where,' Lieutenant Orville pursued, 'is Novi Glad?'

'It's the capital of Vostkojek.' Blanchard waved a hand to indicate someplace far away. 'About five thousand miles from D.C. Past an ocean, and most of Europe.'

'And where were *you* when this ambassador was killed?'

'In D.C.'

Beginning to realize this was not after all going to be a fruitful line of inquiry, Lieutenant Orville segued out of it with one final question: 'Did they ever catch the perpetrator?'

'Oh, sure,' Blanchard said. 'It was political. He was a Bigendian.'

No. No deeper into that blind alley. 'And where were *you* this morning,' Lieutenant Orville abruptly demanded, 'when your *latest* employer was being kidnapped?'

Blanchard pointed at Wooster. 'At my desk there.'

'And what were you doing?'

'Arranging charitable affairs for Mr Hall to take part in.'

Unbelieving, Lieutenant Orville said, 'Monroe Hall needs *charity*?'

'Oh, no,' Blanchard said. 'He *gives* charity. His reputation took a bad hit a little while ago, and we've started the rehabilitation.'

Lieutenant Wooster mildly said, 'My uncle lost everything in the SomniTech affair, everything.'

Turning that bland smile toward Wooster, Blanchard said, 'But I'm sure the family helped out.'

Lieutenant Wooster's mouth opened. He looked completely blank, as though the plug had been pulled on his brain.

Lieutenant Orville said, 'So you were arranging charity this morning. Who with, and where did that person go?'

'A lot of people, by phone.' Blanchard pointed at the immobilized Wooster again. 'The phone log is by your partner's left hand there.'

'Bob,' Lieutenant Orville said, 'let's see that phone log.'

Popping back to life, Lieutenant Wooster picked up the black ledger book, carried it to Lieutenant Orville, and went back to his seat. Lieutenant Orville scowled at the book. When he leafed its pages, they were all there: names, numbers, times. There was no doubt it would all check out.

Slippery son of a bitch, this Blanchard. If only I could get under the surface, Lieutenant Orville told himself. There's *something* going on down in there. He said, 'Until further notice, I don't want you leaving the property.'

Blanchard actually laughed. 'Not me,' he said. 'I wouldn't skip this for a million dollars.'

50

Mark told himself there was no point in having the jitters, not now, not when it was all over. Or at least this part was all over. Monroe Hall had been successfully extricated from his compound – with butler, but never mind – and the two of them, freed of their blindfolds and ropes, were now snugly tucked into separate locked upstairs bedrooms with sheets of plywood over the windows. Mark and Os and the union men were gathered in the main living room, removing dustsheets from the sofas and chairs, making cozy. Os had already filled the refrigerator with beer, some of which had been brought out for a victory toast. So there was no reason any more, if there had ever been, for Mark to have the jitters. And yet, he did.

This feeling of edginess, of nerves unstrung, had started just before the kidnapping. He'd been fine on the trip to borrow the horse and its carrier; he'd been fine getting into the carrier with the others to leave the driving to Mac; he'd even been fine when they'd made it past the guardshack.

When it had started, the butterflies, the twitchiness, the body-out-of-control feeling, was when he put on the ski mask. That awful hot wool against his face had been a kind of shock, a reality check.

This is real! he told himself. We aren't just talking about this, we're *doing* this. Looking around at the others, clustered in the swaying carrier in the semidark, looking at the ridiculous ways they'd chosen to conceal their faces, he'd suddenly thought, We're crazy. People don't do this sort of thing. Why don't we just forget Monroe Hall? Why don't we get over it, get on with our lives?

Well, that was a hell of a moment to come up with such an idea, while driving from the guardshack to Monroe Hall's home. Looking around the interior of the carrier, it had seemed to Mark that everybody else was calm, assured, confident, ready, knowing exactly the dangers and their own skills, like paratroopers clustered at the open doorway of the airplane.

It was only when they'd dashed out of the carrier and laid hands on Hall himself – and the butler, but never mind – and the others had all started shouting like madmen, yelling orders at one another and so on, that he'd realized they were all having the jitters, too. It was not just him. And that knowledge, plus the success of the operation, had calmed him considerably, until Monroe Hall recognized his voice.

That was the moment. That was the moment his mouth opened, his throat closed, his eyes bulged, his heart contracted, and his hands began to shake like fringe on a cowgirl. He had been a wreck ever since, silent except when he had to whisper something to Buddy to say to Hall, and not even Hall's current residence in a locked room nor the presence in his own hand of a full and frosty beer had done much to make him calm.

Recognized my voice!

'Well,' Mac said, dropping into a sofa like a relief package without quite spilling beer, then drinking beer, 'that was one hell of a drive.'

'You did it great,' Buddy assured him.

'We acted, I would say,' Os informed them all, very nearly smiling, 'in the finest traditions of *Mission: Impossible.*'

Mark had things he felt he could say at that moment, but somehow the words didn't come. Somehow, his mouth didn't open.

Recognized my voice!

Buddy said, 'What's the program now?'

'We let Hall go without dinner,' Os said. 'It's four-thirty now. We'll have our own dinner—'

Ace said, 'What about the butler?'

Everybody looked at him. Os said, '*What* about the butler?'

'Does he go without dinner, too?'

'Oh. No, no,' Os said, 'we'll feed him. Soups and things, with plastic spoons and things, so he can't get any ideas.'

'He didn't strike me,' Buddy said, 'as a guy who'd get a lot of ideas.'

'True,' Os said. 'But one can never be too careful.'

'Sure,' Buddy said. 'But after we've had our dinner and the butler's had his dinner and Hall hasn't had his dinner, then what?'

'At around, say, eleven tonight,' Os said, 'we'll go in, all of us properly masked, and we'll lay out the situation to Hall – I'm afraid you'll have to go on doing the talking, Buddy.'

'Make me out a speech. Write it down.'

'Mark will do that,' Os said. 'Won't you, Mark?'

Mark nodded, a bit afraid the gesture would make his head roll off. It didn't, and he stopped nodding.

Os said to the others, 'My expectation is, Hall will refuse tonight. So we'll switch off the electricity to that room and let him think it over in pitch black darkness for tonight. Tomorrow morning, we'll bring up a big breakfast, full of good things to see and smell, like bacon and waffles and maple syrup and orange juice and coffee, and we'll ask him if he's ready to cooperate. My guess is, he'll say no, so we'll take the breakfast away again.

'Good,' Ace said.

'I've got a problem here,' Mac said.

They all gave him their attention. Mildly, Os said, 'Yes, Mac?'

'I got a home and a family,' Mac said.

'That's right,' Buddy said, as though surprised at the reminder.

'In the first place,' Mac said, 'nobody except us in this room knows we're the ones doing what we're doing.'

'As it should be,' Os said, and Mark nodded.

'So we gotta live normal lives,' Mac pointed out. 'We can't be here twenty-four hours a day.'

'I see your point,' Os said. 'I do think it important we make a show of strength tonight. Could you three phone your families and make excuses, why you won't be home till midnight?'

'Eleven,' Ace said. 'Henrietta will go along with bowling or whatever, but the curfew's eleven.'

'Me, too,' Buddy said.

Os said, 'Then we merely move the schedule forward, talk to Hall at nine, then come back tomorrow. No one needs to stay here overnight, though actually I will. Mark and I will return horse and trailer, then I'll come back here. In fact, I do have a right to be here, and I can keep watch.'

Buddy said, 'The idea was, Mark was gonna write out the demands for me to read, because Hall recognized his voice, right?'

'Exactly,' Os said, and Mark shuddered.

Mac said, 'What? Hall knows it's Mark?'

'No,' Os said. 'He knows he knows the voice, that's all. That's why he won't hear Mark any more, and probably shouldn't hear me, either.'

Buddy said, 'My idea is, why don't we just hand him the piece of paper, and he doesn't hear anybody's voice? That'd be scarier, wouldn't it?'

Mac grinned. 'Silent masked men,' he said, 'with a note.'

They all liked that. 'I'll get some more beer,' Ace said, getting to his feet. 'Then make my call.'

51

They sat around another terrific old-country dinner from the kitchens of Tiny, but nobody felt much like eating. 'Everything's completely outa whack,' Tiny commented, frowning at his food.

'It looks to me,' Stan said, 'like we're gonna find out if these IDs we got from whatsisname are gonna stand up.'

Kelp said, 'I've been trying not to think about that.'

'If only we could get outa here,' Stan said.

Well, forget that. Not only did the law have the entire compound shut down tight, but the media was out there like seven-year locusts, just waiting to photograph and question anything that moved. Up till now, the only upside was that three reporters so far had been hospitalized after getting a little too close to the electric fence; apparently, it did pack a mean wallop.

'And tonight,' Tiny grumbled, 'we were gonna be outa here. I'm gonna be alone on the gate, the coast is clear, we're home free. We drive the cars out, we come back and drive the rest of them out, stash them in the place, go home. Josie's expecting me in the morning.'

'Well, now she isn't,' Kelp said. 'This kidnapping thing is all over the news.'

'I'm getting very irritated,' Tiny said.

Stan said, 'You know, I'm beginning to realize. That electric fence is just as good at keeping people in as it is keeping people out.'

'We all noticed that,' Tiny told him.

Kelp said, 'I wonder how John's doing.'

Tiny snorted. 'Dortmunder? Don't worry about Dortmunder, worry about us. He's outa here.'

187

52

I gotta get outa here, Dortmunder thought. But how? This was a kind of a nice bedroom – guestroom, he figured, with its own small attached bath – but it wasn't rich with forms of egress, and yet, Dortmunder didn't want to be in it any more.

He really needed to get out of here. The car heist was supposed to go down tonight; his life as a butler was supposed to be finished by now. But here he was in this *room*.

I should be able to beat this thing, he told himself. What I *do* is get in and out of places. So this is a place, and I've got to get out of it.

What do we have in here? What are the possibilities? Like most bedrooms, this one had a door that opened inward from the hall, so the hinges were on this side, and that should mean he could pop the pins out of the hinges and yank the door open that way. Worry about what was on the other side of the door when *he* was on the other side of the door.

The only trouble was, these hinges had been painted so many times over so many years they were absolutely stuck solid. Maybe if he had pliers, wrenches, hammers, probably a hacksaw, he could make some headway with these hinges, but not with bare fingers. Not after bending one fingernail a little too far back.

So what else do we have here? Two windows, both goodsized, and one smaller window in the bathroom, and all three of them sealed up with plywood attached on the outside. Push on that plywood, nothing happens. Punch it with the heel of your hand, then you get to walk around the next five minutes saying, 'Ow, ow, ow,' with your right hand stuck in your left armpit.

What else? Anything else? The door is locked, with a kind of ordinary old-fashioned lock, the kind where you can bend down or kneel down and look through the keyhole and see some length of wall and another closed door across the way. Maybe Hall was in there. Anyway, there's no getting at this lock in this door, just no way.

And yet, somebody was inserting a key, he could hear it, inserting the key, and turning it.

188

Damn! If he'd known somebody was coming, he could have positioned himself behind the door with a chair poised over his head. Now, it was all happening too quick: key in lock, knob turn, door open.

Oh. Five of them, all in those different kinds of masks. The one with the bandanna around his nose and mouth like a bankrobber in the old West must have been the driver on the trip here. Anyway, a chair was not going to deal with all five of these people, no matter how much advance warning he got.

'Listen,' he said, as they tromped in, 'I gotta get outa here.'

One of them handed him a piece of paper. What? What's this? A handwritten note? Don't these people speak English? Well, of course they do, he'd heard them in the trailer.

Two others were putting things on the low dresser. A sandwich, on a paper plate. Soup in a waxed-paper cup. Ice cream in another waxed-paper cup, with a plastic spoon. They nodded at him, pointed at the food, and turned away.

'Hey,' he said. 'Hey, wait a minute. *I'm* not the one you want, what's the edge in holding on to *me* like this?'

They weren't here to talk. They left, closed the door, turned the key in the lock, took the key away with them.

Damn those people! How could they louse things up so—

What time was it, anyway? He couldn't see out, he didn't have a watch, he had no way to tell if it was day or night or what it was. But the sandwich and the soup and the ice cream suggested – and his stomach was going along with the idea – that it was dinnertime. How long did they figure to keep him in here?

Maybe the note would give him a clue. Opening it, he read:

Dear Mr Butler,

We're sorry we had to bring you along. It was not in the original plan. We need your employer's agreement to a business situation. The discussions may take some little time, and unfortunately we will not be able to release you until their conclusion. In the meantime, we will provide you with food and shelter. We can bring you books or magazines, if you like, or possibly a television set, though the reception in these mountains isn't very good, and of course we can't let you have access to the satellite. If you have any requests for items we could bring you, write them on the back of this note and slip it under the door. We feel we should not engage in conversation with you. Again, please accept our apologies for including you in this operation. We all hope it will be over soon. In the meantime, sit back, relax, and enjoy your unexpected vacation.

Your Friends

Meatheads. Eating the sandwich – ham and swiss on sourdough, with honey mustard and mayo, not bad – Dortmunder brooded at the room, this solid cube he was shut inside.

How?

53

When he heard the *clink* of his pen as it hit the floor, Monroe Hall immediately dropped the metal rod onto the windowsill against the plywood, slid the window shut, and was halfway across the room, glaring, when the door opened and the five buffoons in their varied masks marched in.

'What now?' he demanded, hoping one of them would talk. He needed to hear that voice again, the one he knew damn well he'd heard somewhere in the past. Some unpleasant association, but that didn't help much; most of his conversations the last few years had involved unpleasant associations.

But they didn't speak, none of them. The one wearing a Frankenstein head carried a laptop, and the one in the green ski mask with the elks carried a folded sheet of paper, which he extended toward Hall.

Hall backed away, not taking the paper. 'You people are in a great deal of trouble,' he said. 'You can make it easier for yourselves if you release me now. The longer this goes on—'

Ski Mask moved forward, waving the piece of paper in his face, insisting he take it. Hall folded his arms. 'If you want to talk to me,' he said, 'talk to me.'

In the background, Frankenstein had started a whispered conversation with Bandit's Bandanna, who nodded. So did Paper Bag and the Lone Ranger. Hall, trying to keep an eye on everybody at once while ignoring the sheet of paper, watched Frankenstein and Bandit come this way, passing to either side of Ski Mask. Abruptly, they grabbed Hall's arms, ran him backward, and forced him to sit down hard on the bed.

'What are you— What are you *doing*?'

Frankenstein and Bandit stood to each side of him, to hold him in place. Ski Mask stepped forward, opened the piece of paper, and held it in front of Hall's face.

Hall knew when to quit. 'All right,' he said. 'All *right*, I'll read it. You can let me go, I'll read it by myself.'

So they let him go. Ski Mask handed him the paper, and he read:

191

You will access your offshore accounts. You will transfer cash to other accounts we will describe to you. When the transactions are complete, we will release you.

'Not a chance.'

He glared at them, and they stood in a semicircle, observing him, waiting to see what he would do. He said, 'I will not, now or ever, while you people hold on to me, access anything except nine-one-one. You people must have a very low opinion of me, I must say.'

They looked at one another. A couple of them shrugged, and then they all turned away and moved toward the door.

Hall popped to his feet. 'Make your own money!' he shouted at their backs. 'Don't come sniveling to *me!*'

Out the door they went, carrying the laptop, shut the door, and the key turned in the lock.

Immediately Hall went looking for his pen, which he found against the baseboard, where the door had pushed it when they came in. It was his warning system. Once again, the same as last time, he inserted the end of the pen into the keyhole, balancing it there just far enough inside not to fall back out again, and also far enough inside to be nudged by a key as it was inserted from the other side. The idea had served him well already, and he was sure it would serve him well again.

Alarm system in place, he turned back to the window he'd been working at, and all at once the lights went out.

Oh, yes? In the dark, he made his way around the bed and found the bathroom doorway, and tried the lightswitch there, and that was also out.

It was really pitch black in here, and of course it would go on being pitch black, night and day. He could see their idea. They had no intention of feeding him, of course, and they would leave him alone here in the dark, making their demands until hunger and sense deprivation should force him to go along.

Well, it wasn't going to happen. Hall had triumphed over tougher adversaries than these amateurs. He didn't need light, not for what he had to do.

In the dark, he moved along the wall until he found the window he wanted. He opened it, reached in, and found the rod where he'd dropped it. This was a strong piece of metal about eight inches long, one inch wide, and a quarter inch thick. It had been part of the flushing system in his toilet. He'd have to flush by hand now, but that wouldn't be a problem. Not for as long as he intended to be in this place.

He'd be happier with a larger tougher prybar, but this one would do. Slowly, patiently, relentlesly, he prodded the space between the window frame and the plywood sheeting. Infinitesimally, he could feel it give way. He had no idea how much longer he worked on it, but then all at once he became aware of a difference in the air, a hint of smell, a sense of movement.

Outside air. It was a start.

54

It was panic that saved Flip's bacon, panic and nothing more.

The trouble was, it had never occurred to him that once 'Jay Gilly' kidnapped Monroe Hall, the person who had *recommended* Jay Gilly to Monroe Hall would attract the attention of the police. After all, *he* wouldn't be anywhere around the Hall compound when the deed was done, but would have a solid alibi, being miles away with a client. Thus, it had come as a real shock when the police came beating on his office door at seven that evening. A shock that should have ruined him but that ultimately saved his bacon.

He was in his office at that hour to videotape his stepboard routine for the exercise DVD he planned eventually to release. All at once, a pounding at the door to the front office threw him off his stride, and initially just made him angry. Switching off the camera, fuming, ready to give *somebody* a good tongue-lashing, he stomped through from the gym to the office, yanked open the door, glared at the two men in suits and ties standing there, and barked, '*Now* what?'

They both held up small leather folders with shiny things inside. 'Police,' one of them said. 'Alphonse Morriscone?'

He almost fainted. He nearly fell down in an absolute swoon. He never sweat while doing his routines, but now great beads of perspiration popped out all over him like a tapioca pudding, and he said, 'Puh-puh-puh—'

'We'd like a moment of your time,' the same man said, but he said it in a very disagreeable threatening manner, as though what he *really* were saying was, 'You're under arrest and you'll never be a free man again.'

'Well, I— I don't see— I mean, why would—'

'If we could step inside, Mr Morriscone.'

'I, I, I—'

Somehow, they were inside. Somehow, they were all seated in his office, the talking policeman behind the desk, Flip in the client's chair facing him, the other policeman in the folding chair from the closet. The talking policeman said, 'Tell me about Jay Gilly, Mr Morriscone.'

'Oh, my God!'

They both looked alert. 'Yes, Mr Morriscone?'

'I-I-who?'

'You heard us, Mr Morriscone.'

Deny everything. No, it's too late, they already know. Deny everything anyway. 'I don't, I don't know.'

'You don't know what, Mr Morriscone?'

'Jay Gilly.' Sweat ran into Flip's eyes, but he was afraid to blink.

'Is that so?' The talking policeman smirked. 'And yet somehow,' he said, 'you introduced Jay Gilly to a client of yours, didn't you? Didn't you?'

'Oh, my God.' Too late to deny everything. 'Oh, Mr Hall.'

'You remember now, do you? You don't know Jay Gilly, and yet somehow you introduced him to Monroe Hall, didn't you? Didn't you, Mr Morriscone?'

'I-I-forget.'

'You *forget?*'

'Where I met him,' Flip blurted, as though that's the question he'd been asked, because in the shaken kaleidoscope that his brain had become, he knew that was the question he *would* be asked, and that he didn't have an answer for it. In his mind, he skittered back and forth like a rabbit trying to elude an oncoming truck, trying to figure out how it was that he knew Jay Gilly, and failing to find an answer he could present. Not through a client – the client would deny it. Not through anybody. So, in his panic and desperation, he answered the question that would destroy him before they got around to asking it.

'You forget where you *met* him?'

'He was just— I mean, I don't know, we just talked, and when it was on the news, Mr Hall, I thought, Oh, the *police* are gonna get me!'

Both policemen looked very interested at that. '*Get* you, Mr Morriscone?'

'Because I forget where I met him.' Flip waved arms around, to indicate just how large the planet Earth actually was, with so many places in it where a person might meet a person. 'I mean, we just talked, he just talked to me, he told me he trained people to ride horses, and I said, *Oh, I know somebody who needs somebody to teach him how to ride a horse,* and he said he could do it but he'd bring his own horse, and I said I'll call Mr Hall, and he said fine, and I called Mr Hall, and he said fine, I mean Mr Hall said fine, and I told this Mr Gilly, and he said fine, and I thought no more about it, and then it was on the news, and I thought, Oh, they'll want to know why I talked to Mr Hall about that man, and where did I meet him, and everything about him, and I don't *know* anything, and they're going to find out I'm mad at Mr Hall, and they'll think I did it on purpose, and they'll lock me up—'

'*Mad* at Mr Hall?'

'Oh! No-no-no, I'm not mad at Mr Hall, did I say I was mad at Mr Hall? Well, I used to be mad at Mr Hall, just a little bit mad at Mr Hall, but I got over all that, I mean I'm not mad at him *now*, that was just—'

'*Why* were you mad at Mr Hall?'

Oh, why did I tell them that? Flip demanded of himself. Now I have to tell them I'm a tax cheat, and they'll be convinced I'm a hardened criminal, and—'

'Mr Morriscone?'

My mouth has been open a long time, Flip pointed out to himself, and shut it, then opened it to say, 'He got me into a little trouble with the IRS. I didn't know he was going to report what he paid me, so *I* didn't report what he paid me, and that's the only time in my life I ever did anything like that, and I'll never do it again, and in fact, after I stopped being mad at Mr Hall, and never was really *mad* at him, but then after that I was actually *grateful* to Mr Hall, because I learned my lesson, believe you me.'

He didn't want to stop talking, it seemed to hold the inevitable at bay if he kept talking, but all at once he ran out of things to say, and so he just sat there. His mouth was open again. He thought, should I tell them about the time I cheated on the test in high school? No, they don't want to know about that, they want to know all about Jay Gilly, and I *can't* tell them about that, somehow I have to *not* tell them about Jay Gilly, not the truth, oh, no, not the truth. His mouth closed.

Meanwhile, the talking policeman nodded thoughtfully a while, then turned to the other one and said, 'You see what this is, Bob.'

'I think I do,' the other one said, Flip hearing his voice for the first time.

'They talked to people who knew Hall,' the talking policeman said, 'looking for that weak link.'

'That's the story, all right.'

Weak link? Do they mean *me*?

'Probably met in a bar somewhere,' the talking policeman said, 'something like that.'

I don't go to bars! Fortunately, Flip didn't actually say that, or anything else.

'So this is another blind alley,' the talking policeman said, 'like that foreign embassy.'

Foreign embassy?

'Sure looks like it.'

The talking policeman stood, and then the other policeman stood. The talking policeman said to Flip, 'Well, thank you for your time, Mr Morriscone. Here's my card.'

They're not going to arrest me! Fortunately again, Flip also left that sentence unspoken. Instead, he got to his quaking feet, took the card without looking at it, and waited for whatever would happen next.

'If you remember anything else, give us a call.'

'Oh, yes.'

'And when we get this Jay Gilly, and you can count on it, we will get him—'

'Oh, yes.'

'—we'll ask you to come in to identify him for us.'

'Oh, yes.'

'We'll let ourselves out.'

They did, Flip staring at them in wonder the whole time. It was true! They were letting him go! They weren't suspicious! He was a weak link!

He locked the door after them, hurried back through the gym to the changing room, and took a long, long shower. Partway through, he took off his clothes.

55

The fact is, almost everybody who uses a power drill releases the trigger just a second too late. You or I, if we drive a long thin galvanized screw through three-quarter inch of plywood into a hardwood window frame, will keep going that tiny bit too long after the job is done, to leave the plywood around the screwhead dimpled, dented, with some few of the fibers of the plywood already torn.

This is what had happened at the window where Monroe Hall, with all the obsessive patience and single-mindedness brought on by total darkness, struggled to lever a corner of plywood away from the window frame. The first part was the hardest, as that first tiny damage to the plywood caused by the power drill was worried and pressed, twisted and stressed. More fibers snapped. Air from the outside world seeped into Hall's prison room, and then more air.

None of the screws pulled out of the window frame. They were too deeply embedded in solid wood for that. Instead, slowly, relentlessly, they were pulled *through* the plywood, leaving not quite an inch of sharp-edged screw jutting from the frame, plus a small Etna of splinters that exploded inward from the plywood.

The first to come loose was at the lower-left corner of the window, and then the one a foot above that, and then the one a foot to the right along the windowsill, and then back to the next-higher screw on the side. When the fifth one popped, along the windowsill, he could force one end of his bar into the corner and push the other end up along the complaining face of the plywood until the bar was perpendicular to the building and the plywood was arched backward like a dog-eared page in a book.

Was this enough? Every time he reached over the sill, it seemed, his hands hit either the cutting edges of the exposed screws or the nasty points of the shredded plywood fibers. Also, the tapered opening was still mostly too narrow to permit him to slide through.

So, no; he had to do more. His fingers were bleeding from the work, and the backs of his hands were bleeding from the plywood shreds, but fortunately in the darkness he couldn't see any of that, though he could certainly feel it. After a very brief pause to breathe in the fresh air, he pulled his lever back in and went on to finish the job of freeing the plywood all across the bottom sill. And when he wedged the lever in to make the dog-ear this time, there was much more room to maneuver.

He remembered there'd been an armchair in the room. Stumbling around, cautious but hitting into anonymous things anyway, he found the chair at last and dragged it over to the window. Standing on it, he confronted an opening he really still couldn't see, though there was by now the faintest hint of light from the outside world, and he decided the way to go out was feet first.

It was very awkward, holding on to the window frame, the window, the chairback, the sill, while he maneuvered himself around, but finally there he was, seated on the sill, legs outside the house, nose against the window glass. He had no idea what was outside or how far away the ground might be, but did that matter? No, it did not.

Where were those jutting screws? He felt under his thighs, and there they were, too close together to avoid completely. He'd just have to slide out above them somehow.

Grasping the bottom of the open window with both hands, he leaned far backward into the darkness of the room, then began to hunch himself forward, first on left buttock, then on right, while pulling with the strength of his forearms, upturned hands gripping the window bottom. Outside, his feet kicked in the night air, until he pressed his heels against the side of the house and used that leverage, too.

He was moving. The curl of plywood pressed against his right hip, but he was moving, inexorably moving, and all at once the plywood let him through.

Gravity took over. It took over too soon, before he was ready, before he was clear of the building. Two screws laid tracks of sharp awful pain upward along his torso, and he couldn't twist away. His flailing left hand hit the wedged bar and grabbed it, pulling it loose, and the plywood snapped back down onto him like a mousetrap, scraping the entire upper half of his body as it squeezed him like toothpaste out of the building.

Eleven feet below this window was the ground, dark thin mountainous soil full of boulders and rocks. Most of Hall's parts hit rocks when he landed, most significantly the headsized rock he hit with the back of his own head.

He was unconscious then, but didn't know it. On automatic pilot, he struggled to his feet, straightened, and marched into the wall of the house. Correcting, he spun himself about, lost his balance, found his balance, and headed off downhill, reeling forward, still clutching the metal bar in his left hand, only staying upright because his feet still knew their job was to stay, if possible, directly beneath his head.

Plunging in this way, his head hurtling down the mountain while his feet scrambled to keep up, he legged it some distance from the house, and might even have gone on like that all the way to the valley if his head had only been alert enough to tell his feet to avoid that tree.

Concussed for the second time, Hall dropped onto his back like a delivery of curtain rods. His extremities twitched, then lay still. A frown gradually faded from his brow as, off to his left, the sun at last put in an appearance.

56

Mark got back to the lodge a little after nine in the morning, and the brown Taurus was already there, tucked in next to Os's white Porsche. Putting his mother's hand-me-down Buick Regal in next to the others, he was happy to see that Taurus, because it meant the union guys had not funked.

He himself had almost funked, damn near funked. After yesterday's traumatic experience of having Monroe Hall recognize his voice, on top of the tension and disbelief connected with actually *doing* this thing, he had, after returning the horse and its carrier with Os, spent the rest of a mostly sleepless night in his miserable basement room under his mother's off-limits mansion thinking about what he could possibly do now, and what he'd mainly thought about was funking it. Caving in. Being a quitter. Giving up the whole idea.

Of course, he'd tried not to phrase it in such negative terms during those wakeful hours. He'd tried for a more positive spin in his internal debate, telling himself he could 'start over,' he could 'reinvent himself,' he could 'wipe the slate clean,' he could, in the Mark Twain way, 'light out for the Territories.'

Isn't that, after all, what it really means to be an American? All of the current resistance to a national identification card (and many years ago, for the same reason, to the Social Security number), all of the alarm about the threats to 'privacy,' are based on the simple American conviction, from the very beginning of the immigrant experience, that it was the ultimate right of every American, if circumstances happened to call for such drastic measures, to turn himself into somebody new. The classless society was the ideal partly because, in a classless society, all identity is flexible. Mark, in his sleepless hours of not so much battling funk as welcoming funk aboard, had used every shred of schooling he could dredge out of memory to convince himself that at this point of crisis in his life, it would be not only acceptable, it would be not only guilt-free, but it would be damn near his patriotic duty, to run away and become somebody else.

And yet he hadn't done it. Along toward dawn, he had sunk into a heavy troubled slumber, and when the alarm jolted him awake no time later he knew, grimly, that he wouldn't be doing his patriotic duty as a turn-tail-and-run after all. There are no Territories to light out for, not in this century. It was no longer easy to become the new you. New or old, you were already you.

So that's what it came down to. He was Mark Sterling, of a certain background and a certain position in the community, and he always would be. He had started on this path, and the only thing to do was keep on it. And keep his mouth shut, particularly around Monroe Hall.

So it was a relief to see the Taurus, because it meant they were all in agreement: There *was* no way out of this. If the union men had successfully bagged it, Mark would have felt even worse than before, but they had not, so he felt marginally better.

Entering the house, he found an empty but astonishingly messy living room with faint sounds of activity far ahead. Following those sounds, he came eventually to a kitchen containing all four of his coconspirators, plus more mess than a kindergartner's birthday party. Breakfast was being made, with more enthusiasm than precision, all over the kitchen, using most of the pots, plates, cutting boards, cutlery, silverware, and electric gadgets formerly in the cupboards and on the shelves. Os was the most covered with flour, Ace the most covered with egg in varying degrees of congealment. It was as though they'd been hired by biased researchers to prove male incompetence in the kitchen.

Os noticed Mark first: 'Ah, there you are. We're almost ready here.'

Mac waved toward him a maple-syrup-smeared hand, and said, 'I hope you haven't had breakfast yet.'

'I haven't,' Mark agreed, looking around, 'but I'm not sure I'm hungry.'

'It's gonna be great,' Buddy assured him.

'First, of course,' Os said, 'we have to not feed Monroe Hall, and then feed the butler. Then we can bring most of this back down here – well, not down *here*, I think the dining room would be more welcoming – and tuck in to a hearty meal.'

Mark couldn't help it: 'Like the condemned man?'

Os frowned at him in surprise, 'What's wrong with *you*?'

Mark shook his head. 'Not enough sleep,' he said, knowing it would be impossible to explain that what was wrong with him was that there weren't any Territories any more.

Buddy said, 'You know about the reward?'

'Reward?' All he could think of was receiving a gold star. But who would present it, and for what?

Mac explained, 'Somebody, the wife, I guess, put up fifty thousand dollars for information leading to the return of Monroe Hall.'

'Fifty thousand?' Mark grimaced. 'For Monroe Hall? That's not much.'

Buddy said, 'Ace wants to collect it.'

'And why not?' Ace demanded. 'Fifty grand for information? We *got* the information.'

Mark said, 'Os?'

Os shrugged. 'It's up to his friends in the labor movement,' he said, 'to draw for Ace the direct line between that information and the jail cell.'

'There's a way,' Ace insisted. 'We just haven't thought it through yet.'

Mac said, 'We're ready here.' Pointing, he said, 'That's the breakfast we show Hall but don't let him eat, and that's the breakfast for the butler. And all the rest of it is for us.'

Os said, 'Buddy, why don't you carry the butler's tray, while Ace carries Hall's tray?'

Ace said, 'That's because we're labor, right? And you're management.'

'Of course,' Os said. 'And also why I'll be carrying the laptop.'

Mac said, 'Masks.'

So everybody put the dumb masks on, Buddy picked up a small tray of breakfast while Ace picked up a large tray of breakfast, and they all trooped upstairs. Buddy put the butler's breakfast on a side table in the corridor and Os picked up the laptop from where they'd left it leaning against the wall, while Mark went down to the circuit breaker box at the end of the corridor. He waited there until Os inserted the key into Hall's door and nodded to him, then switched the lights on in Hall's room as Os unlocked the door and everybody pushed in.

Mark came back, entered the room, and saw everybody milling around. He said, 'Where's Hall?'

'Hiding or something,' Os said. He sounded irritable. 'Damn it, Hall!' he said, raising his voice. 'Stop playing the fool!'

'You two shouldn't be talking,' Mac pointed out.

Oops; Mark put fingertips against his mouth.

Ace had put the tray on the bed, then looked under it. They looked into the closet and into the bathroom. Then they stood in the middle of the guest room and looked at one another, baffled and silent, until Mac said, 'How come that window's open?'

They all clustered around the plywood-shielded window. Now that they looked at it, they could see that the plywood was pushed outward from the sill along the bottom and part of the left side, held away by the screws that had once held it down. Tentative, unbelieving, Buddy pushed on the plywood, and it moved.

Mac, in awe, said, 'He got out.'

'Then,' Os said, '*we* had better get out. Who knows how long ago he escaped?'

'I *knew* it!' Mark said. If only he'd funked, after all. If only there were Territories!

They hurried from Monroe Hall's former prison to the corridor, leaving breakfast behind, and turned toward the staircase. Going by the other tray of breakfast, Mark said, 'The butler!'

They all stopped. They all looked at the butler's breakfast, and then at Mark. Mac said, 'Maybe Hall took him along.'

Os said, 'Hall? Look out for somebody else?'

Mark said, 'We have to let him out.'

'Here.' Os pulled the other key from his pocket. 'Do what you want; I'm getting far from here.'

Not far enough, Mark thought. Not all the way to the Territories. Thinking that, he hurried back down the corridor, fumbled with the key in the lock, finally got it to turn, pushed open the door, stepped into the room and, just one second too late, saw that chair swinging like a runaway satellite around the edge of the door, swiftly in his direction at, well, at head height.

57

The slope was steep, but he could hand himself down from treetrunk to treetrunk, most of the time managing to stay on his feet. As the sun rose higher, off to his left, the chill in the air grew less, but he didn't mind the chill, really; the exercise of walking down the mountain kept him warm.

His head ached, and other parts of him hurt, while different parts stung. There was an intermittent buzzing in his ears, and from time to time his eyes lost their focus and he had to cling to a tree until he could see clearly again. But it wasn't so bad, and when he came across the road it got even better.

The road was one lane, dirt, not much more than a pair of rutted grooves angling diagonally across his downward path. It descended leftward, so he followed it, because it was easier to walk on a real road, and he had no clear destination in mind. It was just important, it seemed to him, to walk down from the mountain.

It was just as well there were no mirrors or streams or other ways to see himself along the way, because his appearance had not been improved by recent events. His red-check flannel shirt was redder than before, with dried blood, and sported two irregular long gashes up the back. His tailored blue jeans were ripped here and there, splotched with grass stains, and with the left hip pocket half torn off, to dangle like a warning flag. His dark leather cowboy boots were so mud-stained you could no longer see the pictures of cactus plants on their sides. His hair was a tangled snarl, his face and hands streaked with dirt and dried blood, and his eyes had a strange look, like a fishtank overdue for cleaning.

He walked for a while down the small dirt road, and then it met a slightly larger road, two-lane blacktop, that angled down to the right. Blacktop was better than dirt, so he took it.

The first house he passed had been abandoned a long time ago. Half the roof was collapsed in, and much of the front porch had sagged completely away from the house. He stopped to look at it, slumped there, shadowed by the trees, then decided that wouldn't be a good place to stop, so he kept walking.

After a while, a pickup truck passed him, going the same direction he was; it came down from up behind him, and kept going. He watched it go and thought it would be nice to ride in the pickup truck instead of walking, but he didn't wave or shout or do anything but just kept on as before.

The next vehicle he met was coming up the mountain toward him. It was some sort of police car, with a red dome light on the roof. The dome light was switched off and the car drove uphill at normal speed. It seemed the car would just go on by, like the pickup truck, but then it stopped when it was opposite him and the driver's window lowered.

Beneath the opening window was a picture of a silver badge painted on the door, with SHERIFF in large letters superimposed on it, plus other things in smaller letters. The driver of the car was a rawboned man of forty or fifty or sixty, wearing a brown uniform and a darker brown necktie and the kind of broadbrimmed hat the Parks Department people wear. He looked out and called, 'You OK?'

'Just fine.' He kept walking, slowly, and smiled at the sheriff.

'Hold on there a second.'

He stopped, and the sheriff backed off the road, put his blinker lights on but not the dome light, and got out of the car. He had a handgun in a holster on a separate belt that he adjusted before he walked across the road and said, in a friendly manner, 'You staying around here?'

'Down that way.' He gestured at the road ahead.

'You look as though you been in an accident.'

'Do I?'

'Yes, you do.' The sheriff studied him, particularly his eyes. '*Have* you been in an accident?'

'Well, I don't think so.'

'You don't think so.' The sheriff took a minute to study his boots and his shirt. Then he looked him in the eye again. 'I don't think I recognize your face,' he said. 'We don't get a lot of visitors up in here. Would you mind telling me your name?'

'I don't mind,' he said.

The sheriff waited. Then he looked a little irritated, as though somebody were pulling his leg. 'You don't *mind*? I asked you what your name is.'

'Well,' he said, 'I don't think I know that just right now.'

'You don't know your name?'

'Not this minute, no. Do you think I should?'

'Most people find it a help. Would you have your wallet on you?'

Surprised, he said, 'I don't know.'

'Would you like to take a look? A lot of folk keep it in their right hip pocket.'

'All right.' He patted his right hip pocket. 'There's *something* in there.'

'Why don't we take a look at it?'

'All right.' His fingers stinging, he tugged it out of the pocket and held it open in two hands so he could look down at it. 'It doesn't seem like I can read it.'

'Would you like me to read it for you?'

'Oh, thank you,' he said, and smiled, and handed the thing to the sheriff.

The sheriff dipped his head, and his eyes disappeared behind the brim of his hat as he looked at the wallet.

'Is it all right? Does it tell you what my name is?'

'Oh, yes.' When the sheriff's head lifted, he was smiling. 'What does it say?'

'It says,' the sheriff told him, 'your name is fifty thousand dollars.'

58

Dortmunder followed the chair out of the room as though it had yanked him out, stumbling over the suddenly fallen foe, trying to redirect the chair at the still-vertical masked men all around him, but finding it was a chair with a mind of its own and an intention to do nothing but continue in the same long arc until it embedded a couple of its legs into the corridor wall some way to the left of the room he'd just quit.

The chair's sudden stop sent Dortmunder whirling into an orbit of his own, basically another curve leading farther down the corridor. He lashed his fists out in all directions, trying to connect on this crowd of jumping shouting masked people, but nobody laid a glove on nobody, and there ahead of him was a broad staircase leading down, at which he flung himself as though it were a swimming pool on a hot day.

Three and four steps at a time, he hurtled down the staircase, and there ahead was a big messy lodgeroom in semi-darkness because all its windows were covered, but over there was a half-open door with daylight behind it, and through that door he went, like a light-seeking missile.

Porch. Launch across the porch, *bom bom* down the wide echoing wooden steps, and off he went down the gravel drive, past the three cars parked there, and on. Away. Away from that place, whatever it was, and those people, whoever they were, and away.

The gravel drive went steeply downhill, which was good, since they had arrived here by traveling steeply uphill. So this must be the way to civilization, or at least to somewhere without those idiots back there. He chanced a quick look over his shoulder, and the very large lodge – gee, it was big, and he was seeing it for the first time – looked deserted back there, despite the three cars parked in front of it. He was at least a football field away from the place already, and the strange thing was, nobody was chasing him.

What was going on here? He stopped, breathing very hard, and looked up at the lodge, and for a long minute nothing happened. Then, in a rush, three guys carrying boxes and bags came running out onto the porch and down to the drive, where they stuffed all their goods into the trunk of the

Taurus. Then they jumped into the Taurus themselves.

No, no, not good. They'd get down here in no time. And of course, they must have seen him already. Nevertheless, he turned off the long gravel drive into the neatened woods to his right, and hid himself behind the widest tree he could find, which wasn't actually that wide.

Up the hill, the Taurus coughed into life with a lot of unnecessary revving of engine and grinding of gears. It backed and filled, then came rushing down the drive and on past the semihidden Dortmunder, and away. They never even looked in his direction. They were all without their masks, and all three stared straight ahead, willing themelves to be some-where else.

What was going on here? All of a sudden, they're leaving the place, but not because they want to chase the butler, but for some other reason. What other reason? What's happening?

Dortmunder had started to trudge back out toward the drive from the woods when suddenly here came the white Porsche. The driver, who was also not wearing a mask, had a grim skull-like quality as he glowered at the road ahead. He looked mostly like the officer in charge of Special Punishments at a federal penitentiary. Beside him, a guy lay back as far as the seat would let him. White towels, some of them with red polka dots, covered most of his head and face. One hand held the towels, the other hand lay out of sight beside him. Again, like the first three, they just tore on by, not even bothering to look at him, where he stood completely in the open, just to the side of the road.

What was happening? What were they up to now? And, come to think of it, where was Monroe Hall? They didn't kill him, did they, those clowns?

It was true Dortmunder and his crew meant to do their automobile dealing with the insurance company, but the insurance company, in turn, would have to work with Hall. If Hall was dead, and there was some sort of estate in charge of the cars and everything else, they could just forget it.

But why would he be dead? Why would these people go through all this stuff of the masks and hiding their voices if they just meant to kill him?

Dortmunder looked up at the lodge. Now it *really* seemed empty, even though one car was still parked out front, a kind of goldy-green Buick. But the front door had been left open and there was just that aura up there of a house with nobody inside.

What had they done with Hall? Dortmunder needed Hall; he'd spent a lot of time and effort on this job; he needed the son of a bitch so he could rob him.

There was nothing for it. Sighing, shaking his head, reflecting yet again on the unfairness of life, Dortmunder slogged back up to the lodge, entered it, switched on lights – well, at least the electricity was still on – and proceeded to search the place.

It didn't take long to find the room where Hall had been kept, just down the corridor from his own. Nor did it take long to figure out how Hall had managed his escape. But what had he used to pry with? Talk about unfair; in Dortmunder's room there had been absolutely nothing to pry with, but in this rich guy's room, who's got more than he needs already, what has he got? A prybar.

Dortmunder turned away from the breached window, looked around the room, and saw the big tray of breakfast on the bed. Come to think of it, he was goddamn hungry.

There was a kind of vanity in the room, with a chair in front of it, so Dortmunder put the tray there, sat in front of it, and set to.

The tray hadn't been on the bed for long, so the cold things on it were still cold and the hot things were still hot. Orange juice, excellent. Homemade pancakes, with butter and maple syrup – what could be wrong? Scrambled eggs and bacon, both done just exactly the way he liked it. *Four* pieces of white toast, just enough, with a choice of orange marmalade or strawberry jam. *Very* good coffee. Whoo, you could feel somewhat better about life after a meal like that.

You could also feel like going to the bathroom, which would have been all right except, when he flushed, it wouldn't do it. The thing was broken somehow. Dortmunder lifted the water closet lid, looked in at it, and grew suspicious. Walking down the hall past the chair embedded in the wall and back into his previous room, he entered the bathroom, lifted the water closet lid, and found what Monroe Hall had used as a prybar.

Oh. Hmm. Pretty good, damn it.

59

Zelkev didn't like the ordinary array of targets on the gunnery range. The hulking 'bad guys' sighting down pistols were not for him. He preferred a good Nativity scene, a number of lambs and Magi and so forth to pop with his two trusty Glocks, or possibly a Crucifixion, working his way around from the nails in wrists and ankles to the crown of thorns to a few quick rounds in the sword-slice in the side.

Of course, his absolute favorite was St. Sebastian, he of the soulful look while his entire body was studded with thick long arrow shafts, so that he would mostly make you think of a condominium for birds. Zelkev just loved to pop St. Sebastian, using both Glocks at once, sinking one cartridge into each arrow wound, then finishing with a double hit right in the center of old Seb's nose.

He could shoot St. Sebastians all day, and would, too, even using the same target over and over, around and around, if he didn't know better, know what it could do to him. Control the impulses, don't let yourself get into endless repetitions, the repetitions building the mania, the mania feeding on itself, the St. Sebastians shredding into the unrecognizable and still the desire growing for more, that's where the darkness lay, that was the loss of control that had to be guarded against.

(Upstairs in the embassy, they knew. When it would happen that his laughter, deep and rolling, would rise up from the gunnery range in the embassy's subbasement, louder than the shooting, the security people knew it was time to descend – cautiously – talk with Zelkev, call him by name – 'How are you, Zelkev?' 'When do you think this rain will stop, Zelkev?' 'Are those new shoes, Zelkev?' – until it was possible to disarm him, take him upstairs, medicate him, and not permit him to leave the embassy grounds for three or four days.)

Well, that hadn't happened for months now, six months, seven, something like that. He'd been good; he'd kept himself under control; he'd not let any of the little dark imps run away with him. On the other hand, he hadn't had any work to do either, not for such a long time. You can't practice forever. St. Sebastian fills in for only so long.

211

This afternoon, he rode the elevator up from the gunnery range feeling logy, out of shape and out of sorts, and when he stepped out to the second-floor corridor where his room was, Ulffin was just coming down toward him and stopped to say, 'I was just sent for you.'

'I have done nothing,' Zelkev said.

'Memli wants a word with you,' Ulffin told him,

'I'll wash, and then see him. I've been shooting.' Of course, he'd always been shooting, but it was necessary to say these things.

'I'll tell him,' and Ulffin scuttled off, afraid of him as they all were afraid of him, though when had he ever harmed anyone in the embassy? Never.

His room was a monk's cell, with its hard single bed, small metal dresser, metal table with the television set on it, metal chair. A tall man, angular, with close-cropped blond hair and a square boxlike head featuring unemotional blue eyes, a small sharp-looking nose, and narrow bloodless lips, Zelkev stepped through into his bathroom, washed the shooting from his face and hands, returned to the bedroom to change to a cleaner and more formal shirt and pants, then went downstairs to the main floor and Memli's office. He moved with a certain stiffness, as though at one point he'd been taken apart and then a bit awkwardly put back together again, but in fact he could move with a great deal of grace and control, when necessary.

Memli, who always wore his army uniform in a useless attempt to distract from the sloppiness of his body, was Zelkev's superior officer at the embassy, the military attaché. He looked up from his desk when Zelkev entered his office, tried not to look frightened, and said, 'Ah, Zelkev, good news. Harbin has been found.'

Zelkev smiled, an honest smile of pleasure and anticipation. He seated himself across from Memli and said, 'In America?'

'Oh, yes, he's still in America.' Memli looked with some satisfaction at documents on his desk. 'You remember, we'd learned he'd bought a new identification.'

'Blanchard.'

'Oh, you remember the name, good.'

'He got away from me,' Zelkev said, with remembered annoyance. 'I never forget the ones that get away from me.'

'Well, here's your second chance.' Memli held up a document, gazed from it to Zelkev. 'Fredric Eustace Blanchard. He has taken a position in rural Pennsylvania. There was some criminal activity that got into the newspapers, and a friend noticed Blanchard's name. He is acting as personal private secretary to a disgraced American businessman named Monroe Hall.'

The name meant nothing to Zelkev. Only the name Fredric Eustace Blanchard meant anything to him. He said, 'You have the address?'

'He's in a protected compound.'

'So many of them are.'

'Unfortunately,' Memli said, 'we still don't have a photograph. Not since the plastic surgery was done.'

'I don't care what he looks like,' Zelkev said, and stood to take the document from Memli. 'Good-bye,' he said.

60

Does a kidnapper report a stolen car? On the other hand, did Dortmunder want to go wandering the highways and byways of ruralest Pennsylvania just waiting to catch the eye of some curious cop? Or did he want to slink around in the most out-of-the-way places he could find, on his way to going to ground?

The problem was, he just couldn't see himself slipping back into the role of John Howard Rumsey, butler to the murdered and the kidnapped. There would be cops all over the Hall compound, and for the once-missing butler they'd have a thousand questions. Also, since he'd gone off at the same time as both the kidnappers and the kidnappee, there would certainly be at least one or two of those cops who'd want to know just exactly which of those categories they should place him in. Jim Green's recycled identifications had worked for background checks during the employment phase, but would John Rumsey make it through a total acid-bath investigation? Let's not find out the answer to that.

Having finished Hall's breakfast and his own study of the lodge where he'd been held captive, Dortmunder had gone back outside to inspect the one car those clowns hadn't taken off in, being the greeny-gold Buick Regal. He hotwired it and drove it down from the mountain, getting lost a couple of times on little nothing dirt or gravel roads that seemed to be doing all right until he'd realize they'd gradually veered around and were now headed *uphill*. No, no, we've been uphill, let's find us some valley for a while.

Which he finally did, and then found a blacktop road, and then at last an intersection with signs. The Buick contained a Pennsylvania roadmap in the driver's door pocket, and with its help he made his way across the state to Shickshinny, being very careful to stay on secondary roads. A dubious butler would create suspicion enough; a dubious butler in a hot – and hotwired – car would be just a little too much.

Taking these routes, it was so long before he turned in at the driveway to Chester's house that he was late for lunch, but that wasn't the primary consideration. The small one-car garage was just to the left of the house;

leaving the Buick in front of it, Dortmunder went over to ring the front doorbell, and after a minute the door was opened by Grace Fallon, who gave him a surprised look, then a kind of critical once-over: 'Well, look at *you*.'

Another distraction. 'What about me?'

'Well, you're dressed nice,' she allowed, 'but other than that you look like a bum. Not shaved, dirt all over you, you didn't even comb your hair.'

'I don't have a comb.'

'You've got fingers,' she pointed out.

Enough. Dortmunder said, 'My question is, is Chester here?'

She frowned. 'Why?'

'Because I wanna know if his car is here,' Dortmunder told her, realizing the only way to handle this was to make as open and full a case as he possibly could. 'And the reason I wanna know that is, if his car *isn't* here, I wanna put that Buick over there in the garage, and the reason I wanna do that is because I stole it. We up to speed now?'

'Well, you don't have to get huffy,' she said.

'Is his car in there?'

'No,' she admitted. 'But I'm not sure he'd like you to put a stolen car inside there in its place.'

'He's gonna love it,' Dortmunder said.

Chester's garage was as messy as most garages, which was sort of a surprise. You'd think a driver would have a different attitude toward garages, but apparently not. Still, there was just enough room to squeeze the Buick in, open the door partway until it hit the snowblower and the wheelbarrow and the sack of fertilizer, and squeeze himself out. He shut the garage door, walked back to the house, and she was still standing there in the doorway, arms folded, frowning.

He nodded to her, wanting to make nice. 'I'll move it when Chester gets back,' he said.

'Fine.'

'And you're right, I'm very dirty. If I took a shower, what could I wear afterwards?'

'A different house,' she said.

'Come on,' he said.

She thought about it, then sighed. 'I'll see what I can find,' she said. 'But take those shoes off before you come in.'

'I was gonna do that,' he lied.

61

Saturday was a very busy day for Kelp, but not a happy one. The after-shocks of the Monroe Hall kidnapping just kept coming. Friday he'd been plagued by those two plainclothes cops, who knew they were suspicious of *something* but couldn't figure out exactly what. But then Saturday came along, and the cops became the least of his problems.

The day started before eight o'clock, when he was rousted from sleep in his room in the little green house by Stan, who said, 'The boss's wife is on the phone. She wants you to talk to her and me to drive her some-where.'

He found his way to a phone – there were none in the bedrooms – took a few seconds to remember his name in this context, and then said into the receiver, 'Morning, Mrs Hall, Fred Blanchard here.'

'Oh, Fred, they've found Mr Hall.'

'Well, that's great,' he said, thinking, good, the heist is back on track.

'I'm going to the hospital to see him,' she said.

'Hospital? What, is he wounded?'

'I don't think so. I think it's just observation. I'll need you in the office to take care of things, and I'll phone you later.'

It wasn't until after he'd hung up and was brushing his teeth that it occurred to him she hadn't mentioned the butler. Was Dortmunder in the hospital, too?

No. It was a little after nine when she phoned again, Kelp cooling his heels in the office most of that time, wondering if they were going to get their original plan back on track or not. Tonight, was the concept. Tonight the cars go to Speedshop. Then the phone rang, and it was Mrs Hall, and she said, 'Fred, two people from my law firm are on their way. I know you'll give them all the help you can.'

'Mrs Hall? Is Mr Hall all right?'

'Well . . . It's complicated. Would you also speak to Mrs Parsons?'

Not willingly. 'Sure,' Kelp said.

'Tell her, please, to pack my summer things, and her own.'

'Pack?'

'Tell her we'll be going home,' she said. 'She'll know what I mean: Maryland.'

What the hell is going on here? Kelp thought. What he said was, 'You're going away for a while?'

'Yes, I suppose so. Call security, please, tell them to bring the Pierce-Arrow up to the house, put the luggage in it that Mrs Parsons packs.'

'Will do.'

'The two people from the law firm,' she said, 'are named Julie Cavanaugh and Robert Wills.'

'That's a funny name for a lawyer, Wills.'

'Is it? Please tell the gate to let them in.'

'Sure,' he said. Having written the two lawyer names down, he looked at them and still thought Wills was a funny name for a lawyer. Cavanaugh wasn't, though. 'Mrs Hall.' he said.

'Yes?'

'How's, uh . . .' Could *not* remember the name. 'How's the butler?'

'Rumsey?'

'Rumsey. John Rumsey. Is he in the hospital, too?'

'No one knows where Rumsey is, Fred. Monroe was found wandering around in the woods, but he was alone, and he doesn't know where the kidnappers held him, and Rumsey hasn't appeared anywhere.'

This is worse than I thought, he told himself. There's more to this story, and none of it is good. 'I'll take care of everything,' he promised, and did.

The lawyers were young bird dogs, skinny and focused. They looked like brother and sister, both tall and thin with very sharp features and thick black hair swept straight back as though they used a wind tunnel for hair-care. They were announced from the gate, so Kelp went to the front door to watch the black BMW drive up the road and stop where the horse trans-porter had stopped, just yesterday. A lot had happened since.

'I'm Blanchard,' he told them when they marched together up to the door, the boy lawyer in black suit, white shirt, dark blue tie, the girl lawyer in knee-length black skirt, high neck white blouse, open black jacket with discreet shoulder pads.

'Cavanaugh.'

'Wills.'

Nobody offered to shake hands. I am, after all, Kelp reminded himself, a servant. He said, 'The office is this way.'

Entering the office, Cavanaugh said, 'Oh, good, a partners' desk. Robert? Do you have a preference?'

'I like daylight to my right.'

So they seated themselves facing each other at the partners' desk, as though this had been their office for a hundred years, and Cavanaugh said to Kelp, 'We'll need the list of staff at the compound. And I understand some actually live here?'

'Including me,' Kelp said.

'I'll need a separate list of indwellers,' she told him. 'We have a lot of notifications to give out.'

'Notifications?'

Wills took over the story. 'Mrs Hall is closing the compound, in prospect of marketing the property and its contents.'

'Marketing? You mean, put all this up for sale?'

'Yes, of course.'

Kelp said, 'But if Hall is back, so there's no ransom to pay or anything like that, what's going on?'

The lawyers looked at each other. Cavanaugh shrugged, looked at Kelp, and said, 'This will be common knowledge soon enough. Mr Hall has amnesia. His memory is gone.'

Kelp said, 'Like the soap operas?'

Wills said, 'It was the result of blunt trauma to the head, or multiples thereof. The doctors believe it's irreversible.'

So that's what Mrs Hall had meant when she'd said her husband's condition was 'complicated.' And she'd described him as having been found wandering in the woods. But, in that case, what had happened to John?

Cavanaugh was going on: 'Those resident here will be given until Monday to find housing elsewhere. All staff will be given two weeks' salary, to be mailed to their home address or whatever address they leave with us.'

'Only security stays on,' Wills said.

'So,' Cavanaugh said, 'we'll need to interview staff, one at a time. Would you arrange that?'

'Except for security,' Kelp said.

'And Mrs Parsons,' Cavanaugh said.

Kelp turned away, to go over to his own desk and start making the calls, but then he turned back to say, 'I have to tell you, I still don't get it. Why all of a sudden sell this place?'

Again the lawyers looked at each other, and this time Wills was the one who shrugged, then turned to say to Kelp, 'This is speculation on our part, and we would prefer you not to pass it on.'

'We'll tell you our speculation,' Cavanaugh explained, 'because you are being impacted by what's happening here.'

'Mr Hall's assets are controlled by the courts,' Wills said, 'and yet, he lived here beyond what means he should have had. There is a theory he had additional assets in offshore accounts.'

Cavanaugh said, 'No one knows that for sure.'

'But,' Wills said, '*if* those accounts exist, Monroe Hall would be the only one who could access them. Who would know the numbers, the passwords.'

'Oh,' Kelp said, 'and he's lost his memory.'

Kelp sat at his desk across the room from the lawyers and fielded phone calls and arranged for staff to come in for their farewell interviews, which several of them took badly, pointing out years of faithful service, sacrifices made, the decision to stay on with Hall even after the world had turned against him, but what was anybody to do? This party was over. Those few human beings in the world not yet shafted by Monroe Hall were now getting their turn.

Including, Kelp realized, the wife. It was Hall's bone-deep selfishness that would have kept him from protecting Mrs Hall, providing for her, writing down those secret account numbers and passwords and leaving them somewhere for her to find. But what would *he* care what happened, if he wasn't around? In Kelp's mind's eye, a whole lot of hundred-dollar bills with wings attached flew across a blue sky and disappeared over a black mountain in the distance. No, thousand-dollar bills. Gone. Forever.

It was eleven-thirty, and the lawyers were just finishing the last of the staff interviews when the phone rang and Kelp answered, as usual, 'Hall residence.'

'Robert Wills, please.'

'Who's calling?'

'Frank Simmons of Automotive Heritage Museum.'

What? What can this mean? Nothing good. Bland as ever, Kelp turned in his chair and said to Wills across the room, 'For you. Frank Simmons of Automotive Heritage Museum.'

'Yes, got it, thank you.'

It was very hard for Kelp to hang up, not listen to this conversation, but he managed. Wills spoke briefly, then hung up and said to Kelp, 'Blanchard, call the gate, will you? There'll be some flatbed trucks arriving, in about half an hour.'

Worse and worse. Reaching for the phone, Kelp said, 'Sure. Uh, what are they for?'

'The antique cars,' Wills said. 'You know about the antique cars stored on the property here?'

'I've heard of them,' Kelp acknowledged.

'Technically, since the bankruptcy proceedings,' Wills said, 'they've belonged to the Automotive Heritage Museum. With the changed situation here, the museum wants to move them to their own property, for safekeeping.'

'Their own property.'

'Yes, in Florida. I understand it's a beautiful place, glass-walled buildings, views of the Gulf, all completely climate-controlled.'

'They've been wanting to get their hands on these cars for years,' Cavanaugh said. 'Hall always managed to fend them off, but that's over now.'

'I guess it is,' Kelp agreed.

'It's a better place for them, really,' Cavanaugh said. 'They have thousands of visitors a year. Here, no one ever got to see the cars.'

'Yeah, that's right,' Kelp said, and turned away to call the gate, while the lawyers finished their final interview, with a raspy-voiced housemaid who now announced this firing was the best thing ever happened to *her*, she was going to her *own* climate-controlled glass-walled building in Florida and live on her sister for a while.

Who did this? Kelp silently demanded of the world, as he made the call to the gate. What clown had to go and *kidnap* Monroe Hall and louse up what was going to be a very beautiful piece of work? May he suffer, the louse.

62

It was the best day's sleep Mark had had in a good long time, maybe ever. Partly it was the hospital bed, infinitely adjustable, beautifully comforting, but mostly it was because, at long last, his conscience was clear.

When Os had driven Mark down the mountain from that lodge, Mark had known he was in deep trouble, both physically and legally. Physically, as it turned out in the hospital's emergency room, that chair had given him a broken jaw, broken nose, and torn ear. But legally, as he was painfully aware, he was in even worse shape.

Monroe Hall and the butler were both gone, escaped from the lodge. Both could identify the lodge, which would mean the authorities would soon find Os, a relative of the lodge's owner and a sworn enemy of Hall. Even if Os didn't immediately give them Mark – and why wouldn't he? Mark knew game theory as well as Os, and the first to turn gets the best deal – but even if Os did the unlikely and even selfless thing and kept his mouth shut, sooner or later the authorities would come to Mark, as Os's closest associate, and insist he speak out loud in Monroe Hall's presence. 'That's him! That's the voice I heard!'

After the jaw and the nose had been set and the ear sewed up, Mark had been moved from the emergency room to this plain-to-barren single room, where he'd had nothing to do but think about the position he was in. A television set hung from the wall opposite the bed, reminding him unhappily of the butler's chair jutting from the wall at the lodge, but it wouldn't function until his credit card cleared, which, a self-satisfied nurse informed him, would be in twenty-four hours. You can buy a Cartier watch and only have to wait thirty seconds after the card has been swiped along the doohickey, but in a hospital it takes twenty-four hours. And they talk about advances in medicine.

Well, it was just as well he didn't have television to distract him, or so he thought. It gave him time to consider his position, and his options. Not that he needed a whole lot of time, nor did he have, on reflection, a whole lot of options. Fifteen minutes after he was left alone in the room he reached for the telephone on his bedside table, grateful that at least this appliance didn't need twenty-four hours to be activated, and phoned his lawyer.

'Iss is Ark,' he told the receptionist, which is what the jaw would now permit him to say. 'Ark Sterling.'

The ensuing conversation was slow and difficult, but he did at last convince Dan Richards, his family attorney, that he needed a lawyer by his bedside, Saturday or no Saturday, before the cops arrived, as inevitably they would. Dan promised to send someone good from a firm closer at hand, but no lawyer had yet appeared when the plainclothes cop came in, unmistakable even without the badge on its leather carrier dangling from his shirt pocket. A bored, slender guy with black hair, short for a cop, grinned at Mark and said, 'I'm Detective Cohan, Quentin Cohan.'

'I'll talk,' Mark said, not entirely accurately, 'en ny lawyer gets ere.'

'Oh, really.' Detective Cohan was both surprised and pleased, not having expected juice from this interview. No longer bored, he said, 'Fine by me, Mr Sterling. I got nothing but time.'

Seating himself in one of the two visitors' chairs, Detective Cohan pulled a crossword puzzle magazine from his casual jacket pocket and amused himself for half an hour until a man who looked like central casting's idea of a lawyer walked in. Bald head on top, black gorse around the ears. Pinstripe suit, white shirt, patterned red-and-yellow tie. Black briefcase dangling from left hand. Skinny black-framed eyeglasses that reflected the light. Watch on left wrist big enough and shiny enough to be the entire control panel on a *Star Trek* ship. Looking from Mark to Detective Cohan, apparently unable to sort them out, he said, 'Mark Sterling?'

'Ere,' Mark said, and raised a hand.

'Eldron Gold,' the lawyer said. 'The Richards firm sent me. Is this police officer arresting you?'

'Not yet,' Detective Cohan said, with a happy smile, as he stood and put away his crossword puzzles.

Eldron Gold said to Mark, 'Would you like to speak to me privately before you answer the officer's questions?'

'No,' Mark said. 'I just ant to get it other ith.'

Detective Cohan stepped closer, still smiling, opening a small notebook. 'Good idea,' he said.

Mark took a deep breath. 'Thor other theothle and I kidnathed Nonroe Hall,' he said.

'Wait!' shouted Eldron, over some pleased exclamation of Cohan's. 'Are you *sure* we shouldn't talk first?'

'No, it's all right,' Mark assured him. 'You'll see.' To Detective Cohan he said, 'Thigh oth us kidnathed Nonroe Hall.'

'This is *completely* unacceptable,' Eldron interrupted. 'In a hospital setting, my client is sedated, he's not responsible for his statements, absolutely *none* of this would be acceptable in a court of law.'

'It's OK, it's OK,' Mark told his mouthpiece, patting the bed to calm the lawyer down.

'Objections noted, Counselor,' Detective Cohan said. He didn't seem troubled.

Mark said to Eldron, 'I hath to get this out. This isn't easy thor ne to say.'

Detective Cohan smiled upon him. 'We know that,' he assured him. 'Go on, Mark.'

'All right.' Mark took a deep breath as his lawyer hopped around like the boy on the burning deck, and went on. 'We kett Hall at my thriend's thanily lodge uh-state thon ere. We also took the utt-ler, utt that was an accident. They oath got away. The utt-ler hit ne with a chair.'

At last Gold interrupted, saying, 'Sterling, are you *sure* we shouldn't discuss this, you and I? *Just* you and I?'

'A little late, Counselor,' the happy Detective Cohan said. 'Tell us about the other four, Mark.'

'Don't!'

Ignoring Eldron, Mark said, 'One is ny izness thartner, Osthourne Thaulk. The other three are, uh, union nenthers. I don't know the union.'

'Their names will do,' Detective Cohan said.

'Well, they're Nac, Thuddy and Ace.'

Both Eldron and Detective Cohan leaned in closer. Detective Cohan said, 'Would that be Mac, Buddy, and Ace?'

'Yes. Os knows Thuddy's real nane, I think, I don't know ith he knows the others.' Then Mark sighed, his story told, happy to be unburdened.

It took Detective Cohan a while to realize the story was now complete. He had another half hour of questions, intermixed with useless objections from Lawyer Gold, but Mark had essentially told the whole story right at the beginning. Once he'd done so, he felt much better about things. He knew he'd been first to turn state's evidence, which would mean they'd come to him first for testimony against the others, which meant he would be treated more leniently than everybody else. What a relief.

Such a relief, in fact, that when Detective Cohan and Lawyer Gold finally left, Mark fell immediately and deeply asleep, and remained asleep for most of the day. The shadows outside the hospital room window were long and amber when at last he stirred, stretched, smiled, stopped smiling because it made his jaw hurt, and then remembered where he was and everything that had happened.

What a terrific sleep, after so much tension and worry! That was the moment he told himself it was probably the best day's sleep of his life, and just the fact of it reassured him he'd made the right decision. Betraying one's friends and associates, it turned out, wasn't something to agonize over or regret. No, it was merely an unfortunate possibility in life, as much so for Os and the union men as for himself. One was sorry to find that one had reached that point in one's life, but then one accepted the reality and got on with it. He had got on with it, and everything was better – for him – as a result.

Smiling again, though more carefully, he turned his head, and there was Detective Cohan, smiling right back at him from the visitor's chair. He was a very happy boy.

'So you're awake, are you?'

'Oh, yes. God, I theel rested.'

'Good.' Detective Cohan rose and came over to smile down on Mark. 'A lot has happened while you've been asleep,' he said.

'I thought it would.'

'We went looking for this Osbourne Faulk,' Detective Cohan told him, 'and it turns out, he'd already fled the country.'

Mark blinked. 'Thled?'

'Went straight to Brazil. I doubt we'll ever get our hands on him.'

'Di-ruh— Thra—' No; impossible to say the name of that country. 'Why not?' he asked instead.

'Well, there's no extradition treaty between the United States and Brazil,' Detective Cohan explained. 'Once he's there, there's no way we can get our hands on him.'

'There *are* Territories!' Mark cried.

'Sure,' Detective Cohan said, 'a number of territories around the world without that extradition treaty. Most of them you wouldn't want to go to, but Brazil isn't bad. Rio, you know. Very tall women in bikinis, the way I understand it.'

'What athout— What athout Nac and Thuddy and Ace?'

'Well, you don't know their real names, and you don't know what union they're in,' Detective Cohan pointed out. 'Your friend Osbourne may have known at least one real name, but he's long gone, and believe me, there are dozens of Macs and Buddies and Aces in every union in the United States.'

'So I'm the only one you've got.'

'I'm afraid it gets worse, Mark,' Detective Cohan said, with his pleasant smile.

Mark had always hated it when policemen called him by his first name, thinking they were doing it only because he was upper-class and they weren't, but he suspected this was not the time to make an issue of it. He said, 'How could it get worse?'

'Well, they found Monroe Hall,' Detective Cohan told him. 'Found him wandering around, had some concussions, hit his head a lot.'

'I didn't do that. None oth us did that.'

'No, no, nobody's accusing you, don't worry about that. The point is, all those bumps to the head, Monroe Hall's got amnesia.'

'Well, if anythody deserthes—' But then it hit him. 'He *what?*'

'No memory,' Detective Cohan said, and waved a hand beside his head as though saying good-bye to his brain. 'The doctors say, he'll never get his memory back, it's all gone.'

'Inthossi— Inthoss—'

'But true. Also, just by the way, it seems the butler has disappeared. John Howard Rumsey. Nowhere to be found. It's beginning to look like, up there in the wilderness where he ran away from you people, a city man like that, something went wrong. Maybe he fell in a mountain tarn, or could be he met up with a bear. Anyway, gone. We'll keep looking, but it doesn't seem hopeful.'

'Tough,' Mark said, not seeing any connection with himself, and already bitter about not learning of Monroe Hall's amnesia until too late.

But Detective Cohan was not finished with his cheerful smiles and his bad news. 'All in all, Mark,' he said, 'it's a good thing you spoke. Without you, we'd *never* have found that lodge, or you, or your friend Faulk's name, or anything. Yes, sir, Mark, without you coming forward the way you did, the entire Monroe Hall kidnapping would have remained a complete mystery forever. I'll send your lawyer in now, shall I?'

63

At least when he chauffeured Mrs Hall, Stan got to drive a good car, a black Daimler like a sofa converted to a tank. Also, while she was in the hospital and while she was at her lawyer's office, instead of trailing after her as with Mrs Parsons, he got to stay at the wheel and read his newspaper, his wrong-size hat on the seat beside him. And driving between the hospital and the lawyer's office, he got to hear at least parts of her several telephone conversations, which didn't sound at all good.

She told more than one person that 'poor Monroe' had lost his memory forever, and it wasn't ever coming back, and that meant there was permanently no way to get at 'you know,' which he guessed would be money in banks where she didn't know the secret word. She also talked about 'liquidating' this and that, which from a mob guy would have meant somebody was gonna die but which from a respectable married lady meant something along the lines of a visit to the hockshop. She also told a few people she'd be 'coming home,' which after a while he realized didn't mean the compound but somewhere else.

But the main thing she kept saying, in conversation after conversation, was that she wanted this or that 'taken care of today. I mean today. I know it's Saturday, but I don't want to have to still be in that compound tomorrow. Or any other day. So I want it taken care of today.'

She said that several times, and though she never raised her voice or sounded angry, Stan somehow had the feeling she was going to get her way. Whatever it was she wanted done today, it would get itself done today.

What it added up to, when he put it all together, there was no Monroe Hall any more. Everything that had been fixed tight around him, his wife, his compound, his employees, the people there to steal his cars, everything was now untied, off and away, as though Hall's gravity had been turned off.

So far as Stan could see, this was bad news for the heist. He supposed they could still do it, still collect the cars, deal with the insurance company, but somehow it felt different now. How would the other guys feel about it? How would Chester feel about it? It was Chester's need for revenge against Hall that had got them into this thing in the first place.

On the other hand, did they want to go through all this for nothing?

It was just after twelve-thirty when they got back to the compound, sailing past the guardshack where the brown-uniformed plug-ugly on duty saluted, not very well, when he saw Mrs Hall in the backseat. Stan drove her up to the house, got out, opened her door, and when she climbed out she looked very sad, 'I believe this is good-bye, Warren,' she said.

On a sudden impulse, he said, 'My friend's call me Stan.'

She liked that. Smiling, she said, 'Then I hope we've become friends, in this very short time.' She stuck her hand out. 'Good-bye, Stan.'

She had a strong handclasp, but he treated it gently anyway. 'Good-bye, Mrs Hall,' he said, and walked down the road, heading for the green house and lunch, when ahead of him, out of the side road, came a flatbed truck with a yellow convertible Triumph Stag on it, its black hardtop in place. Stan had studied the list of Hall's cars, and remembered that one; it was from 1976.

But where was it going? Toward the gate. As he walked on, Stan watched the truck go through the gate, out to the county road, and turn left.

Stan turned left, too, onto the side road toward the green house, and here came another flatbed, this one bearing a 1958 Studebaker Golden Hawk, creamy white with black trim on its roof, hood, and tail fins. The truck driver, a skinny guy in a straw cowboy hat, gave Stan a casual wave on the way by. Automatically, but not really meaning it, Stan waved back.

What was going *on* here? Where were they taking those cars? Come *on* here, Stan thought, those are *our* cars.

He walked faster, hoping Kelp or Tiny would be at the house to tell him what was going on. Or maybe Dortmunder would be back by now. Ahead of him he saw the house, and then saw, on its tiny porch, Kelp and Tiny standing against the rail, like people watching a parade.

Well, they *were* watching a parade. Another flatbed truck, this one bearing a 1967 Lamborghini Miura, all gleaming white, a flat-nosed front like a predator fish, was next in line. This truck, like the ones before it, had Pennsylvania license plates, so they'd been hired locally. But where were they going?

Stan was practically running by the time he reached the house. The bitter expressions on Kelp's and Tiny's faces were not encouraging. As a black Lincoln Continental Club Coupe from 1940 sailed by, the vehicle Frank Lloyd Wright once described as 'the most beautiful car in the world,' and that the Museum of Modert Art chose as one of the top eight automobile designs in history, Stan said, 'What's going on?'

'Our heist,' Kelp said, 'Out the window.'

'Off the property,' Tiny said. He looked as if he wanted to eat that Lincoln, flatbed truck and all.

Stan said, 'But where *to*?'

'Florida,' Kelp said. 'A car museum in Florida.'

Tiny growled, and the red 1955 Morgan Plus 4 was trucked by. Stan said, 'All of them?'

'Every last one,' Kelp said. 'Except the Pierce-Arrow. The missus is taking that with *her* to Maryland.'

'They're closin shop,' Tiny said.

Stan found it hard to look at the cars going past, but then it was even harder not to look. Frowning at the house instead, he said, 'John not back?'

'Nobody knows where he is,' Kelp said.

'Dortmunder always shows up,' Tiny said. Clearly, he didn't want anything to deflect from his irritation.

'Well, wherever he is, he's better off than here,' Stan said. The 1950 Healey Silverstone, white, the car Mrs Hall most often drove, was next. Stan shook his head. 'John wouldn't like to see this,' he said.

64

One good thing about Hal Mellon: his cell phone didn't ring. When Chester drove him on his rounds, Mellon kept his cell phone in his shirt pocket, over his heart, set to vibrate rather than ring when he got a call. 'Getting me ready for the pacemaker,' he said, which might have been another joke.

But there was a different joke coming at Chester this sunny Saturday afternoon in June, though he didn't know it yet. He knew Monroe Hall had been kidnapped from his compound yesterday, because the *world* knew Monroe Hall had been kidnapped from his compound yesterday. He also knew they had grabbed the butler as well, but wouldn't that be Dortmunder? He hoped Dortmunder would get himself away from those people, whoever they were, and he sure hoped the police presence at Hall's compound wouldn't screw up the grand auto theft planned for tonight. He didn't want to be stuck in this car with Hal Mellon forever, Tuesdays through Saturdays, because, in Hal's world, the managers he needed to schmooze with were likelier to be in the office on Saturday than Monday.

'Young couple walking in a graveyard,' Mellon said. 'Oops, hold on.' And he dove into his shirt pocket for his phone.

Another couple, Chester thought, in another graveyard. Why don't they spend their time at horror movies, like all the other young couples in the world?

Mellon murmured briefly into his phone, then broke the connection, pocketed the phone, and said, 'Canceled the appointment, the son of a bitch. Who cares if he's got pneumonia? I've got product to move. Ah, well.'

Mellon looked at the dashboard clock, so Chester did, too: 3:24.

Mellon sighed. 'Let's call it a day,' he said. 'That was my last real appointment anyway, I was just gonna do drop-ins after that.'

'Sure thing,' Chester said, and U-turned in front of two trucks, an ambulance, and a cement mixer.

Mellon no longer blinked when Chester did things like that. Sitting back, half-smiling out the windshield as he took the vodka bottle from the

229

pocket in the door, he said, 'Couple pass a gravestone, says, "Here lies John Jones, a lawyer and an honest man". Girl says, "Is that legal, three men in one grave"?'

When Chester drooped into his house at four-thirty, Hal's baseball teams and frogmen fading slowly from his brain, Dortmunder himself was seated in Chester's living room, on Chester's sofa, watching Chester's television set, and wearing Chester's overcoat and, apparently, nothing else. 'What the hell is *this*?' Chester demanded.

'Disaster,' Dortmunder told him, and gestured at the screen.

Chester moved around the room to where he could see the television screen. Between the crawl at the bottom of the picture and the CNN logo and some other stuff at the top was a photo of a hangdog-looking guy in black suit, white shirt, and narrow black tie, giving the camera a distrustful look. 'That's you,' Chester said.

'They made us take mug shots when we got the jobs,' Dortmunder said. 'Tiny was gonna cop them when we left.'

'Missing butler,' Chester read from the crawl, then gave Dortmunder-in-the-flesh the once-over. 'Missing clothes, too, I see,' he said. 'Where are they?'

'In your drier,' Dortmunder said. 'They used to be in your washing machine. But I need something except that suit, I can't wear that suit after it's been all over CNN. Two, three billion people have now seen that suit.'

'There's also the face,' Chester pointed out.

'I can squint or wear glasses or something. Listen, Chester, I couldn't call over to the compound because maybe the wrong person says hello, recognizes my voice. You could call.'

'Why?'

'Find Andy or Tiny or somebody. Get my clothes from the house there. I can't go back there anyway, the cops'd ask me questions for a year. I thought I'd wait till the cars moved tonight, but I can't sit here in your overcoat like this.'

'I agree.'

'So maybe somebody could bring me my stuff over to me now. Is that asking too much?'

'I'll find out,' Chester said, and made the call, and somebody with nails in his throat said, 'Front gate.'

'I'm looking for, uh, Fred Blanchard.'

'He's at his house, I'll forward you.'

Waiting, Chester said to Dortmunder, 'Calls didn't used to get answered at the front gate. Suppose something's happening over there?'

'Yes,' Dortmunder said.

It was Kelp who answered the phone, sounding aggravated: 'Yeah?'

'An – I mean, Fred, it's Chester.'

'I don't care what you call me.'

'Listen, I got John here, over at my house, you know what I mean?'

'John? There? What's he doing *there*?'

'Sitting in my overcoat. He says would one of you guys bring him his stuff from his room, he isn't going back over there.'

'Good idea,' Kelp said, though he sounded angry when he said it. 'We'll bring everybody's stuff. See you in a little while.'

Chester hung up, and Dortmunder nodded at the screen, saying, 'They got one of them.'

The photo on the screen now was of a very upright businessman type in a suit and tie – a corporate headshot. The off-camera announcer was saying, 'Forty-two-year-old Mark Sterling, now in police custody, has admitted his part in the kidnapping. One other alleged perpetrator, a business associate of Mark Sterling's named Osbourne Faulk, is said by police to have fled the country. Another three conspirators are thought to have been involved, but little is known of them except that they are alleged to have belonged to the same labor union.

'There you go,' Dortmunder said. 'Now the kidnappers got a union.'

65

'Little is known of us,' Mac said. 'You hear that?'

'We're royally screwed,' Ace insisted. 'That guy Faulk was right. What *we* gotta do is flee the country.'

'To where?' Mac wanted to know. 'And using what for cash? We wouldn't last a week, Ace, in some foreign country, and once they look at us and start to wonder how come we're on the lam, then we *are* screwed.'

The television had moved on to commercials. 'More beer,' Buddy said, offed the set, and got heavily to his feet. So far, he hadn't come down on one side or the other in the current dispute over whether, in the current crisis, they should (1) vamoose, or (2) do nothing.

They were in Buddy's rec room again, and with some trepidation they'd been watching CNN on the old rabbit-ears antenna television set against the unfinished wall under the big silk banner that lived here when it wasn't being used at union rallies or on picket lines. Against a royal blue background, the bright yellow words curved above and below the initials:

Amalgamated Conglomerated Workers
A C W F F A
Factory Floor Alliance

As Buddy went to the World War II refrigerator for some up-to-date beer, Ace said, 'If that guy Faulk thinks *he* oughta run, we oughta listen. Those were smart guys, educated guys, remember? Harvard, or maybe Buddy's right, Dartmouth, but not dummies.'

Passing right over the blatant attempt to suck up to the uncommitted Buddy, 'One of them's arrested,' Mac pointed out, 'which is how smart *he* is. And the other one skipped because Mark knows him and can identify him, and according to the TV, Mark even gave the cops Osbourne Faulk's name.'

Buddy, distributing cans of beer and resuming his seat, said, 'Not a good way to treat a pal.'

'And the point is,' Mac said, 'if he'd give them Faulk, he'd give them *us* twice as fast but he didn't. And you know why?'

'They didn't get around to it yet,' Ace said.

'Oh, they got around to it,' Mac said. 'Little is known of us, that's what the guy said, except we're in the same union together.'

'Which means,' Ace said, 'they know enough that they're probably already on the way. Canada, Mac, we could disappear in Canada.'

'They're not on the way,' Mac insisted, 'because Mark doesn't know our names.'

'Sure he does,' Ace said.

Pointing at each of them, and then at himself, Mac said, 'Ace, Buddy, Mac. That's not name enough to lead anybody to *us*.'

Buddy said, 'Mac, they knew *my* name, from the registration on the car.'

'Faulk did,' Mac said, 'and he's fled. Ace, if you make a move, you'll just draw attention to us.'

Looking around, Buddy said, 'Come to think of it, you know, I can't go anywhere until I finish this room.'

'Exactly,' Mac said, and that took care of that.

66

Dortmunder was drinking coffee, though what he would rather be drinking was anything that started with 'B.' But tonight was when, at long last, the heist would go down, and he should be at his quick-witted best for the occasion. Some time after midnight, with Tiny alone on guard duty at the entrance to the compound and with the cops gone from the place because the kidnapping was over and solved and done with, at last they could go in and get the goddamn cars and deliver them to the Speedshop. And *then* Dortmunder could get out of Pennsylvania, back to New York, back to a cozy living room with his faithful companion, May, and drink everything in the house that started with 'B.' Something to look forward to.

In the meantime, he was seated here in Chester's living room, with Chester and *his* faithful companion, Grace, all of them drinking coffee and waiting for Dortmunder's clothes to get here. Chester's overcoat wasn't bad, but it didn't really fit all that well, and it was uncomfortable having to worry about your coattails all the time.

They'd stopped watching television, because it was obvious the story was over, even though the newspeople were prepared to go on beating it into the ground for several hours yet. Monroe Hall had been kidnapped, then found, then found to have lost his memory. His butler had been kidnapped with him, and was now disappeared. One of the five kidnappers had been nabbed, one had skipped the country, and the other three would never be rounded up unless they put signs on their backs saying, 'I did it.' So it was over, all except the swiping of the cars.

Ding-dong. Ten minutes to six, and Dortmunder watched eagerly as Grace Fallon went over to open the door, though he didn't stand yet, just in case this was somebody other than somebody with his clothes.

But, no, here came Andy Kelp, with two suitcases, only one of them Dortmunder's. And behind him Stan, with a suitcase. And behind him Tiny, with a duffel bag.

Dortmunder stood, coattails forgotten. 'Everybody?' he asked. 'And packed?'

'It's over, John,' Kelp said, and handed Dortmunder his suitcase.

Dortmunder wanted to go to some other room and change into actual clothing, but he had to know: 'Over? What's over?'

Stan answered, 'Forget the cars.'

Dortmunder shook his head. 'Forget the cars? After all this? Why?'

Stan said, 'Because they aren't there any more.'

Kelp said, 'It was awful, John. We stood there and watched them go.'

'On trucks,' Tiny said. He sounded as though the trucks themselves were an insult.

Dortmunder said, 'I don't get it.'

Chester said, 'John, do us all a favor. Get dressed. Use our bedroom.'

'Don't say anything till I get back,' Dortmunder warned them, and was gone a very short period of time, to come back dressed like a person, not like either a refugee or a butler. He said, 'OK, now what?'

Kelp said, 'Because Monroe Hall lost his memory, his wife can't get at the money he had stashed, so she's selling everything.'

'Starting with the cars?'

'Turns out,' Kelp said, 'Hall really didn't own those cars. A museum does.'

'That was a scam,' Chester said, 'so he could keep the cars and not have to turn them over to the bankruptcy court.'

Kelp said, 'Well, it was a scam and it wasn't a scam. This car museum in Florida really does own them all, but Hall got to keep them at his place. Now, with the situation like it is, the museum wants their cars. So today, they left.'

Dortmunder said, 'So that's it? We plan, we prepare, we do everything right, and it's *over*? Just like that?'

Stan said, 'There's still some of that other stuff Arnie Albright said he'd take.'

Dortmunder shook his head. 'I did not come here to load a car with music boxes,' he said. 'I am not a pilferer, I got my dignity. If there's no cars there, there's no reason to go there.'

Kelp said, 'That's why we all packed up and came over.'

Tiny said, 'I'm not going back to that place. If I did, I'd break something.'

Dortmunder sat down on the sofa, where he'd been for so long in the overcoat. 'I've been drinking coffee,' he said.

Grace Fallon said, 'I believe we have some bourbon.'

'Thank you,' he said simply.

After getting concurring nods from everybody else, she left the room and Stan said, 'One drink, and we might as well drive back to the city.'

'Forever,' Chester said. 'That's how long I'm gonna listen to Hal Mellon's jokes.'

Dortmunder said, 'You know, I'm beginning to realize what the worst of it is.'

Kelp looked interested, but apprehensive. 'There's a worst of it?'

'If we're not pulling a heist here tonight,' Dortmunder told him, 'you know what we've been doing the last three days? We've been having *jobs*.'

67

Sunday afternoon. Chuck Yancey had never had to stand guard duty himself at the gate before, and he didn't like it. It was demeaning. It was beneath him. And it was only necessary because Judson Swope had pulled a bunk. Out of here some time yesterday afternoon, never showed up for his midnight tour on the gate. Frantic last-minute calls in all directions, and finally they got Mort Pessle to fill in, but that meant Mort wasn't available for his normal tour today. Shorthanded without Swope, Chuck Yancey found himself doing gate duty with Heck Fiedler. At least it gave him an opportunity to make Heck's life miserable, but it was still a comedown.

Also boring. There'd never been much traffic through this entrance on weekends, and now that Mrs H was shutting the place down, laying off everybody but Yancey and his crew, there was no traffic at all, not for the first six hours.

But then, at five minutes to two, an unremarkable sedan turned in and stopped at the bar, and Yancey's spirits rose for just a second, until he saw the occupants; the two plainclothesmen from CID, making such pests of themselves on Friday. Lieutenant Orville, who was driving, and the other one.

Yancey stepped out of the shack to see what these two wanted – the case was over, wasn't it? – and Orville said, 'We want to talk to Fred Blanchard.'

'I'll see if he's around,' Yancey said, because in truth he hadn't seen anybody from the main house today. Back inside the shack, he called the main house and got no answer at all, then tried the house where Blanchard and Swope and a couple others were living and got the same result.

Back outside the shack, he reported as much: 'Nobody around.'

Orville nodded as though some deep suspicion had been confirmed. 'He's been living here, hasn't he?'

'Until tomorrow, that's right.'

'We'll want to see his place.'

'I'll have to escort you,' Yancey said, and called in to Heck, 'Be right back.'

Heck smiled and nodded, glad to see him go, and Yancey got into the backseat of the cops' car to direct them to the green house, and along the way Orville, looking too often at Yancey in the mirror for somebody supposed to be steering a car, said, 'You may wonder why I'm still after Fred Blanchard, what with Hall being found and the case over.'

'I may,' Yancey agreed.

'You may say,' Orville said, 'that Lieutenant Orville, he's just got his nose out of joint because *he* didn't catch up with that Mark Sterling fella, but that would not be the case, would it, Bob?'

'Absolutely not,' said the other one.

'Mark Sterling just fell into their laps,' Orville explained. 'I never even got a *look* at him. So that's one of the kidnappers, but there's at least four more. And don't forget the butler.'

'I won't,' Yancey promised.

'And who did the butler used to work with, down in Washington, D.C.?'

'Blanchard,' Yancey told him.

'Exactly! I didn't trust Blanchard from the second I saw him. I knew he was hiding something, and I am *going* to find it.'

When they stopped in front of the green house, it had an empty look to it even before they got out, hammered on the door, opened the door, stood in the living room, and yelled, 'Hello?'

'Nobody here,' Yancey said.

'Which is Blanchard's room?'

'I would have no idea.'

'Well, Bob, I guess we'll search the whole place.'

Yancey thought of mentioning warrants, but it was no skin off his nose. Nor, as it turned out, was it to be much of a search. The house had been stripped of all personal possessions. Nothing left but rumpled sheets and open closet doors.

'So they all went,' Yancey said, as they trooped back down the stairs.

Orville said, 'All?'

'The new hires.'

'The new hires!'

'My security guy Swope, Blanchard, the new chauffeur, and the butler. Of course, the butler was already gone.'

Orville said, '*With* his personal property?'

'Well, somebody packed it up and took it away,' Yancey said, and the phone rang, echoing in the empty house. 'I'll get it,' Yancey said. 'Probably Heck at the gate.'

It was. 'Got a guy here,' Heck said. 'Old friend of Blanchard's, wants to talk to him.'

'We'll be right there.'

★

The old friend of Blanchard's didn't look like anybody's old friend. Tall and bony, he had yellow hair close-cropped like Yancey's, but somehow looking more menacing on this bozo, and mean blue eyes that studied them as though they were meat and this was lunchtime.

Before anybody else could speak, the bozo turned those eyes on Orville and the other one and said, 'Fred Blanchard?' Yancey wondered why his right hand was up by his jacket lapel.

It had seemed to Yancey the bozo had been asking which of the plain-clothesmen was Blanchard, but maybe not. Orville hadn't taken it that way, anyway, because he said, 'So you're an old friend of Blanchard's, are you?'

'Oh, yes,' the bozo said. He had some kind of accent that made him sound like a knife sharpener. 'It has been too long since we have met.'

Yancey said, 'Lieutenant, he's got a weapon under that jacket. Heck, stay behind him.'

'Oh, yeah.'

The bozo looked startled. 'I have done nothing.'

Orville might be slow, but he could catch up eventually, because all at once his own pistol was in his hand and he was saying, 'Lieutenant Orville, CID. Put your hands on top of your head.'

'I have done—'

'Now!'

'I shall go away,' the bozo suggested, but he did put his hands on his head. 'I shall come back another time.'

'Bob, frisk him.'

'No, I go away.'

'Heck, shoot him in the leg if he takes a step toward the door.'

'You bet!'

So the other one frisked the bozo, and he turned out to have two loaded Glocks on him. Also three wallets, each with different ID, but all showing photos of this same guy.

Orville could not have been happier. He was practically kissing himself on both cheeks. 'I knew we'd get to the bottom of it,' he chortled. 'And I knew, when we *did* get to the bottom of it, we would find Fred Blanchard.'

'I have diplomatic immunity.' the bozo said.

'Not here you don't,' Orville told him. 'But you're a diplomat, are you? Bob, it's that foreign embassy again.'

'I think you're right,' the other one said.

Orville, suddenly even more excited, jabbed a finger at the bozo and said, 'You and Fred Blanchard and the butler and your whole crowd, you probably killed the ambassador, too!'

From the flinch the bozo gave, and the sudden skittery look in his eyes, Yancey guessed that, whether they were thinking of the same ambassador or not, in some way or another Orville was right.

'All right, my friend,' Orville told the bozo, 'I'm taking you in for questioning, and before I'm done with you, you'll spill everything you know about Fred Blanchard. Put the cuffs on him, Bob.'

As the other one put the cuffs on the bozo, Orville looked out the guardshack window at the county road, but he was clearly seeing much farther. 'I knew I was gonna get you, Fred Blanchard! You won't hide from me! Nowhere on Earth, Fred Blanchard, will you be safe from Lieutenant Wilbur Orville! Let's go, Bob. This is a wrap.'